I07633888

Steve Zell

TRUE CREATURE

TRUE CREATURE

Steve Zell

Edited by Leigh Anne Beresford

This book is a work of fiction, set in a time several decades ago; it is not intended to be an accurate description of actual events or locales. Spider-Man and Peter Parker are creations of Marvel Comics. All characters depicted (with the exception of those associated with *The Wallace and Ladmo Show*) are fictitious, and any resemblance to other real persons living or dead is coincidental.

Steve Zell
Please visit my website: www.talesfromzell.com

Printed in the United States of America

First Printing March 2019
Tales From Zell, Inc.™
Portland, Oregon

ISBN-13: 978-0-9847468-7-3

LCCN: 2019900962

This book is dedicated to the wonderful cast and crew, living and not, of *The Wallace and Ladmo Show*. No matter how hot *or scary* life was – you always made us laugh.

Thank you, Leigh Anne for once again bringing order to my random thoughts; to my daughter, Vicki, for your help in deciding which way to go on the publishing side; and special thanks to my wife, Nina, for granting me all the time I've spent inside this book.

Contents

Foreword

True Creature takes place in a setting that may not be familiar to most even though Phoenix, Arizona is and has always been a winter destination for many folks from the North and Midwest.

For those of us raised in Phoenix during the 1950s through '70s, the fact we lived in the middle of a mortally-hostile desert environment where summer days could reach 121 degrees and the only consistent water source was man-made, wasn't any more frightening than going to school, or for those of us who attended Catholic schools – the nuns. We had no idea we were part of an experiment, or of the political machinations required to bring water and life to the city.

We were kids.

Sure, it was hot as Hell – but we had *Wallace and Ladmo, Legend City* and *Big Surf,* movie houses, and quite a few public and private swimming pools to keep our skin temperature down and our moods high. Parents who dared to have grass lawns used an irrigation system not far removed from the one the Hohokam left us. Experiment that we were, we were the testing ground for every fast-food franchise and every new bit of marketing there was – so there was plenty of neat stuff to eat and play with. And heck...if you teed off at 5AM in the summer – you could golf year-round. As hot as it was for us kids...Phoenix back then had its own sort of *cool.*

But underneath all of that...*there was always something else.*

Chapter 1
Paradise

Once you come to believe you have nothing more to lose, you'll lose one more thing.

The spring in your step. A few degrees of motion in your fingers, your knees, a measure of clarity in your vision. The loss is rarely sudden, more often something you become aware of gradually.

And, little by little, you'll begin to realize that at one time, youth firmly in hand, you lived in paradise.

But you had no idea you'd been there until you looked back.

And now you wonder if others who began this journey with you knew just where you were. You realize that many must have. They knew, and they took full advantage of it.

But for you paradise wasn't to be found in the "here and now." It was only to be enjoyed once you'd circumvented all the pretty traps and snares of the present.

Back then you dreamed of, and lived for, the future.

Paradise.

But every day you lost a little more.

And finally, weary of walking toward a future that seemed ever more uncertain; you decided you had walked long enough, far enough.

And only when you were tired and old did the truth become clear…that this very time and this very place…

This is what you sacrificed paradise for…

- Dark Warrior

Arizona
May 2, 1968

A breath! Air whistled down his sandpaper throat; another rattling and painful breath. *Awake.* His eyes were dry, his sight smoky, motes like large winged bats swirled across the narrow tunnel of his vision. *Cold.* His powder blue blanket, the one with the cowboy hats and lassos was gone.

Where was his bookshelf filled with picture books? Where was his fielder's mitt?

He saw that shelf now at the far wall of the room. But who moved it?

Where were the curtains printed with drawings of other kids playing – figures that often scared him at night...*because sometimes those kids seem to move...to really play.*

The windows on the south side of his room were gone; only one thin window high up that far wall and fogged white.

This isn't my room. It's not my bed!

"Ma-" A cry for his mom couldn't escape his parched, cracked lips. His tongue was a leathery, useless thing in his mouth.

The hand he raised was fragile, the fingers long and white with knobby knuckles, barely more than bones with skin; *not my hand.*

This isn't me.

A brittle scream that couldn't possibly have come from him and then...darkness.

He dreamed.

No. *He remembered...*

June 2, 1953

Choking dust. Deep sand sucked at his sneakers, slowed him down, weakened him. But he kept pumping his arms, kept running. The full moon led him up and away from the others, guided him past the cactus and the sharp, unstable rocks. But it couldn't *hide* him because the moon led *them* too.

They'd seen him, and he had no idea where he was running to but the lake. *And then what?* What would he do? Swim away from them?

He had never run this hard. He was hungry and cold – with nothing inside to fuel him but terror.

The boy's legs pistoned and pumped and finally, failed him. He wasn't fast enough; *he wasn't strong enough to escape.* He dropped to the sand.

The stench of decay, something dead nearby – a bird, a jack-rabbit…

"This way!"

Tommy! His friend stood atop a small mountain of boulders well-guarded by Cholla, what they called "jumping cactus" - the *worst* cactus of all – because Cholla needles were so long, so sharp, they were in your skin before you even knew you'd touched them.

"Through here! This way!"

Tommy waved his arm toward the awful stand of Cholla.

Joey stood, wiping the sandy snot from his face. He couldn't make it through that cactus. *No way.* But he could hear the pounding footfalls behind him. He had to go somewhere! In the blink of the eye, Tommy was gone.

Why did he come here, what did he expect to see?

Nothing like what he'd seen tonight, nothing like this!

He heard his brother shout, *"Joey, stop!"*

His brother would be angrier than anyone if he caught him.

Tears poured down Joey's cheeks. He sucked his lips into his teeth. *And ran for his life.*

Pain slammed his ribs. His fevered eyes saw only stars, and then...Chuck Webb, nearly twice Joey's age and massive - the fetid odor of sweat and something the boy was far too young to know.

"You didn't see nothin'! You hear me? You didn't see nothin'!"

The Lily Murders

May, 1968

Phoenix, Arizona

"Charlie?"

Melissa Webb swirled the plastic sword within her frosted glass and stabbed another salty olive, plucking it from the bottom. The martini was sour and not nearly dirty enough. *Damn it.* Vermouth should only *touch* the glass, be swirled for a bit and dumped out. It was the olive juice, the salt she savored.

"Charlie..."

Charlie knew better. What was he thinking?

She slipped from her sandals, relishing the feel of cool marble beneath her feet as she crossed the kitchen floor to the patio.

Beyond the sliding door, rectangles of aqua light from the pool danced along the terrazzo, painted the wrought-iron benches, the meticulously clipped lawn, and high stone wall that protected their yard and their pool.

And there was Charlie himself. King of his castle. Lord of his pool, his rotund form distorted by the sheets of water sluicing down the faux rocks above him, those beefy white feet dangling in the churning water. His martini rested safely just beyond the flow.

Melissa downed the last of her far-too-sour martini, slipped the robe from her shoulders and dove naked into the warm pool. Her breath slipped away in silver bubbles as she glided effortlessly across its length.

Charlie had been a varsity fullback when they'd met. So powerful, *so handsome.*

That was fifteen years ago. And here he was now…

Things had changed…Charlie had definitely changed. He'd grown fat and bald. To be fair, neither of them had lived up to their physical expectations she supposed. She'd miscarried the child who had tied them inextricably together back then and picked up thirty pounds of sadness herself from the experience…

But she loved big Chuck today the same way she always had.

Through the churning surface, through the bubbles, there were those big feet, the sunrise tattoo on his ankle glowed a garish purple in the aquamarine pool lights.

She clasped his tree trunk ankles in her hands and began to pull herself up to him.

His feet slipped from the ledge. Charlie's body toppled headlong into the pool.

-=-=-=-=-=-=-=-

Ross Tennet worked *so hard.*

Jo Anne had cleaned the Burl & Tennet Agency office nightly for ten years, she'd long ago stopped counting the times she'd found Mister Tennet asleep at his desk.

She knew he had children. She knew he'd been divorced – at least twice. Outside of that, she knew he lived only for the agency.

He was a quiet man, but a good man as far as Jo Anne knew. He smiled often.

She clicked off the vacuum before she made her way down the hall past the stone waterfall that trickled softly, beside his office. There was no need to wake him. The man was meticulous. Anything she found there she could handle just fine with a dust cloth and pan.

The clock near the bookshelf read 8:13 PM.

At 8:25 PM Jo Anne had swept, dusted, and tidied everything but Mister Tennet's desk. It wasn't until she reached for his empty water glass that she realized Mister Tennet wasn't breathing.

-=-=-=-=-=-=-=-

Los Angeles, California

“What the fuck?”

Sara Poole raised her gloved hands. The rotund, naked form on the examination table before her settled slowly onto his back.

“Is that a rhetorical question?” Ben glanced up from his clipboard.

“This wasn't an overdose…” she said. “I’m thinking murder.”

Ben shook his head, and read the report back to her again. "The deceased, Richard Bilken, was found in bed by his roommate with a needle in his arm. He’s a known heroin addict.” He added, “with an arrest and conviction record longer than your girlfriend's clit."

Sara, a good four inches taller than Ben, her body molded by years of competitive diving and martial arts, smiled benignly at this attempt at humor from the squirrel-like twerp, as she usually did. In the macabre world of forensic pathology, you found humor where you could.

“I'm thinking he was drowned and placed.”

Ben tilted his chin toward the bags of clothing their customer had come in with, freshly bagged on the counter awaiting tags.

“His PJ’s are dry.”

“Come on. Give me a hand here.”

Checking a customer's back for signs of trauma was a necessary part of the Medical Examiner’s job, the “heavy lifting” part. Sara was strong enough, and with her natural leverage, a good steady pull of the arm was usually enough to roll a corpse, but Bilken was a large man. A large, dead weight.

“Take his shoulder. One. Two...three.”

With a gurgle and a moan, the dead man rolled toward her, a gory mix of water and blood sputtered from his open mouth and nostrils into the gutters...and just kept coming. Two liters or more by the time he was done.

“Again...I'm thinking murder. By drowning.”

-=-=-=-=-=-=-=-

"I seen her stuffin,' Alice. Candy - she's hidin' it on you, sweetie."

"I know that, Crystal. Where does she hide it?"

"Come on, sweetie...just a taste, okay?"

"Shit, Crystal..."

"I'm not a snitch, baby...you know I'm not like this -"

"Where, Crystal? Where does she put it?"

"I got two babies, Alice. I'm just...you know, I'm just messed up now, just now, you know?"

"I know...*I know how that is, honey."*

Out on the floor where, at this moment, Candy was making sweet love to the brass pole under the adoring gaze of three fans, actual music played. In here, Alice's "nest," with its carpeted door and walls, there was only thumping bass, deep rhythm, a dark pulse. In here, all melody was lost and the only light was a watery purple glow from the aquariums.

The snow-streaked face in the mirror resting below him, the one with the rolled fifty dollar bill up its nose, mascara highlighting his long black lashes, that face didn't belong to him, it was an homage to his favorite act, Alice Cooper; a caricature of a caricature.

His real name was Cecil. That had become "Cee-Cee" early on. Now it was Alice.

Nothing was his. Not even Candy. Not even the money she made off his good nature.

He ran the paper along the mirror resting on Crystal's backside, skimming the sweet powder, sucking its cold-burning life into his nose until a drop of red blood spattered the remaining dust.

Oh, feel that cold, medicinal, burn...

His lips curled, for a moment he could feel his gums pull back with them, felt his teeth grow long and sharp.

Oh, if only he could be that monster he wanted to be.

"Just a taste, okay. That's all I need, okay, sweetie? That's all."

A ghost of a face, a flickering purple, a face that might have been that of a sweet child in the light of a summer not long ago, that face looked back at him with equal parts hope and terror.

He took two bottles from the shabby desk behind them. One, Peppermint Schnapps, the other, Tabasco.

"I'll give you a taste, honey."

He dumped a white pile onto the mirror, swirled in schnapps, Tabasco, and his own blood...

Her eyes grew wide.

"Where does she hide it?"

-=-=-=-=-=-=-=-

The rat-a-tat machine-gun fire of southern California rain pounded against the metal door. Alice was spent, burning, freezing...and flying.

It had been a *fabulous* night after all.

Heartbreaking, yes. Candy had cut him deep. A love like that didn't come cheap. The breakup had been expensive in every way.

Oh, and it burned...it burned deeply, *wonderfully.*

He hugged the fiery, wet crotch of his slacks.

Well, passion burns, honey. And breaking up is very, very hard to do.

He found her stash afterwards. A pocket stitched into the black curtains backstage. Alice had some mending to do tomorrow.

Before that, he'd taken a good, solid fist of cash from the safe, and marinated it in his special love potion while Candy writhed through two turns onstage, and warmed the laps of her three johns in the private rooms.

Only then had he waved her, smiling, to his nest.

He yanked the door open and burst, arms wide, into the rain-filled night. *She'd passed, screaming through this same door only moments before.* The thought made him feel good, *powerful.* The sounds of his sweet revenge still echoed through the steely, rapid fire, of the LA torrent. That felt good too, cooled the burn.

The heavy rain had formed black rivers, they swept the trash of LA's backside, before him.

Wadded bills swept and rolled past his feet. The very thought of a trail of soiled bills stretching as long as Candy could waddle and run, screaming, hands plastered to her bottom, brought a snicker and a snort from him.

He let the bills go. *At first he did.*

The money wasn't important to him, not really. It was the pain she'd caused him, the lies, the disrespect. She'd stolen from him, taken advantage of his goodness, his charity, *like so many had.*

It wasn't until he reached the dumpster behind the dilapidated club, where his VW love bus awaited him, that Alice finally bent to recover a nastily-stained $100 bill.

"Huh?"

A black raincoat rode along the surface of the river before him, sweeping that bill and several others with it. And just past the coat -

Alice recoiled in terror.

A tall, no, *gargantuan* man stood naked beside the dumpster.

Alice fled, sloshing through the rainwater, back to the door, his hands slipped, tugged, clawed at the knob.

Locked. Of course it was locked. It would have locked the moment it closed.

"Aa!" was all Alice could manage.

He looked back to see the man collapse in a splash of foam to the asphalt, like a wave crashing to a sandy beach.

He was gone.

Coke? What was in that fucking coke? Fucking LSD?

This was no fucking joke. The coke was fucking laced.

His knees gave way. He would fucking kill his pusher. *Lance was fucking dead.*

No joke.

He fumbled for his keys, they dropped to the river of muck and bills at his feet and he stooped, quickly, to retrieve them, along with a few sodden bills while he was down there. His eyes blinked, raced from keys to dumpster, to sidewalk and to the refuse of East LA beyond. No apparitions this time. No naked giants.

I don't deserve this!

I don't!

His keys sparkled in the slowly rising creek at his feet - but before his hand could scoop them up -

Another hand did. A *huge* hand.

It rose up to his face faster than his coked-up reflexes could dodge it, and then Alice was flying backwards. He slammed the metal door with rib-snapping force.

His scream strangled with water, his nostrils, throat, and lungs burned and filled with it. The water filled his lungs to the point of bursting, *then beyond.*

The creature's eyes, *two blue stars of pain,* stabbed into his.

And then there was only pain.

-=-=-=-=-=-=-=-

"Got a real *Sunday night special* for you this morning, Sara. Meet, Cecil Benson, alias, *Alice.*"

Sara thumbed an extra dab of peppermint oil just below her nostrils, as she made her way between the tables. The oil didn't help.

"Peppermint won't help with *this* stinker."

"Thanks for that, Ben."

"Probably, make you more nauseated than you already are."

"Again, thank you."

She'd had a good night, but a rough one too – last night's White Russians mixed with the odor of mint intertwining with the powerful stench of feces and whatever *devil's cologne* the stinker had splashed on the day he'd perished nearly made her puke.

"Ah... let me guess," Ben wafted the air around her with his latex-clad palm. "White Russians?"

"I bow to your genius. What happened to his eyes?"

Ben nodded toward the cylindrical jar resting between the man's legs. Two brown eyes stared crazily at her from their formalin bath.

"I don't mean where are they *now* – why aren't they *in* him?"

The man's empty lids, streaked with mascara and blood, had sunk deep into the pits beneath them.

"That *is* the real question. Cops had to chase them down the street before they saw El Segundo for the last time."

Sara nodded, continuing down his body.

"Throat and abdomen are *extremely* distended, he lay face-down for a while, purple with lividity all the way down to...*fucks' sake-"*

The man's penis, still erect, was fiery red.

"And *that* is the primary source of today's atmosphere."

"Jesus. What did he do?"

"Apparently he delivered a *hot mint poker* to a friend."

"What the hell is *that?"*

"It's a mix of Schnapps and hot sauce. It's a form of *figging*?"

"Figging?"

"That's where you use a shaved ginger root for an anal plug. Keeps your partner from clenching – it was all the rage...somewhere back in the Renaissance."

"Maybe that's why I failed art history."

"With a hot mint poker, one usually rubs the mixture *over* the condom, a gift you *give*, not receive. But...apparently, this one was a giver *and* a taker."

"That can't feel good for *anyone.* I'd rip his eyes out too."

"You never know until you try."

"Remind me again why we don't hang out after work. Oh, that's right - you just did.

"That's a weird scar."

Just over the customer's carefully-shaved pubis, a cluster of bluish lines, slightly raised. She moved her gloved index finger lightly over it.

"Yeah. Noted that. No stitch or burn marks. Could be a birthmark."

"Huh. I think it's a tat, just really badly done. Likely caused an infection."

"Nasty place for body art."

"Well...I'd say this fellow wasn't too discerning. So who was Mr. Benson's last date? Anyone out there missing a freak?"

"Perp wasn't hard to find. She showed up at Mercy Hospital with severe Colo-rectal distress at 2:12 AM, a few minutes after they found him."

"Well...let's see what *else* she did to him," she said, "Check his back, I'll get his arm."

"Watch that hand..."

It too was bright red and stunk to high heaven.

"Jesus. What a bastard," she muttered.

"This one could be messy inside. From the looks of him, she shoved a hand grenade up his ass."

"Yeah?" Sara said, with a glance at his flaming erection, "She deserves a medal for heroism. One. Two. *Three.*"

The man's unhinged jaw flopped wide open; a torrent of water, mud and gore gushed onto the table, cascaded over the troughs.

The force of the liquid was so shocking that, for an instant, they both stood, flabbergasted, leaving the man on his side as the effluence fire-hosed out of him.

Just as suddenly, the filth and water separated, the water seemed, almost, to slither over the sludge.

Beneath the table, the five-liter collection bottle filled with it.

"Get another bottle!"

Ben crashed into the corner of the table. The cylinder with the eyes teetered, the balls inside twirling, and Sara caught it with one hand as she fought to disconnect the collection bottle, just as Ben slid a new one in place.

She capped it, or tried to. The cap didn't fit – *no, it did* – she just couldn't twist it down far enough to catch the thread.

"What the fuck is this?!"

Sara grasped it with both hands. She shoved down with all her weight.

The big plastic bottle swelled beneath her. Beside her, another bottle filled.

"Damn it!" It throbbed, pushed back against her as she forced the cap down.

Then it burst!

She shielded her face with her arms as the water slapped into her, knocked her back, painfully, against the next table. The second bottle exploded beneath the collection pipe, soaked her.

"Fuck!"

The water slid off her in one thick sheet then dropped to the floor.

"Plug the drain!"

Ben pulled the control with everything he had – *it wasn't enough.*

They watched helpless to stop it, as the water slid through the grate of the floor drain. And then the floor was dry, *completely* dry.

Sara looked at her gloves, her coat. *Dry.*

They looked at each other, stunned. From the table, the dead-man groaned as the eyeless corpse collapsed onto its back once again.

Chapter 2
Lake Pleasant

"It is my distinct honor to introduce the next senator from the great state of Arizona, Todd Worwick!" crowed Sondra Tucker, one-time assistant to the creative director, of the Burl & Tennet Agency, and now that former director's campaign manager.

It was 96 degrees Fahrenheit with no clouds in the sky and no hint of relief from the few wispy clouds above. Todd Worwick, former Arizona State University quarterback and NFL hopeful, practically squirted sweat through every possible pore and orifice of his six-foot-five frame. He had tossed the blazer over one shoulder, pulled down the tie – but he was still a layer too hot in his dress shirt and slacks.

He towered center-stage at the microphone on a wide platform before the sun-drenched Lake Pleasant, flanked by councilmen, children from a local school, and several Pima Indians dressed in ancient Hohokam garb. A dust-devil sent a blast of sand swirling across the stage, upsetting the sun screens and flapping the curtains behind him.

The candidate himself was unflappable.

"Hey Arizona - how the heck are you?" He shouted.

"Worwick's our man! Worwick's our man! Worwick for *President!"*

He waved and shook his head.

"No – that was my opponent's idea, not mine. A bad idea for him too! We know where Barry Goldwater's heart is – we all know he still wants to be President someday. He doesn't care about us anymore. But until Washington comes to Arizona, my home is right where I was born – right here in Phoenix. I'm an Arizonan! I'll ALWAYS be an Arizonan!"

That brought an even louder cheer.

"Water!!! Bring us the water!!!"

"That's going to take leadership, my friends! Leadership we'll never get from that failure, Barry Goldwater.

"It is time for a change, Arizona. Todd Worwick will work for you. I will work *with* Washington *for* Arizona. We all know that water is everything."

"Real water...not that "gold-colored" stuff!" Someone shouted.

Todd raised his hands and shook his head.

"Now come on. Let's be civil," but he couldn't help but smile.

"Lakes like *Pleasant* hold the lifeblood of Arizona – the lifeblood of agriculture. Agriculture is Arizona's heart."

"The Central Arizona Water Project will pump that blood into our economy. That will bring the jobs we need, the prosperity we *deserve.* But that is a grand project my friends. Hat's off to the Hohokam and the beautiful canals they built...but after a thousand years or so, their irrigation system needs a little work, don't you think?"

On cue, the faux "Hohokam" turned to him and shook their fists.

"Whoa there, Chief! I didn't mean any disrespect!"

Laughter erupted from the audience.

"Completion of CAP, the Central Arizona Water Project, will take money and lots of it. And, unlike my Republican opponent in this race, I will not saddle Arizonans with that burden. I will work with my good friend, President Lyndon Baines Johnson to bring Federal money to bear!"

"Bring us the money, Todd! Bring us water!"

"You know I will! And speaking of water! I don't know about you," he crooned into the microphone, "– but I can't think of anything better than catching a wave in the desert, can you? And the great folks at Great Wave have brought surfing to us right here at Lake Pleasant. How about that? What do you think Arizona?"

Right on cue, the curtains behind him parted and a dozen local teens in jams and bikinis Boogalooed onto the stage, surfboards in tow. The opening phrase of the iconic Beach Boys hit, *Catch a Wave*, thundered over the public address system.

The assembled crowd hurrahed. Todd waved and turned toward the shade, and large whirling fans located backstage.

“Keep waving, the cameras are rolling,” Sondra said.

Todd turned back, smiling even wider, brighter than before, waving with renewed vigor. Blue eyes and impeccably capped ivories gleaming. *There were worse things than being here.* Even if he couldn't think of any just now. He was at Lake Pleasant – possibly the most ill-named, god forsaken body of water in the great US of A as far as Worwick was concerned, stuck in the middle of the desert north of Phoenix. There was nothing remotely *pleasant* about the steaming sand hole – not late in May. But submerging the old Waddell Dam was a key piece in the Central Arizona Water Project, and the fact that an Arizona company, Great Wave, had figured out a way to put an artificial ocean wave, or some-such apparatus that forced something *resembling* an ocean wave onto a man-made beach in a man-made bay in man-made Lake Pleasant – had turned the idea of kicking off his *water for Arizona* platform here an opportunity his campaign couldn't pass up.

“Your boat’s ready to launch right after you start the first wave. Sun cover and all the tackle you could ever want.”

“Fishing is good. Cassie loves it, but is it really necessary, today?” he said through his smile. “I can't just…you know…slip out once they flush that wave out?”

“Not if you want to be Senator." Sondra said through her own tight smile. “Our next senator is a happily married father.”

“Right.”

He raised his hands, and shouted over the music, “Time to turn the mic over to a couple great friends of mine I don't have to introduce – but I will! From your favorite Channel Five show, it’s Wallace and Ladmo!!!”

Two men in twenties-style body-covering swimwear, one pudgy in bright polka-dots, the other tall and skinny with wide stripes on his baggy swimwear accented by a wide tie and top hat, hopped onto the stage - the kids in the audience went wild!

“Hey kids! Give a big Wallace and Ladmo cheer to our next Senator, Todd Worwick!” The pudgy Wallace said, taking the mic as skinny sidekick Ladmo offered Todd his top hat – which Todd proudly donned to the cheers of the kids, tipped, then handed back to Ladmo as he headed, waving, offstage to a smaller platform on the brand new artificial Lake Pleasant beach where a giant turquoise button emblazoned with the turquoise Great Wave logo, stood atop a pedestal. The crowd and cameras followed closely behind.

The surfers had already begun paddling out to a line of buoys marked by brightly colored flags. Todd squinted into the dancing diamonds of sunlight glinting off the lake.

"How does this thing work?"

"Submerged pumps, they tell me." Sondra said. "Think of Lake Pleasant as a huge toilet."

"Not that difficult."

"Same principle – when enough water gets pumped into this bay to create a siphon it flushes – we get a wave."

Todd considered that.

"You know, CAP goes through…a couple years from now this whole bay is underwater."

"Not a problem. The pumps are mobile. The lake moves – the bay moves. Blasting a new beach out here is easy enough; plenty of rock and sand."

"And, soon enough - all the water they'll ever want."

Tall Ladmo took the mic, one long, lanky arm waving to the surfers, who waved wildly back. "Okie dokie, surfers! Ready to hang – five?"

Wallace took the mic back, "That's ten, Ladmo!"

Ladmo slapped his palms to his hat, "Dang!"

"Let's hope Gerald doesn't come along and ruin it…OH NO!"

A man dressed in velvet knickers, spectacles, water-wings, and a Dutch-Boy blonde wig sauntered out to them, carrying a small, Styrofoam surfboard and a mic of his own.

The crowed jeered.

Todd snickered, "Gerald tries to ruin everything. All these years…still gets me."

"Me too." Sondra laughed.

Spoiled rich kid *Gerald,* was actually Pat McMahon, a local KPHO talk-show host, and a regular on the Wallace and Ladmo Show – McMahon played other characters on the show – including a kid-hating clown. Todd always thought he was a hoot.

"I'm rich. I own this lake," Gerald said. "I get the first wave."

"No you don't, Gerald. This lake belongs to everybody!"

Ladmo, had moved behind Gerald, directing the crowd, and Todd, with outstretched fingers.

"ONE!"

Todd raised his palm over the big blue button.

Gerald stomped his feet, *"No! No! No!"*

"Two!"

"Damn thing better work," Todd said, sideways at Sondra through his wide smile.

"No! No! No!"

"THREE!!!"

Todd slapped the button down.

For Todd Worwick, a moment of utter silence. He blinked. *He was alone.*

Out on the water, the surfers, the brightly colored floating flags, were gone. All around him, only the desert, and the lake. The water.

He stood atop a huge boulder overlooking the dam. Staring at that place where the water lapped the concrete wall...

With a shudder and roar – it all came rushing back. The cheering crowd, the Beach Boys. Just beyond the buoys, a long blue swell began to rise, bringing a collective gasp from the crowd. The surfers paddled toward the rising wall and turned back to the beach.

The wall of water sheered and a great wave began to curl toward the shore, bringing the best of the surfers along with it.

The crowd went wild!

"Holy cow!" Sondra laughed. "It really works! Todd?"

His skin was ashen beneath his sunglasses.

"Todd?"

"Somethin' else," he said.

-=-=-=-=-=-=-=-

"How you doin' over there, kid?"

Cassie sat at the back of the boat, her tan legs tucked beneath her as she watched the red and white bobber float over still waters some twenty feet closer to the shore. Her blonde hair was pulled into a ponytail that flowed from the back of her baseball cap. Her wayfarers glinted the sun back at him.

"I'm good."

She turned back to her quarry, the great big bass she knew to be swimming inches from that little worm knotted around her hook.

"Not getting too much sun?"

"I like the sun."

Todd nodded from his well-shaded seat beneath the canopy.

"'Kay."

"Todd?"

He took the beer Sondra offered. She dutifully twisted the can till his palm covered the label.

"Long-range telephoto on the shore."

"Got it." Todd, smiled at the rocky bluff above the beach where a cadre of photographers perched.

"They gone for a while?" He was referring to the KPHO boat that had followed them out here for a special, *the senatorial hopeful parts the sea, creates an ocean wave; then spends a quiet morning fishing with his twelve-year-old daughter*. A sweet slice of life news story and publicity you couldn't pay for, though he was certain Sondra, and his campaign, had paid dearly.

"For now. They'll be back – to cover the big catch."

"They planning to bring that *big catch* with them?"

She raised her beer to the ice-filled Coleman beside them.

"Done."

"You don't know my Cassie – she'll pull one in twice the size of that cooler."

"Insurance never hurts. And keep your hand over the label -

They toasted. The cold beer felt good, *real good*, going down.

"You've done well, she's a good kid, Todd."

"That's her mommy, not me."

"She's going to be a heart-breaker – I can tell."

The second long gulp felt even better.

"...like I said."

"Hey! Hey!" At the back of the boat, Cassie's reel ratcheted and sang, her rod bowed and dipped wildly with the *big catch* dance.

Todd set down his beer and swept up the net.

"Reel him in, honey!" He winked at Sondra, "Told you."

-=-=-=-=-=-=-=-

"Mind if I hitch a ride?"

"*Arizona Tribune* too cheap to hire a boat?"

"*Tucson Gazette* these days, Mick."

"Hard times hit us all, I guess." Mick swung his gear into the boat and squinted into the sun at the shapely silhouette on the pier above him. He extended a crusty hand which the woman took easily as she stepped onto the gunwale.

"Well, I could give you the whole company run-down on liability insurance and our lack of it if you're interested," he grimaced and shook his head "no" while he said it and she mirrored his gesture.

"Nah, I'm good, Mick."

"I'll take that for verbal acceptance."

He tossed a life-jacket toward her from the open bench beside him and pulled her onboard.

"You're a peach," she said.

"Hey, no passen-" If not for the straps holding them around his neck, Dan Brigg, KPHO's Second Unit Director, would have dropped his binoculars.

"*Deanne!*"

"Afternoon, Dan."

Mick clucked his tongue.

"I'm sure you two'd rather swap spit all day – but what d'ya say we get a shot in before the day's over? Looks like that kid hooked something."

Dan tossed the tie-line from the gunwale. He twirled his hand overhead, shouting to the captain,

"We're movin'!"

Mick clipped on his harness, hefting the big camera to his shoulder in one swift move, and Deanne barely had time to pull on her life-jacket and drop to the bench beside him as the twin motors revved and the boat roared away from the pier.

-=-=-=-=-=-=-=-

The clip shot from that boat, the one they ran on KPHO that night, and across the nation not long after – was full of sunlight, bright wide smiles, and fatherly pride. The sort of good-natured "they're just like us" slice of family life – that warmed our hearts only a few years back – before John F. Kennedy waved us all goodbye from that convertible in Dallas.

Carefully planned, carefully executed. Carefully candid.

Tahoma knew the real story, at least how it began, and he was working hard on a conclusion.

He watched that reel through the dirty ribbon of smoke from his cigarette, a noxious plume that intertwined with all the others around him into a thick haze.

"You want another, hon?"

Two impossibly long fingers barely recognizable as his own tapped the smudged glass sitting next to three others on the sweat-smudged bar.

A glass dropped next to its companions, a bottle clicked its dirty rim, an echo, a glug, and the alcohol flowed out. Clear like water, but not water. Not water at all.

The woman who poured it might have been young, might even have been pretty once. At one time that would have meant something to Tahoma. A flicker of something...what? Regret that it no longer did?

"You know," the bartender glanced up at the television nested between the garishly lit bottles. "He's going to be president one day."

Tahoma downed the contents of his glass in one swallow, as he always did, and stood to leave. He shook his head.

No...he is not.

-=-=-=-=-=-=-=-

"Deanne Mulhenney."

Todd peered at the pretty woman from beneath his sunglasses, he took her extended hand as the KPHO News team stowed their gear behind her.

"With *The Arizona Tribune*?"

"Formerly," Sondra corrected, with a distaste she didn't attempt to hide.

"Formerly," Deanne acknowledged, "*Gazette* now."

"I've read your work. Good to put a pretty face with the byline."

"I know this is family time..." she said.

"Why don't you call our office," Sondra handed her a card. "I'm sure we can find some -"

"We have some time before they flush the big toilet again, don't we?" He winked at Deanne, for the off-color reference. "We off the record now?"

"Are we ever, really?"

He smiled warily, unsure if she was joking or not. Slowly, she returned the smile. He nodded.

"...before they perform another wave test?" He corrected.

Sondra nearly protested, but stopped herself before she started – there are times when "no" means "no," and other times when it means absolutely nothing, and this was clearly the latter. She bit her lip.

"Yes," she said, "We have a few minutes."

Deanne glanced at the boat beside them, where Mick had just zipped up his equipment bag. He stood next to it and not-so-patiently folded his arms.

"I'll keep it short. My ride is almost on its way back to shore."

Sondra considered it a minor victory, at least, when Todd didn't offer the woman their boat for the afternoon.

"Why do you want this project so badly?" Deanne asked.

"That's sort of a softball question, isn't it? Is that really all you want to know?"

"That depends on the answer."

"Well that's easy, Miss Mulhenney, CAP is what Arizona needs and Arizona can't fund it alone. I know it's going to take federal money and no, I'm not doing it to curry favor with Lyndon – or to make points for higher office."

"Really? This isn't a shot toward Washington? And *Deanne* is fine."

He shook his head.

"Deanne, really. I'm -"

"An Arizonan, I know. An ASU Sun-Devil."

"You a Wildcat?" He quipped.

"Bear Down," she acknowledged with his rival Alma-mater's fight call. "But I can be fair – as long as we're not talking football."

His laugh came easily.

"Arizona needs water for crops and cattle. The reservoir needs to hold more water for that to happen, a lot more, and the Agua Fria's tapped out. This lake will run dry before we even irrigate Glendale, let alone Phoenix."

"That's it? You have no plans for higher office? Everyone *else* thinks you do."

"I'm not even *Senator* Worwick – yet. Help me with that – and you'll help Arizona Agriculture get the water it needs."

"I don't campaign I report. Truth doesn't have an angle."

His sideways boyish smile, the lucky rabbit's foot of charm that had warmed and broken hearts of opposition since kindergarten, broke out before he could even hope to stop it.

"The truth will help me, Deanne."

"It was good meeting you, Miss Mulhenney," Sondra tilted her chin toward the KPHO boat, where Mick leaned heavily back on his equipment pack – he let out a deep sigh.

"Thank you." Deanne produced her own card which she handed directly to

Worwick. "Call me if you'd like to elaborate."

"I'll do that."

"Call my office if you have more questions," Sondra said.

"Thank you, I will."

"I do have one more question for you, Mr. Worwick."

"Todd is fine, shoot away."

"Todd. You were practically a partner at Burl & Tennet. Ross Tennet's funeral was this morning."

"And Friday I made a generous contribution to The Children's Fund in his name. Ross was a strong supporter of CAP. His wife, Nan, understands why I'm here today, and Ross would too."

As the KPHO boat headed toward shore, Worwick handed the card over to Sondra – but not before he'd memorized Deanne Mulhenney's number.

"Careful with that one, Todd. Her last series didn't help anyone or anything - least of all her career."

Todd knew exactly what series Sondra referred to – it was a frank assessment of child abuse in the church, accused priests moved from parish to parish. Probably should have won a Pulitzer, instead, it had cost her her job.

"Heck, Sondra, she's a scrapper. She took a hit and she's still at it – good for her. If she gets the real story out it's a good thing for us."

"She's a wrecking ball...*with lipstick."*

"Daddy, I'm hungry."

Oww! He mimed a clawing cat back at Sondra and hugged his suddenly rowdy girl.

"Want me to fillet that monster, Cass?"

"Grodie! *No way!"*

"Awe come on, sweetcakes," he tugged the stringer, "let's see if that big fella's ready for lunch."

"No!" She half-giggled, half-screamed as she pulled at her father's waist, trying to drag the tall man away, *"leave him in the lake!"*

He tugged again...and the stringer came up *much too easily.*

Only a large fish head remained, hooked through the gill. It dangled, loosely for a moment before Todd dropped the stringer back into the water. He turned quickly back to his daughter.

She was still laughing, she hadn't seen it.

In the distance, the dingy concrete wall of the Waddell Dam loomed like the gray ghost of a beached battleship.

"You're right, Cass. Let's leave him be for now. There's a bucket of Kentucky Fried in that bench front of the boat. Save me a 'stick, okay?"

He turned back to the lake and stared into the water, deep into it.

"Todd?"

He barely acknowledged Sondra as his daughter scrambled to the front of the boat.

"Crawdads," he said, quietly. "Crawdads got him. Don't tell her."

"Crawdads?"

"Damn lake's full of them. They'll take your whole catch if you're not watching. I should've known better than to keep him in the water." He quickly pulled the stringer up and released the odd fruit that hung there. Blank eyes stared glassily up at him as the head twirled slowly into the greenish depths below.

Sondra winced.

"Well..." she nodded toward Cassie, who was happily plowing into fried drumsticks like a champ at the bow. "She probably shouldn't eat too much of that chicken if she's going to swim."

"She's not swimming."

"In twenty minutes they're running another wave test *just for her* -"

"I said, *'no,'* didn't I?"

And this time, 'no' meant exactly that.

Chapter 3

"Aww - what're you looking at? She's stuck up. Forget about it!"

"Nothing. *I'm not looking at nothing."*

"Yeah, right."

But he *was* looking at her. As she collected her books from the back seat of the big Lincoln Towncar, Donovan *couldn't stop looking at her.* He probably hadn't quit looking at her since his family moved to this side of town and he'd wound up at Saint Bartholomew.

"Donnie's got a girlfriend!"

"Shut up!"

Terry could be a jerk sometimes.

He was probably right though. Cassandra Worwick had never once looked Donnie's way. But today, Donovan O'Malley *had the ticket.*

The orange crate on the sidewalk behind him had already attracted a small crowd of the curious.

Today was *show-and-tell* and in 4th period, right after lunch, Donovan would unveil the best show-and-tell item ever. The big brown paper bag, slowly rustled and crunched inside the crate. He'd masking-taped the top, giving his pet just enough air, without giving away just what was rustling around inside.

One kid, Jim Richards, had produced a yardstick from an open classroom, he poked the bag. Two girls squealed.

"Hey! Stop that!"

He took one look back at the big car as the chauffeur shut the door behind her. With all the commotion, had Cassandra looked his way? Sure she had!

He smiled as he hefted up the crate and ran, clumsily, just making it to the end of the line in front of his home room as the morning bell rang.

-=-=-=-=-=-=-=-

Did Yertle have enough air?

It was a typical spring day in Phoenix. Hot. Even with the big swamp cooler, whose fan rattled and spit above him in the classroom, it was stifling in here. The swamp coolers did little more than waft humidity over them.

Show-and-tell had started five-minutes into Civics and they were moving slowly, alphabetically, through the class.

Jesus, Bobby Milbanks was taking forever with his dumb *Visible Man* doll – he'd actually dumped most of the guts out. Now he dryly named each organ, holding each tiny plastic piece up to the class before replacing it, painstakingly, in its proper location within the clear cavity.

At the front of the row to Donovan's right, Cassandra Worwick had taken advantage of several absences and moved to the front row for the demonstrations. Donovan was pretty sure she liked Bobby. She leaned forward into her desktop, watching the dull reverse autopsy with rapt interest.

Donovan grimaced.

The big clock at the front of the room read, 1:41. In nine minutes they'd be breaking for art class.

Next to the windows, way back at the end of the shelf that ran the length of the classroom, Yertle's orange crate had gone strangely silent.

Was he asleep?

Polite applause from the classroom as Bobby proudly snapped the plastic chest plate back onto his *finally* reassembled doll.

"Thank you, Robert." Sr. Mary Augusta, smiled brightly from her desk, "That was educational."

"Mr. O'Malley. What have you brought for us today?"

"Um." Skinny and taller than most in his class, his overly long thigh struck the desktop as he stood, the desk lifted and dropped loudly, bringing a few guffaws from the class. *Cassandra Worwick was looking at him.*

"Uh." He practically sprinted to the back of the room. "I have something you don't see every day – even though, he...uh is right at home here in the desert."

Donovan hefted the crate. His heart leapt as he felt Yertle shift with the sudden movement. *He's still alive! Thank you, God!*

The special treat he'd given Yertle was gone too, so he hadn't been too terrorized by the box to eat.

Donovan hurried to the front of the classroom, taking as much care as he could not to conk any heads with the crate along the way.

Normally, he'd feed Yertle half a lettuce head as a treat every few days. Knowing it would be a long day in a cramped space, Donovan had been especially generous this morning. He'd dropped a whole lettuce head in the bag before he'd taped it shut. In the darkness of the bag, with a belly full of breakfast, Yertle had likely settled in for a long nap.

Donovan set the crate carefully onto the floor at the front of the room. His classmates stood and leaned forward – the rustling crate had been an object of fascination for them all morning – even Sister Augusta had left her desk to look.

Best of all, Cassandra Worwick was all the way up on her elbows to look. Their eyes met. Heat flashed in Donovan's cheeks. Something told him *look away!*

But he didn't. Not right away.

"Mr. O'Malley?"

He quickly knelt beside the crate, ripped open the bag and reached inside.

"Um. Let me introduce to you, Yertle. The desert tortoise!"

He pulled the sleepy tortoise from its dark cell, hefted it up and slowly twirled the creature overhead giving a good look, scaly head, foot to tail.

The boys, *"oooo"*ed. Some of the girls, *"ugggh"*ed.

Yertle's big snake of a neck craned suddenly, his beaky face gaped, suddenly awake, and as Donovan turned Yertle's scaly, twitching tail toward the class...

Yertle let loose.

Anyone who grows up in the Sonoran desert has a favorite Mexican food dish. For Donovan O'Malley, that was the sour cream enchilada. Stuffed with cheese, rimmed with lettuce and sour cream, it's a cooling desert delight. It also looks like tortoise poop.

Yertle's blast showered nun habit, desk, shirts, blouses and patent leather shoes alike across the front of the classroom.

And Cassandra Worwick was ground zero.

Chapter 4

"I'm not a queer!"

He couldn't do it. He wanted to. Sure he did.

The moon was full, so bright. Why did it have to be so bright? Everything glowed bright silver and it was so, so clear.

His heart beat so hard and fast he felt like it had broken free, had leaped straight up his throat.

You didn't do something like this in the open; you didn't do this where everyone could see...

"I'm not a - !"

Barney woke with a rattling cough, but the cough was swallowed as a train roared by. His house shook in sympathy with the nearby tracks.

"Oh God."

Barney pulled the chain on the tattered lamp that sat on the wooden chair beside his cot. It threw dim yellow light across the room.

The little man sat at the side of his bed, his toes barely reaching the threadbare carpet. He bent nearly in half to lift the bottle he found there. He unscrewed the cap, and drank.

The bottle had maybe half a day left inside. He took another bottle with him.

Ten minutes later, Barney was in his rust-bucket of a truck, an International Harvester bought from a junkyard way back when he could afford such things, driving drunk, at a well-practiced, police-safe speed, past the strip bars and detritus at the southwest end of the Phoenix suburban sprawl.

It didn't take long to reach his destination. He parked, pushed open the door and dropped to the ground, feeling every bit of that drop in his knees, and trudged into the cemetery as he had each Sunday for a long, long time.

A bare hint of daylight defined the worn monuments ahead of him, just enough to purple the blueish moonlight. At one time this had been the cemetery of rich and poor alike, but that was a long, long time ago. The rich were mostly buried in Scottsdale, on the east side these days, and the memorials left him slim pickings. Still, he managed to fashion a small bouquet of lilies as he staggered deep into the world of the dead.

The grave he delivered the dying flowers to was poorly tended, strewn with dead flowers, but otherwise bald. All these years, and the grass had never healed the wound. Despite the little creek that ran behind the grave, patches of cracked earth showed between his widening blanket of limp lilies.

"I know you're there." Barney said.

He was staring at the cheap slice of concrete before him, but he was talking to the creek.

One half hour later, Barney completed his Sunday morning ritual. The little man pushed his way through the dressed-for-mass families, ignoring the pious deference of most, the outright disgust of others, to his favorite seat at Bill Johnson's Big Apple.

Other than the hooch, Sunday hash browns, bacon and a sunny-side up egg were Barney's main indulgence these days.

"Same as always, Barney?"

He nodded as the sidearm toting waitress placed a steaming cup of black coffee before him.

"Want that paper?" She said, as she cleared the dishes for him.

Creased, folded, and stained with coffee and grease, she began to pull it away. But Barney placed his hand over it when a photo caught his eye.

"I'll take it."

"'Kay, hon."

He fumbled dirty glasses from his pocket, lifted them shakily in place.

It was the Democrat-leaning Tucson paper, *The Tucson Gazette.* These days, the Republican's newspaper of choice, *The Arizona Tribune,* featured nothing but Barry Goldwater, Arizona's Republican Golden Boy and one-time presidential candidate, who hoped to make his big comeback as Senator once again.

The retirement of long-time Democrat, Carl Hayden, left a vacuum Goldwater was only-too-happy to fill.

But the *Gazette's* front page featured a tall, handsome man standing with his cute kid on a big boat. The girl was proudly hefting a large-mouth bass half her size.

The photo brought hot bile to Barney's perpetually raw throat. He coughed.

That his *old friend,* Todd Worwick, was running for Senator wasn't news to Barney, though he'd tried his best to ignore it. The cut-line below the photo read, "Senatorial hopeful, Todd Worwick with daughter, Cassandra, at Lake Pleasant."

He quickly scanned the article below it entitled: "Does Todd Worwick Have Bigger Fish in Mind?" A black & white halftone of a young woman, Deanne Mulhenney, sat beside the byline.

He pushed himself away from the table and headed for the door.

"I just put your order in, Barney."

"Not hungry."

He pulled exactly $3.75 from the change and wadded bills in his pocket and slid them next to his coffee.

"You don't have to -"

But he was already gone.

Chapter 5

It was a typical spring day in Phoenix. Not a cloud in the sky and hot as Hell.

Still, Legend City, Arizona's own western-themed version of Disneyland, was crowded with kids. Saint Bartholomew students bused by their Parish Youth Organization mixed with families on the midway. They rushed to the rides, to pan for gold, to eat dogs and burgers and to take a boat along a manufactured river for an exploration of Apache warrior Cochise's desert stronghold.

Soon they'd be lining up to see the antics of their favorite cartoon show hosts, Wallace and Ladmo.

Donovan and his friends had opted to take the scary ride into Cochise's violent territory first, and as they jumped back onto dry land, laughing and squealing, Terry grabbed his stomach and screamed.

"Ow! Ow! Ow! There's an arrow in my belly!"

"Just yank it out!" Donovan laughed, grabbing the other end of the long Red Vines candy Terry was holding to his stomach.

"I can't, it's got an arrowhead on the end!"

"I'll get it!" Donovan swung his foot up to Terry's hip, and shoved.

"OW! Ow! *OW!!!*"

"Got it!" Donovan greedily stuffed the ends of two Red Vines in his mouth.

"Hey – just take one, Piggy!"

He bit off the ends and handed one back.

"You guys are dorks!" their friend Cindy Tapper shouted.

They'd practically run from the ride – a boat trip that took them through Cochise's Stronghold - complete with the aftermath of an

Indian attack featuring a bloody white man robot, writhing in pain, trying unsuccessfully to remove an arrow from his gut.

"That was grodie!"

"Laugh my butt off every time I see it." Terry's sugar-glazed eyes were wide, "Oh man have you been to the Wax Museum in Scottsdale?"

Cindy hadn't.

Donovan had – he knew exactly where Terry was going with this one. He grabbed Terry's red hair.

"Me scalp-'em!"

"Hah! Yeah – they got a guy getting scalped!"

Donovan released him, and Terry rubbed his scalp vigorously.

"Yeah," Donovan elaborated, "You see blood and, like, you know the skin underneath his hair."

Cindy's entire face scrunched up.

"How can you even look at that stuff?"

"What about that other guy getting skinned alive?"

"Oh man!" Terry pulled his lower lip down, exposing gums and globs of shiny Red Vine goo. "They rip his lip down – and they slice -"

"God! Stop it!" Cindy shouted. But she was laughing too, not at the gruesome images – but at the idea that these two boys *thought* they were funny.

A dust-devil swirled sand, dust, and hot dog wrappers across the midway and kids were running from it laughing and screaming like it was just one more ride, covering their dogs and soft drinks and having a great time doing it.

Their friend, Dave, had rushed to the boys' room immediately after the ride. He trotted back to them now. Dave had the bladder God gave a flea.

"What do we do next?" He asked.

"It's 1:15 now - Wallace and Ladmo show starts at 2:00."

"I want a Ladmo-bag!" Terry said.

"When does the bus leave?"

"Six O'clock," Donovan said.

"But we have to be at the gate by five-thirty," Cindy always seemed to know the full story.

St. Bartholomew's Parish Youth Organization had co-sponsored the day and provided the bus from the parking lot to the park.

"Okay – I say we do the Sky Ride."

"Yeah – we can get over to the other side of the park, get on the train and be back at the stage before the show."

In a flash, the group was headed toward the Sky Ride, but the closer they got to the knot of kids waiting in line, the slower Donovan walked. Fake guts and Indian attacks were one thing, being suspended in a gondola, basically a big bucket, a hundred or more feet in the air was another. *Sure, you'd get a great view of the park and the Phoenix Zoo beyond...*

But the truth was, Donovan was afraid of heights.

Deathly afraid.

Up ahead, their little group had already met up with another knot of friends from school. Donovan's long legs, which normally carried him a step or more ahead of everyone if he didn't purposely slow down for them, had other plans now, and moving toward certain death wasn't in those plans.

"Hey, slowpoke!" Terry yelled back at him.

"I'm gonna...get a Coke," Donovan said.

"Come on, man! We can do that after!"

"I think...I'm gonna get one now."

The knot of kids unfolded into a rag-tag line at the gate as a gondola swung toward them. Doors opened to let kids out, and others scrambled happily in. Way...way up in the air, thin cables carried bucket-loads of screaming kids over the park.

Why couldn't he just do that and laugh like everyone else?

He shook his head.

The others were still calling his name as they joined the line; all but Cindy.

Finally, Cindy walked back to him.

"I think there's a hot-dog shack over by the theater," she said. "I'm thirsty too."

Donovan nodded.

Before he knew it they were walking silently together toward the park entrance.

It occurred to him he should say something. Why couldn't he think of anything? Talking was never a problem with Dave and Terry.

Cindy's hair was shiny and black, and her skin was absolutely white – except for a sprinkle of reddish-brown freckles over her nose and cheeks. The contrast of her skin and hair was striking, the first thing you noticed about her. In Arizona where you couldn't escape the sun if you tried, it was practically a miracle. She had wide blue eyes, a pert nose, and was actually really pretty when it came right down to it.

Why hadn't he noticed that before? Maybe he had.

Why did it matter?

He'd never walked alone with a girl before. Not even Cindy. It was awkward.

They were friends, as much as girls *could* be friends in the circle of boys he'd run around with since kindergarten. Somewhere around third grade, he figured, Cindy had quietly joined that circle.

"The arrow thing IS kind of grodie, isn't it?" He said, finally.

"Yes. It IS!" she chortled, before the back of her hand could reach up and suppress it.

The sound she made started him laughing too.

"You'd never see *that* at Disneyland!" She said.

He supposed she was right about that. Disneyland, which he guessed Legend City was supposed to be for Arizona, would *never* have a ride like Cochise's Stronghold. Not with all the blood and arrows and stuff.

"I don't think Walt Disney would want it – but you gotta admit, the Lincoln robot is kind of creepy."

He was referring to the "Great Moments with Mister Lincoln" exhibit off Disneyland's Main Street. The robot Lincoln that had scared him stiff the first time he'd seen it.

"Yes! That is too! Did you notice how his mouth doesn't always match his words?"

"Yeah! Sometimes it's way off – like those robots in the *Carousel of Progress*. *There's a great big beautiful tomorrow...*" He sang, moving his mouth and arms out of sequence with the tune, *"...shining at the end of every day..."*

"That's funny!"

Her hand came up again – but not in time to hide the flash of metal from her new braces. That's why she did that, covered her mouth, he realized now. She was self-conscious about the braces and somehow, that was...*cute.*

"That big eyeball in the Monsanto ride is pretty creepy too."

"Man; that IS creepy!"

He nearly brought them back to the Great Moments with Mister Lincoln show – to say how funny it might be to have a John Wilkes Booth robot appear behind the curtain – but wisely decided Cindy might not find that funny at all.

Their conversation had carried them to the refreshment stand. He checked the prices. He had three dollars on him. He wondered if he should buy her drink too.

She pulled a small hand purse from her back pocket. "What do you want? I'll get it."

"Uh..."

"Two Cokes and hot dogs." She said to the frazzled, overheated kid behind the counter, before Donovan could answer.

"You could eat one, right?" She asked.

"Yeah...sure."

They sat on one of the few well-shaded benches, washing down big chomps of sweet dog and relish. She'd eaten her dog bare, handing the mustard-filled bun off to Donovan, which he practically inhaled without a second thought. They laughed at the kids pulling their moms and dads from ride to ride, and made fun of the nuns back at "Saint Farts" which had quickly degraded from their first nickname for the school, "Saint Bart's." Magically, right now *everything* was funny.

She checked her watch and announced, "One-thirty-five. Terry and Dave should be headed back this way. Let's do another ride before Wallace and Ladmo"

"Okay." They were on the midway now, this was where the usual carnival sort of rides were, basically the ones without *old west* themes.

"What haven't we done yet?"

"Oh! Oh! Oh!" she said, *"The Rage Cage! Let's do The Rage Cage!"*

Rat crap. No.

Scared of small, tight places as he was of heights, The Rage Cage was the last thing Donovan ever wanted to ride, but there was no way he could turn her down.

The Rage Cage stood alone before them now as though every other ride in the huge park had disintegrated and blown away in a Phoenix dust-devil.

A tall Ferris-wheel of sorts, but rather than benches moving slowly around a big wheel, this ride consisted of mobile cages riding a chain which itself moved over the edge of a long lever. If you picture a chainsaw blade – the cages were the teeth. Now picture that blade flipping end over end. As if that weren't enough – the cages themselves could flip and spin nauseatingly on their own if you liked, or lock in place, manually operated by a stainless steel ring on the “safety” bar that held you in.

If the Sky Ride was a bad dream for the deathly acrophobic, the Rage Cage was their worst nightmare.

A few feet away, two wobbly-legged kids led themselves out of the wire-cage-of-death they’d just left. The smell of something sick and sour cut through that of axle grease, oil, and fried food in the air. *Vomit*.

Before Donovan could think of a way out that didn't make him look like a complete wuss, the ride operator, some college kid who no doubt took pleasure in torture, swung the door open to Donovan's certain death.

Reluctantly, Donovan took his seat beside Cindy, with that shiny steel ring right before them. The operator slammed the mesh door home with a *“Clang!”* that sounded very much like a jail cell slamming shut, and locked them inside.

A quick jolt followed by a ratcheting that could have come from raising the anchor chain of the Titanic, and Donovan felt the cage swing suddenly free. It lifted them just even with the roof of the hot dog stand then stopped, briefly, to take on another cage load of fresh victims.

“Let's see if we can flip it!” Cindy took a firm grip on the ring.

“I don't know -”

“Come on – put your weight into it! *Like this!”*

Cindy threw her weight back, tugging the ring toward them as she did so – their knees rose over their heads. A momentary feeling of weightlessness, a complete loss of control...and over they went.

Actually, the feeling wasn't half bad. In fact...*it was fun!*

“Wow!”

They rocked it together as the last cage was loaded beneath them.

Two flips this time!

“Yeah!!!”

The ratcheting sound began in earnest now. Crazy calliope music swelled loud as they rose, higher and higher into the sun. The theater, the boat ride, he could even see the Phoenix Zoo now as they rocked and spun. Now the rooftops of the food shacks and attractions, now sky...and then the great lever, the chainsaw blade from which the spinning cages dangled like strange fruit, lifted them even higher and faster through the air.

And suddenly he realized he was in a tight cage that spun freely in space with the ground rushing up to meet them – and then the sky – and then the ground.

Sweat broke from every pore, his body went rigid, and he would have screamed if he had the breath to do it, but he couldn't take that breath -

The music stopped. The ratcheting slowed. Mysteriously, the Rage Cage cranked to a stop, mid-ride.

Oh, the dog and drink had not been a good idea...all that mustard...

"Oh man!" Cindy protested. *"It's not even half-way through!"*

Down on the midway, Donovan glimpsed a pink T-shirt and blonde hair. *Cassandra Worwick*, making her way between the rides and refreshments just like all the other kids. She had turned to see why the cacophony of the Rage Cage had abruptly ended.

For a moment, he was sure *she saw him.*

A putrid rain spattered down on them.

Cindy pulled the ring and threw her weight back before Donovan could lift a hand, utter a word to stop her!

And just like that, they were upside down, looking straight up through the floor of their steel cage, to the midsection of the cage above them. That cage wobbled and rocked uneasily as the stricken kids inside showed *exactly why* downing hot dogs and pop before a ride on the Rage Cage was a really, *really bad idea.*

"Cindy, let go of the ring!" He cried. *"Jesus! Let go!"*

But Cindy's fingers were frozen to it; her eyes *saucer-wide.*

And then the motion-sick kids above them really let loose -

"Damn it, Cindy!"

He pried her fingers away just as what must have been five buckets of putrid hot dogs and soda and half-digested treats unknown sluiced over them.

Eventually their cage on the ride Donovan would never ride again locked into the unload position and they were free once again to stumble, sticky and stinky, back onto stable asphalt. The crowd of kids quickly opened a wide space for them to move through... And just when Donovan was sure he couldn't possibly feel worse *he saw Cassandra Worwick walking quickly away from them.*

The ride operator groaned behind them. Sadistic or not, that kid would have to clean the cages.

Good for him.

Cindy, small shoulders slumped, shiny black hair matted with yellow-nastiness looked like a latrine-drenched rodent. Donovan knew he looked pretty much the same. They both stank to high-heaven as they slunk to their respective restrooms.

Bathing, then washing your clothes in the sink of a public restroom is likely an art, especially for the unusually tall.

Donovan quickly realized he had no talent for it. The desert sun was a godsend today – at least his shirt and shorts would be dry before the end of the next ride, *if he could even handle another ride...*

The fun had drained out of the day.

What a dweeb he was. What a doofuss. Every time Cassandra saw him he did something gross.

He checked his watch. It was almost time for the Wallace and Ladmo show. Everybody would be there. He sniffed his already drying shirt. The soap had only added stiffness, and a weird sweetness to the putrid odor. *Oh, man.*

The sun burst into his eyes as he opened the door.

When his sight came back, there was Cindy, wet hair dangling and drying on her forehead. She wore a brand new Legend City T-Shirt with a picture of Wallace and Ladmo emblazoned on the front. She held a similar one out to him.

"Man, thank you…"

He liked Wallace and Ladmo, but a shirt with their faces on it was kind of a "little kid" thing...still, he tore his stinking shirt off and tossed it into a nearby trash can without too much regret. He pulled the new one on.

But he still only had three dollars on him.

"Geez, how much do I owe you?"
"Nothing. Cassie Worwick bought them."

-=-=-=-=-=-=-=-

"Come in, Pat. Door's not locked."

"Maybe it *should be.* Anyone could just walk in here."

Deanne uncurled herself from the sedan, setting her glasses on top of the newspapers piled on the coffee table. She slid last night's watery drink out of sight as she stretched some life into her stiff back.

Her cousin's visit was the perfect excuse for a fresh pot of coffee.

Barely nine AM on a Saturday morning and it had already been a long day for her.

Father Patrick Mulhenney, looking distinctly unpriestly this morning in Bermuda shorts and a T-shirt, carried the saddest-looking bouquet of lilies she'd ever seen through her entryway.

"What's *that* for?" She lifted her coffee mug toward him as she made her way to the kitchen, and he followed her.

"Sure...I'll take a cup." He said. "These aren't from me. They were on your doorstep. One of your many fans, I'm sure."

Now she realized his comment about locking her door wasn't just one of his quips.

"I have no fans."

"Apparently."

He laid the limp bouquet next to the stone sink.

"I'm pretty sure those are past needing water," she said, dumping fresh grounds in the basket. She turned up the heat and took a good look at the sad bouquet; a mix of pink, white, and red lilies in various stages of decline. Seven in all.

"Who sends anyone lilies? Let alone, me?" She said.

"A lovesick boy longing for mommy?"

"Hah! None of *those* in my immediate circle."

"Well. One thing is certain – they weren't delivered by a florist. These were unceremoniously dropped in front of your door – I just gathered them up."

"Okay...that *IS* creepy. I *will* start locking that door. No note?"

"I just saw the flowers, but I wasn't really looking for one."

Behind her, the pot began to perk.

"You sure you want coffee?" She asked.

"I'll take what *you* were having."

"Is it that obvious?"

He raised his eyebrows.

"Straight up or on the rocks?" She popped the door on the overhead cabinet, revealing a wealth of colorful bottles. "Sure you wouldn't rather have a Bloody Mary?"

"I'd *love* one. Lots of pepper; no salt, I need to watch that."

"You got it."

"I know you didn't come by to scrape a bunch of dead flowers off my doorstep – but, since you did...and I know you like a mystery – seven flowers - anything you can think of?"

"Plenty of things... if you're looking for a religious answer: The Seven Deadly Sins, if you include the day God took to recover from it The Creation really took seven days, the Sabbath being of course, the seventh day. Have any Seventh Day Adventist friends?"

"Can rule that one out."

"Well...maybe it isn't the number. I mean...*lilies.* Lilies have associations themselves. Easter. Funerals. Death, resurrection, the return to innocence."

"Okay. Now I'm getting a *bolt* on that door too."

"Seriously, Deanne. You have, well, pissed a lot of people off."

"A lot of *your* people, *Father* Pat."

"You attacked the Church."

"I attacked abuse, Pat. The Church owned those crimes when it covered them up. That's on the Catholic Church not me."

"Are you going to make those drinks now or later?"

She pulled two glasses from the cupboard, withdrew a stalk of celery and a half-empty pitcher from the refrigerator. She snapped the stalk in half, poked one in each glass, dropped in ice and poured.

She shook black pepper into both and handed him a glass.

"Let's look for a note."

There wasn't one. Not under the doormat, nor the Terracotta planters.

Beyond her low adobe wall, the Praying Monk, a lone outcropping of rock that also comprised the "eyelash" of the *resting camel* that gave Camelback Mountain its name, continued his endless devotion.

It was already hot, the early morning sun already whitening the sandstone, glaring off it. They retreated inside, back to the kitchen and the wilted offering on her counter.

"Weird joke?" Pat mused.

"Maybe."

But the sleuth in neither of them believed it.

"So...no weird boyfriend."

"If there were one he most likely would be...but no."

"Well, you've been covering the Worwick campaign. You'll find this hard to believe, I know...but not everybody likes what you write. Maybe he doesn't either."

They toasted.

"There isn't anything new I can find on Goldwater. So…like they say, *Worwick's Our Man.*"

"Todd Worwick is a good looking fellow though, isn't he?"

"Spare me. But I haven't found a good angle there either."

"But you *are* devoting a lot of ink to him."

"Come on, Pat. I work for *The Tucson Gazette.* He's a Democrat, they love him."

"Well...maybe that's what those flowers are about. Maybe someone *doesn't* love him so much. Maybe that's the message. They *are* lilies after all - a flower associated with death."

"They're pretty much dead themselves. *Jesus, Pat,*" she said without a hint of concern he'd take offense at her casual blasphemy. "What if someone is using *me* to announce an assassination attempt? It's only been five years since Dallas."

"Good Lord, *I touched them...*" Her cousin blanched. "*I just carried them in!*"

"I'm just throwing it out there. They're just dead flowers. There's no crime...*yet.*"

Still, Deanne retrieved the camera gear from her bedroom.

As she snapped pictures of the flowers from various angles, the various stages of their decline, of death, became even more obvious.

These flowers had been picked several days apart.

Chapter 6

"Cassie?"

Cassandra's door opened into a room still princess pink.

It made Todd smile. She was still his princess. For how much longer he wondered? One day this door would be locked.

A poster of the sexually-harmless Davy Jones from The Monkees still dominated that space beneath her doll shelf these days.

"Let her sleep, Todd," Sondra whispered over his shoulder. "*She's* had a full day of fun."

He took in the slow, even rise of his daughter's breathing; a sound more purr than snore, and the sweet cascade of golden hair over her pillow. He nodded, closing the door gently behind him.

The call he'd been waiting for had come – and it had come not from one of LBJ's lackeys, *but from Lyndon himself.* Vietnam, the rising tide of civil unrest, the old man finally had enough. Johnson wouldn't be running for President. He would announce his abdication in a matter of days.

Sondra stood at the end of the hallway, thin robe loosely tied at her hip. She held a tumbler in each hand. Behind her, the panoramic window opened to mountains silhouetted against a blanket of stars. A cooling breeze swept sweet spring desert air over the narrow pool at her bare feet, rippling its surface.

"We have a lot to consider," she said. "This is good for you."

But was it? Todd Worwick had caught the attention of party bosses and of Lyndon Johnson in particular with his support of the Central Arizona Water Project. Positioned as a centerpiece of an even broader infrastructure initiative, CAP, as they were calling it, was a source of pride, and even more important, a source of income and control of even broader initiatives going forward. It had brought Todd very far in a very short period of time – but without Lyndon Johnson to back it, where would the party's priorities be?

CAP couldn't die on the political vine. *It had to happen.*

Todd wasn't ready for this. His looks, his ability to read others and exploit weakness when he could had brought him this far, but he was a political novice at best.

Once more in his life he stood on the brink of disaster.

The red Samurai mask glowered at him from its pedestal on the stone mantle.

Did he still have enough of the warrior in him to do this? Was this sudden vacuum in the party really good for him?

With Lyndon on the way out and the convention only months away, it was that *little shit* Bobby's show now. Bobby had the Kennedy pedigree not to mention a deadly powerful political machine. Civil Rights, not make-work projects like CAP, would be his platform.

Still, Todd nodded, taking her hand with the glass she'd offered as he guided it to his lips. The bourbon was sweet and her hand was warm and soft against his lips.

"Good for *us,*" he corrected.

Cassandra's eyes were wide open now.

Whispers had given way to open talk as her father had closed her bedroom door and *that woman* had walked with him down the hall. Words she couldn't quite make out, and then the words had given way to other sounds from the pool outside. *Lovemaking.*

She thought of her mom. The thoughts came in colors, sometimes hot red colors, but mostly sad purples and blues.

She pulled Penny, the stuffed pony who had been her friend for as long as she could remember, to her chest and filled her head with images from her day, the smells, frights and wonders, the laughter, the candy and hot dogs, the rides. The images were yellow-white with sun. Behind the tints of color – she saw the tall boy, Donovan, who always seemed to make her laugh. He was like Wallace and Ladmo, or even a cartoon character. No matter what he tried to do, he always wound up in some sort of trouble, in the middle of something embarrassing, even gross.

The tortoise thing was *really* gross and embarrassing for her too – but it made her laugh, even though she had to replace her shoes.

She wished she could laugh now.

Outside, in the pool...it was getting really loud now...

Cassandra closed her eyes, crying softly as she drifted into the dull gray of her dreams.

-=-=-=-=-=-=-=-

Deanne urged her fire-engine red Starfire convertible up the hill and eased it into a space just below Sedona's Chapel of the Cross. From here the view of the red rock formations dotted with juniper, mesquite and chaparral, was stunning.

She'd kept the top up this morning. It was a cold spring day by Arizona standards, and as she popped open the door and stepped out of the car, Deanne wished she'd grabbed more than a scarf before she'd made the trek north.

She climbed the hill quickly, huffing a bit more than she should.

When she pulled open the door and stood before the altar, all her childhood feelings of awe and dread of the crucified *Christus* came as powerfully, as darkly, as they had the first time she'd seen this frightening statue.

Growing up Catholic she was used to images of martyred saints, and of the Crucifixion. Even through the agony of arrows, stones, and fire, a certain serenity, a promise of eternal life always came through the faces of the martyred – but there was no such promise with the Christus over the altar in the Chapel of the Cross. This was Christ as though he never had, never *could* rise again. A rotted twist of tendon and bone, his chest cavity a wide, black, open wound of decay, the sculpture had sparked both horror and praise from the moment it was installed.

A teenage girl knelt in the first pew, a tiara of desert flowers adorned her raven black hair.

The girl rose when she noticed Deanne and the already diaphanous dress she wore, also strung with flowers, nearly evaporated in the powerful sunlight that poured through the panoramic window.

The naked paganism of the girl beneath the Christus was nothing short of shocking. Deanne felt herself draw a breath, take an involuntary, unsteady step backwards.

Circled by the unmistakable scents of pot and strawberry incense, the girl smiled up at her with stoned green eyes.

"I'm Deanne Mulhenney. I was expecting Susan Worwick."

The girl leaned in and kissed her cheek, the pungency of the *flower girl* came along with the kiss.

"I know. I'll take you to Susan," she said.

Down into the lush tangle of Oak Creek and winding westward into the red hills beyond, the girl coughed short commands of "tighty-righty," for "turn right," and "hang a Louie," for left, barely glancing upward from a ring of manzanita, reeds, and feathers in her lap as she busily weaved reeds, vines and beaded feathers into a wreath.

"It's a *dreamcatcher,*" the girl explained. "The Navajo came up with the idea."

Deanne smiled.

"Who told you that?"

"Porter."

"So you're Agnetha. You're Porter Hudson's daughter?"

"Aggie, please. But, uh huh."

"You call your father by his first name?"

"Of course," she smiled vacantly up at Deanne. "That's his name."

Deanne shook her head, "I guess you go with what you're taught."

"'Guess."

"I'm pretty sure it was the Chippewa or Sioux."

"Who?"

"The Indians who began weaving Dreamcatchers."

"Oh," the girl said as though the distinction made no difference at all. "Hang a Louie on Sluice Road."

The road was narrow, barely more than a steep, gravel-filled crack between the pines and oak. With trepidation, Deanne nosed the big car over the edge, the rear wheels kicked rocks and dirt, hammering the wheel wells and sending clouds of dust high into the air. Deanne wondered if the Starfire would keep any of its paint through this day.

Dust and pine gave way to a disheveled hillside studded with mounds of rock, and crosses. A taller, rockier hill beyond, held the rust-crumbling maw of an abandoned mine. Just below the cemetery, a single street lined with what could have been the decrepit remains of an abandoned Hollywood western set.

"You live *here?"*

"Cool, huh?" the girl said with no trace of sarcasm. "Welcome to Piñon Rim."

They sat outside on the back balcony of what the old-west goldminers likely called a "house of ill-repute." Open walls revealed a re-piping and wiring work-in-progress. Other than that, the wainscoted, gaudily-papered original insides, the pressed-tin ceiling, seemed more or less intact. A gas-powered generator chugged just below the deck, and chickens pecked and ran freely in the grassed area beyond.

A breeze brought the clink and bong of clay and bronze wind chimes. Bright rainbow-colored shapes danced over every surface, cast from crystals dangling like sparkly stalactites from every available perch.

If you didn't mind the spooky cemetery and rotted out mine several hundred yards from the balcony, their view of the forest and rock formations, the clear blue sky rising above them, was as spectacular a sight as any she'd seen.

"It's beautiful isn't it?"

"It *is* that."

"But...it's a *ghost town,* yes." Porter Hudson, his button down shirt open to reveal gray chest wool that matched his mutton-chops, served tea in fine bone china. "Susan is finishing her sun salutations. Would you like breakfast? I was just scrambling eggs. They're fresh."

Just at the mention, her stomach growled. She'd left early. Her breakfast had been coffee this morning.

"If it's no trouble, thank you – I'd love some. And yes, as pretty as it is, there is literally *nothing* living here but your family and those chickens."

"Oh – there is plenty of life," he laughed. "We have everything here. Mountain lions, wolves, quail – you name it."

"People?"

"Better than people – *spirits*! The *spirit world* is all around us here – and the harmonics are wonderful. You can feel the *convergence* here, can't you? There is an Indian word for it – *orenda.* This area has *orenda.*"

Deanne knew that was an Iroquois word for spiritual power, really more about *internal* spiritual struggle – but going back to the misinformation he'd fed his daughter about the origin of the dreamcatcher, Deanne couldn't help wondering where Porter Hudson, the trust-fund baby of a wealthy east-coast real-estate mogul, had first seen the word. Had it been scratched into a chip of soapstone he'd found in a souvenir store on the way here from New York?

On the small patch of well-groomed grass below, his daughter was dancing barefoot to music only she heard.

"Aggie's a *free-spirit."* He said, as if the description was necessary.

Deanne nodded, "She seems to be." *Free-spirited or not, how the hell could you drop your half-naked daughter at an empty church miles away to wait for a stranger?* That was a question she kept herself from asking, at least for now. Susan Worwick was the reason she was here. It wouldn't do to make an enemy.

Right on cue, patting unseen sweat from her perfect cheekbones, a cascade of shimmering blonde hair cascading over her bare shoulders, Susan Worwick, dressed in dance tights and a terrycloth robe, took a cup of tea from Porter on his way to the kitchen.

"Miss Mulhenney, it's a pleasure to meet you."

"Thank you for agreeing to see me, Mrs. Worwick."

"Thank you for coming all this way." She swept effortlessly across the floor to the balcony as if gliding over air, seated herself on the bench beside Deanne and crossed her legs, yogi style.

"Always nice to get out of the valley."

"Well, now that we've gotten that out of the way. Can we stick with first names, Deanne?"

"Happy to, Susan."

"I know I'm not your reason for being here, so let's get a few other things out of the way too. I love my husband. If you're here for anything salacious, I have nothing for you. Porter's a friend, not my lover."

Susan smiled with nary a crease marking her face and, though Deanne knew Susan Worwick was only two months from twenty-nine, it struck Deanne just how youthful the woman looked. She'd only seen Cassandra that one time on the boat, but Susan truly could have been her older sister.

"I'm not here to tear anyone down," Deanne assured her.

"You *have* done that before."

"Not intentionally, but facts can be harsh. I'd like to believe your husband is the best statesman Arizona has ever seen, and if that's true I want Arizonans to know *why* he is."

"But here *I* am, and no *good* wife leaves a good husband. If I'm not bad, he *must* be."

"No nonsense."

"Nonsense has its place. I left mine in high school. I partied, I fell in love."

"You got pregnant."

"I did."

"So why leave now? Not just your husband...your daughter."

Susan Worwick produced dark, horn-rimmed, glasses from her robe as the rising sun burnt the sandstone cliffs beyond. "Would you like a pair, the air is clear here, much cleaner than it is down in the valley. The sun here can burn very deeply."

"I'm good."

"You have what you were looking for, Deanne. *I'm* the bad one. Not Todd."

Porter reappeared from the kitchen. He set two plates of scrambled eggs with sausage, wedges of orange and grapefruit arranged like the sunrise before them.

"The water here is wonderful," Porter said, placing a glass of water beside her plate. "I'm sure you noticed the well when you parked."

"You came for the waters?" Deanne smiled; glad to break the sudden freeze with the quote, *"were you misinformed?"*

But neither Porter nor Susan caught the *Casablanca* reference.

"No. We weren't misinformed at all. It *is* wonderful. It comes straight from a mountain spring; absolutely pure."

"Completely disconnected from the Colorado and Agua Fria rivers," Susan added. "A source all its own."

"Why is that important?"

Porter and Susan exchanged a glance.

"River water, uggh!" Porter exclaimed, "*Fish fuck in it!*"

Deanne nearly spit her eggs across the table. They all broke into laughter.

Porter waved his hand toward the torn up walls, the bare wires and pipe, "All of this is temporary. Once Arcosanti gets going, we'll be moving there to help Paulo build it."

He tapped a clay bell hanging from a nearby hook, along with the mellow sound of its chime; Deanne noted a signature on the bell itself, *P. Soleri.*

"We're old friends," Porter called over his shoulder on his way back to the kitchen.

Paulo Soleri was an Italian architect whose radical socialistic designs for community reformation were reflected in his designs. With his move to Arizona, the man had been a controversial topic for her former colleagues at the *Arizona Tribune*. Like most, she had assumed the creation of Arcosanti, a densely populated Paulo Soleri "city" in the high desert not far from where they now sat was an impossible dream. The *Tucson Gazette* hailed him as not only a major artist, but something of a populist hero.

From what she had already learned of Porter Hudson, the fact he was on board with the building of Arcosanti wasn't surprising – but the contrast of the royal lifestyle awaiting Susan Worwick if her husband's political bid was successful made her choice even more perplexing.

The woman-child, Susan Worwick, picked at her fruit, her gaze more often than not toward the hills and beyond; obviously more uncomfortable with this discussion than she'd been earlier.

This isn't her choice.

"Building a self-sustaining community in the middle of the desert; has that been a dream of yours, Susan?"

"You don't *know* him, Deanne," Susan pivoted, "And you won't. Not from me."

"Paulo Soleri?"

A wry smile lit Susan's face.

"Todd's a tall, charismatic and handsome man; smooth and brash at the same time. Easy to fall in love with. *But you'll never know him."*

"I've only spoken with him once, but I'm hoping to set up -"

"I *know* you haven't slept with him, Deanne."

And where had *that* come from?

The jealous but forbearing political wife, it was a role that Jackie Kennedy had tragically turned into an art form. Deanne was well aware of the power of her own looks; she had willingly used that power to gain entry where doors were locked tight maybe more often than she'd needed to. Still, it was a slap. She disappointed herself when, with all her journalistic experience and skill, she could only manage a weak,

"What?" in return.

A quiet laugh that was more of a sigh from the woman-child who suddenly seemed much more sharp-edged than Deanne would have imagined.

"I know...because *you* haven't heard his screams. *I'd know if you had."*

And now, here at mid-morning during an Arizona spring, a definite chill had settled suddenly in.

"His *screams?"*

Susan shook her head, looking very much like someone in urgent need of a cigarette, or a stiff drink. The latter was a feeling Deanne knew very, very well.

"I still can't believe he took our daughter to...*that lake."*

"Lake Pleasant? Did something happen there?"

"When they were kids Todd's little brother drowned there, near the dam. It was a terrible tragedy."

Deanne knew he'd had a brother who died young, but she knew very little beyond that.

"Todd couldn't save him. He was traumatized. I've spent a long time trying to help him deal with that; it's part of him."

Deanne couldn't help seeing the sad irony there.

"The Central Arizona Water Project," Deanne said. "He's backing a program that will make that lake even bigger, more accessible than ever."

Susan shook her head.

"He's not making it bigger, Deanne. He's drowning it."

"Free-spirit," Aggie had taken her dance to the rock-walled well near Deanne's car.

Susan Worwick joined Deanne at the back steps of the old hotel/brothel turned "temporary" home. Porter waved from the top of the stairway, as Deanne returned an unexpected goodbye hug from Susan.

"I'm sorry you came all this way for so little," Susan said.

"Not at all, thank you for your time, and your perspective."

"There may actually be someone who could give you even more perspective...that is if he even exists."

Just when Deanne thought the day couldn't be more odd.

"Todd sometimes mentions another name along with Joey's," Susan said. "A Navajo boy - Tommy Red Hawk."

"What do you know about him?"

"Nothing really. Todd was shocked I mentioned the name – but he called Red Hawk Joey's *imaginary friend.* Look, this is more than I should say – and certainly not for print. Todd's not just some run-of-the mill cardboard cutout politician. He's a good man, a caring man who wants to make a difference."

"You think he blames himself for his brother's death?"

"I *know* he does. He has...*night terrors.* It's as if he's talking to Joey, and Red Hawk. I honestly don't know what he believes or chooses to believe about that day."

"I'll see what I can find on Red Hawk."

Before Susan headed back upstairs, she took a resigned, deep breath, looked deeply into Deanne's eyes. Even through the shades, those eyes looked tired and much older now.

"I know what your job is. Please don't hurt Todd."

What could she say? Maybe the truth would hurt him, maybe it wouldn't. Sometimes her job sucked either way.

And with that, Susan Worwick headed back upstairs to her temporary ghost town home.

Aggie leaned into the well, her head cocked sideways as she listened to whatever echoes might be playing within the stony wetness below.

Without looking up, she asked,

"You know your way back to the highway?"

"Hang a Louie by the cactus," Deanne said, "Couple tighty righties at the pines."

"You got it. The water really *is* better here, you know."

"More pure?"

Now Aggie did look back at Deanne, and her eyes were dead serious when she said,

"No monsters."

-=-=-=-=-=-=-=-

Deanne came home to a new gift lying in a loose bunch at her front door: four limp and long-dead lilies.

She photographed them before dumping them into the waste bin beneath her sink. A good long bath beckoned. Only mid-afternoon and it had already been a long day.

She passed the kitchen phone on the way to a heavenly soak. She sighed. Her day wasn't finished yet. She walked back to the phone and dialed the *Gazette's* desk for her messages.

She was happy to hear Tricia Parks, a fresh grad from the University of Arizona's Journalism Department. Perky and ambitious with a good eye for detail, the kid wouldn't stay long in the secretarial pool.

"One message from Todd Worwick's office. A dinner invite."

"From his campaign manager?"

"From the man himself."

"Oh." Even Deanne didn't believe her own feigned nonchalance.

She took the number, and quickly checked it against the one Sondra had given her for the campaign office. They didn't match. His private line? A dinner invite?

"Thanks, Trish."

It was a potential gold mine and a professional minefield rolled into one – not to mention a *personal* minefield. Worwick was a handsome, recently-estranged husband, with a politician's ego and a notorious off-the-field reputation from his college football career.

She'd need to keep her wits about her. One glass of wine tops.

Deanne dialed, trying not to sound startled when the new blood of the Democratic Party, senatorial candidate, Todd Worwick, answered the phone himself.

"Worwick."

"Deanne Mulhenney, from *The Tucson Gazette.*"

"Deanne. Great! I'd like to give you a scoop – how about dinner this evening with a few friends?"

"I could do that. Just -"

"No speeches, no campaign, just dinner and a round of goofy golf."

That last part caught her completely by surprise. A round of goofy golf? He didn't give her time to pause.

"Green Gables, 6:00, it's Cassie's birthday - she likes you."

"Ah – great. I'll be there."

"Outstanding! See you there. Oh, and no presents."

"Okay -"

The line clicked off.

Ah-great. I'll be there?

Jesus, Deanne.

How many ethical questions did this entire situation raise? Not to mention the most important question of all: what to wear?

In the end, she'd settled on a shift, cool, easy to move, not too low cut, sassy but not too short. She'd never actually had dinner at Green Gables, the Camelot-themed restaurant with its stone parapets and the armored knight mounted on horseback who greeted dinner guests. Like every kid she knew, she'd played the miniature golf course behind it. As kitschy as the restaurant looked she knew it was also fancy and expensive.

Security was appropriately visible in their jackets and sun-glasses as the knight rode his white horse directly to her car to greet her with a flourish of trumpets.

A valet dressed like Robin Hood drove her car away.

It was cool and dark inside. She was met by the pleasant aroma of roasting beef and vegetables as Lady Guinevere led her past walls filled with coats of arms, swords and crossbows, to a private dining room.

The happy chatter of kids cut through it all.

She barely recognized Cassandra Worwick, looking very much the young Brigitte Bardot in makeup and a party dress now, her thick blonde hair brushed up and sprayed in place, a stark contrast to the little girl Deanne had seen only days earlier out on the lake. *Had I even once been that well put-together at that age,* Deanne wondered? Had she been anything but awkward? No, not that she remembered.

A no-doubt *carefully* chosen group of friends were just now seating themselves at the table, it was most likely not the first time most in *this* group had seen their names on place cards.

She noticed one boy in particular; tall, gawkily handsome, he never took his eyes off Cassandra.

Smitten.

Seated across from him, a very pretty girl with porcelain smooth white skin and raven-black hair. She eyed him with the same not-so-secret enthusiasm.

With a tug of the heart, Deanne drew the obvious triangle between them. It was impossible not to.

No, she didn't miss adolescence one bit.

A smattering of adults Deanne couldn't place – and two she recognized immediately and was shocked to see at this table – Don Broadwell and his second wife, Barbara. Broadwell, long known for building communities in Arizona, was also a longtime friend of Republican Barry Goldwater.

Of course it shouldn't have been a surprise really, water and Worwick's play for federal dollars to pay for it, played heavily into building communities out here. Politics made for strange bedfellows. Broadwell was smartly hedging his bets.

Candidate Worwick rose, smiling broadly when he saw her, and his ever-present shadow and campaign manager, Sondra Tucker, left her seat to give her a hug. Sondra leaned in as if for a European-style peck on her cheek – whereupon she set the ground rules.

"Everything you hear tonight is off-the-record. This is a private family event," she whispered, "nothing more."

Then why am I, a reporter and decidedly not family, here? And...Don Broadwell, really?

"Of course."

"Deanne!" Todd said, "Glad you could make it. This is Cassandra's Uncle Don and Auntie Barb, and our neighbors, David and Louise, Devon and Michelle – and, of course, the neighborhood street urchins – and scoundrels from Cassie's school."

He not only called each child by name, he had their nicknames down as well. Outside of "Uncle Don and Auntie Barb," and a couple of Cassie's friends, these really were, for the most part, his neighbors and friends – and it wasn't hard to see by their reactions to him they really knew and loved him. Could it be that the ambitious and drop-dead gorgeous candidate Todd Worwick really was just the regular family guy he projected?

"Hi, Deanne!" Cassandra chirped, seeming genuinely pleased to see her, *"She likes you,"* Worwick had said on their brief call this afternoon, never mind she and Cassie had never actually *met* on the boat – the girl, laser-focused on fishing that day, hadn't given her so much as a nod. *Or had she.*

Deanne's intuition quickly drew one more obvious Cassie triangle, this one included Daddy and *not-my-mommy Sondra.* Perhaps it was more than Todd's campaign pretty Sondra was managing and Cassie knew it. Just maybe Cassie was looking for someone, *anyone,* to break that connection. If so, this was one complex little girl. *Welcome, Todd, to your newly-minted female teen.*

"Happy birthday, Cassie."

Cassie beamed up at her.

You are good, kid.

Deanne took her seat between Todd and Sondra. That Deanne's place card was printed like all the others, not hastily signed, confirmed her suspicion – Cassandra had a plan. The invite wasn't Todd's idea, though he'd gone along with it.

The waiter quickly filled her glass with champagne.

Barbara, the new, "Mrs. Broadwell," an attractive, confident woman, breached a question for her husband's benefit, with a hesitant smile.

"You're a reporter, aren't you?"

"I'm a family friend tonight – like you."

A story featuring well-known Republican backers with a Democrat candidate could be problematic for all concerned, and certainly Todd and Sondra knew that, and still…here she was.

Don, twice as confident, but obviously caught off guard, shot Todd a glance.

Todd simply rose, glass in hand.

"To an amazing incredible thirteen years with the love of my life, my reason for being. Cassie, I am so proud of you. Happy thirteen, kid." She stood and he swept her up in bear hug so warm, Deanne couldn't help but feel her own father's arms around her, *the familiar, comforting smell of Old Spice, soap, leather and the fresh laundry of his always neatly pressed uniform...*

"That's Seven-Up in your glass, right, Cass?"

"Daddy..." She laughed and the others joined in.

The conversations over perfectly roasted beef, carrots, and potatoes, were easy, family and neighbor oriented, there was nothing remotely political, no mention of a campaign at all. The champagne flowed into stronger fare – and Deanne all-too-easily countermanded her earlier self-orders.

Before she knew it, Cassandra blew out the thirteen candles on the biggest birthday cake (chocolate, strawberry with whipped-cream icing) that Deanne had ever seen, and was handed a sword to cut it – and moments later Deanne found herself in the cool, dry evening air, among a gaggle of very happy, very normal people selecting putters and choosing up foursomes to play goofy golf.

The miniature course behind the restaurant was like no other "goofy golf" ever. Meticulously planned and constructed with castles made of real stone blocks, vine covered bridges and mossy waterways filled with goldfish, it had always been a magical, happy place for her.

She realized, with an odd mix of joy and sadness, that here at thirty-one – in the midst of digging around a political campaign - was the first true family, true neighborhood, experience she could remember since her father's death.

What the hell had happened to her life?

No wonder Pat wants me to get a pet.

"Deanne, you're with me, we are gonna beat the pants off Don and Barb."

Don swung his putter up to his shoulder, quickly looked down the shaft as though sighting a gun barrel then pretended to holster the thing.

"We'll see about that."

Barbara giggled in her pearls.

Okay, I'm getting ready to play miniature golf with a senatorial candidate whose campaign I'm covering, and two of the wealthiest people in the state if not the country. And we're in a fake, medieval world.

Surreal didn't begin to cover it.

Todd said, "Huddle up." He placed a paw lightly on her shoulder, glancing quickly over his own shoulder at the other couple before he grinned down at Deanne.

"Okay...I'm not a golfer. I'm no good at this at all. So it's up to *you. Break!"*

"Hah!" She actually guffawed.

She saw Sondra in a foursome of parents just teeing off up ahead, laughing and playing hostess. The kids, groups chosen, were already a good ways down the course, banking putts, cheering, and yakking it up. She noticed the tall boy she'd seen earlier – he was in the *second* foursome – obviously not on Cassandra's A-list yet, but a person of interest. Cassandra was, of course, in the first group to tee off – a group which included the porcelain-skinned beauty who'd sat beside her across from the tall boy.

Keeping your friends close and your enemies closer. Good girl.

Barbara was up first in the Todd Worwick foursome. She quickly placed the ball directly in the middle of the mat and gave it a solid whack that nearly sent the thing into orbit.

It struck the fairway lip, popped onto the pathway, rebounded off a castle wall...and magically found its way back onto the green three feet from the hole.

"Yay!" she chirped.

"It's all in the technique," Don chided.

"Hard to argue with success," Todd said. "Show us what you got, Deanne."

"A long straight road is the safest way," Deanne read aloud from a banner near the tee box, *"but a tap of the stone, can make one's day."*

She placed her ball to the far right and aimed for a red dot painted beneath a large stone halfway down the left side of the fairway. After a straight, measured back-swing, she sent the ball on its way with a smooth forward stroke.

The ball traveled surely down the carpet, tapped the dot, changed direction, then disappeared beneath a castle gate. It reappeared moments later on the green below the fairway, rolling straight for the hole. It dropped in with a satisfying, "plunk."

"Holy mother," Todd said.

"You brought a ringer," Don scoffed, "All bets are off."

"Cheap bastard."

And so it went.

The Broadwells bid their farewells after the first nine.

Deanne and Todd were a twosome now, refreshments in hand, watching the kids and the adults who were acting like kids and having a great time doing it.

Todd sighed as he watched Cassandra and her friends finishing out a hole on a green several fairways away. The kids were egging each other on, laughing, some purposely missing shots – others dead serious – kids being kids.

"So...what do you think's going on there?"

"What do you mean?"

He pointed his chin toward the tall boy, lining up a putt on the green behind Cassandra's foursome.

"You think he's trouble?" Todd asked.

"Ah," she sipped a perfect Manhattan. Feeling oddly comfortable with this perfectly odd evening. Perhaps the next Senator from the great state of Arizona, a man who just might be running for President of the United States in the not too distant future, was asking her opinion of a boy who just might be in the running for something even *more* important – the attentions of Worwick's daughter.

"I think she's thirteen. I'm guessing he's close to the same."

"Not sure if I like that answer."

"I haven't spent time with your daughter. But from what I've seen she's already got a pretty good sense of things."

He winced as he looked down at her.

"I think I like *that* even less."

"Candidate Worwick..."

"*Todd.*"

"There are some questions I'd like to ask you, but I won't tonight. Thank you – and Cassandra – for the invite."

He looked surprised, and disappointed at the abrupt goodbye.

"Did I say something...?"

Finally, she had remembered herself.

You're a reporter, Deanne, not a friend. And still, she could feel heat flushing into her cheeks, the thump of her own heart loud in her ears.

"No, not at all. I just need to go. It *has* been fun – I really mean that, and I do thank you. I haven't had a family night in a long, long time. I'm assuming I can use the number you gave me to set up some time to talk?"

"Of course."

She started to go, but then she turned back. There was one piece of information she needed before she saw him again.

"I spoke to Susan."

"That's fair game. The state of my marriage could be an issue with voters."

"It's not that. She said you wanted to *drown* Lake Pleasant. Why would she say that?"

He stood straight and for a moment the boyish good-nature he seemed to carry like a lucky charm was gone. Finally, he shook his head.

"I don't *blame the lake* for what happened to my brother. Susan...obviously, isn't tremendously happy with me at this point. People who hold grudges tend to think *everybody* does. "

She nodded, filing away another bit of important information from that comment, one she'd already suspected, that Susan wasn't someone to trifle with.

"Is Tommy Red Hawk a real person?"

Worwick glanced skyward, when he faced her again he looked years older, and very tired.

"Joey thought so."

Chapter 7

A fiery red sunset was growing purple as Deanne called The Tucson Gazette's desk for her messages.

A week of calls to the Bureau of Indian Affairs, hours squinting at microfiche birth-records confirmed that Tommy Red Hawk was, in fact, a child's imaginary friend – until an old friend at the University of Arizona Press had given her the name of someone who'd once worked at the Phoenix Indian School. That friend knew another who knew a "kid who'd called himself Red Hawk." More records and calls had given her a location, an ice-house near the train station. A place where another friend had worked nights with "a big Indian guy" they called Red Hawk.

No known residence, no vehicle registration, and no guarantee he had known Joey Worwick.

"No. Nothing from Indian Affairs, and nothing from the Worwick campaign," Tricia, her proficient receptionist, reported. "A few cranks. I took notes and numbers. Sent them to Investigations for follow up."

"Good – you never know. Keep a copy for me."

"Will do – two urgent calls from a Medical Examiner at the Los Angeles County Crime Lab. Name is Sara Poole. No message, she wants to talk to you directly. Her second call was from a motel up there in Phoenix."

"She came here...to talk to *me?*"

"Apparently. The Maricopa County Medical Examiner didn't have anything for me, I checked on conventions in Phoenix this week, nothing related to forensics I could find. She could have family here, though."

"Good work – give me the number."

She scrawled it down watching the sunset falter. It was nearly gone now. The ice-house was located on the far southwest side, through the lawless district of downtown they called *The Deuce. It was where her dad, a beat cop in his final years, had been murdered in the street* – a terrible enough place to be in daylight, nowhere to be at night. The late shift would be starting now. She'd call her later. Deanne tore off the number, and stuffed it down the front pocket of her slacks.

The disdain for *"LA-style"* freeways here in Phoenix made every crosstown drive feel like a cross-country road trip. As much as Arizonans turned longingly to the west coast for entertainment, with Legend City being the *Arizona-fide* version of Disneyland, and the newly-installed "Great Wave" at Lake Pleasant, the *desert-ized* version of a southern California beach, they pushed hard against the "LA-ification" of their roadways. How much longer, she wondered, before Phoenicians finally bit the bullet and cut a few highways through this carefully gridded but growing-up-way-too-fast metropolis?

The Los Angeles County Crime Lab? What would they want with her?

Alec, her crazy older brother was somewhere near San Diego chasing his own demons. Like cousin, Pat, he was a Catholic priest. Unlike Pat, he was certifiably insane. If anything had happened to him, surely the medical examiner wouldn't come all the way out here to contact her...she pushed that thought aside. Alec and Pat were the only family she had.

Hell, they're the only friends you have.

Patrick's idea, that she badly needed a pet of some kind, made her smile...if sadly.

An LA medical examiner – coming all the way out to Phoenix to see her?

Of course, the woman could have family here, many Californians did, but she was staying at a motel.

Eventually, Deanne found herself at the far edge of Phoenix. The shiny new buildings and roads, the few tall buildings of the Phoenix skyline had given way to the old, the shambling. Broken down structures and broken down people.

Her father had worked, and died, not far from here.

Her rambling thoughts broke; an odd tingle of warning took their place. The congestion of downtown Phoenix was gone and there were very few cars on the road here – which made the dark sedan following her that much more obvious.

It could be midnight blue, it could be black, it was hard to tell. But for a while now that same car had traced her route, keeping pace a safe distance behind her.

And almost as if the driver had read her thoughts, the car turned off into another crumbling adobe and Prickly Pear neighborhood.

Awfully nice car for these parts.

Somewhere back there someone had pulled their shiny new Pontiac right into the carport of their two-room, crumbling adobe mansion – surely *wifey* had cocktails in hand…

But who the hell had time to follow *her?*

No one. She was being paranoid.

Finally she came to the tracks and box cars.

Her car shook and bounced over the railed cowcatcher in the road, it seemed even unhappier, more uncomfortable navigating the tracks beyond. She eased her beast another half block and parked beside a haphazard row of much sadder vehicles parked near the tracks.

What the hell am I doing here?

She put that thought away as she gathered her press credential, notebook and pen from her glove compartment. She'd locked her purse in the trunk before she left – a habit she'd developed early on.

You're here for a story, Deanne.

Arizona had been run by the old guard for a long time – Goldwater and Hayden – Republican or Democrat they were a dried up part of the old west. Now Todd Worwick promised a chance for something, someone, new. A brash new sheriff was in town. *A messiah.* He genuinely wanted to bring this one-horse town to the next level – literally bring water to the desert.

But behind all that could be a tragic back-story, another driving force. Yeah, it could be a *hell* of a story. And a Navajo named Tommy Red Hawk could be the key.

This could be the story to put Deanne Mulhenney's byline back where it belonged.

It has nothing at all to do with the fact Todd's charming and handsome, and the deep tug in her chest she felt when she saw the way he looked at his daughter, the protectiveness...the genuine love he had...

Did she *want* him to succeed? Did she *want* the story to end well?

That can't be part of this. Handsome or not, good or evil, her personal feelings couldn't enter into it. She would remain impartial.

She made her way across the poorly lit packed-earth lot, the smell of motor oil and iron, heavy in the air. She felt dangerously small negotiating the multiple tracks in unsuitable shoes, under the clack and thunder of the big Santa Fe engines as they pulled boxcar after boxcar past her on either side.

The doors to some of these cars opened to an inky black maw inside. Her father had told her of migrant men, hobos who traveled cross-country, hopping car to car. Some were simply displaced or looking for a free ride from the dirt-poor towns of their birth to a promise of something better at the end of these tracks.

Others...escaping incarceration, or worse, were looking for a new name, a fresh start and new victims. The knowledge that most of them learned quickly to avoid the brutality of the railroad security guards by jumping on or off well clear of the city, wasn't as comforting as it might be. She knew there were others spoiling for a fight, looking for pain, to give it or take it, men who lay in wait eager to prove themselves tougher, more brutal than the men working for the railroad.

With that thought, the story she didn't want to write tonight, she reached the literal polar opposite of Dante's Inferno.

Cold bit through the massive doorway of the huge building before her, right through the flimsy jacket she wore even before she'd even stepped in to find:

Hell frozen over.

Massive blocks of ice slammed together and split apart with the sound and fury of war, spinning saws sprayed arcs of blue-white chips high into the frigid air. She saw freshly sawed suitcase-sized fragments carried toward the waiting boxcars by a tortuous network of chains fed by powerfully built men wielding giant tongs.

The high-pitched whine and bite of the saws, the hammering of ice against steel and beams of wood, outmatched the shake and rattle of the trains moving slowly through.

Rough eyes moved over her, some registering surprise to see a female here – others with clear and very dark intentions.

She didn't feel like the only woman on the news staff here – she felt like the only female in a prison filled with men.

Deanne found one crusty man with a clipboard who looked to be in charge, and waved her press credentials.

"I need to speak with a Thomas Red Hawk who works here," she shouted over the din.

"Good luck. *He's mute."*

Well, that put more than a small crimp in her plan. When she didn't immediately respond he explained,

"He can't talk."

Yes, she was a woman after all. She wouldn't know what a big word like "mute" meant. She ignored the slight, the man was plainly incapable of irony or sarcasm.

"Could you tell me which one he is?"

"The big fella'. Way over there."

He pointed to a boxcar which may have been a city block away. But even from here it was easy to see exactly who the foreman meant.

The man was *gigantic*, his shoulders completely visible over the heads of the men around him. He wore what looked to be a fisherman's rain slick, a black braid protruded from beneath the hood.

"Thank you."

"Don't hold him up long. He's my best loader."

Clearly.

While the others pushed the massive ice blocks to him by guiding the overhead chains, the big man released them, lifted and loaded each into the car by hand.

She approached, as quickly as caution allowed, over a wooden floor slick with oil and ice. Sliding blocks, rapidly moving men heaving and pushing to their limit, were mortal collisions waiting to happen. Some "clear" pathways had been painted green on the floor some time ago. Other areas, striped in black and yellow, were clearly no-go zones where skull-crushing pillars of ice followed those heavy chains toward the saws.

And everywhere, there were eyes. Hoots, catcalls, and whistles, loud, but thankfully only barely audible in this frozen nightmare.

What the hell am I doing here? She asked herself again… It was becoming a mantra.

As she neared her intended target, men signaled to Red Hawk – pointing out the intruder headed his way.

He turned full on toward her.

His face might have been chiseled from cherry wood. Even from here she could see his black eyes. Without a moment's hesitation and with little effort, he hopped into the car, pulled a nearby cord, apparently a signal the half-empty car was fully loaded, and a whistle sounded. The train began slowly pulling away into the dark night beyond the doorway.

"No wait!" she shouted.

She ran after him, or tried to, but her shoes slipped and slowed her. Men, and countless other obstacles blocked her way.

By the time she'd reached the doorway, the boxcar had cleared the building.

In the moonlight she could see him lean from the car. He waved.

"Shit," she coughed. Breathing heavily from the effort. Her feet and ankles were killing her. *Why did I wear these stupid shoes?*

She crossed the track he'd left on, no doubt an unsafe maneuver – but so was every other maneuver she'd made so far tonight. She followed that with one more unsafe maneuver, crossing a set of tracks that skirted the north wall of the building.

But as long as this building was, there was no way she was going back inside to face those men again.

Finally she turned the corner and began the long hike back to her car, leaving the awful cacophony within that building behind her.

So many rail and ties to navigate. Boxcars on tracks all around her. Some in motion, though most were still.

Once again, she became very, very aware of her smallness compared to the tall, wide city of boxcars she maneuvered through.

It was quiet enough to hear something drop to the gravel behind her. *Someone had jumped from a boxcar.*

She heard another.

Her car was a hundred yards or more away. She picked up her step.

A ragged cough. Someone spat into the dirt not far behind her, *not far at all.*

It was suddenly difficult to draw a good, deep breath. Her heart was pounding.

What the hell have I done?

She'd *suspected* someone had been watching her, following her for a few days now. The dark sedan had proved that. *Why hadn't she followed her intuition? No story was worth dying for.*

Another, heavier crunch of gravel, *and another.*

She broke into a run.

"No call to run off, miss!"

Her shoes slipped off, the sting of sharp rocks against the tender pads and bones of her feet.

God. Dear God, no!

"Why don't you just be nice, *have a drink with us?"*

The nearby clack-clack of a moving train.

"*Ain't nowhere to run to."*

She ran full out now, ignoring the pain in her feet, sucking in whatever breath she could.

"Just be nice and have a couple sips, huh?"

That voice was close. She shot a glance over her shoulder and saw two men running behind her, another one simply walking, obviously feeling no need to hurry, the glow of his cigarette arced upward to his lips.

She smelled sour sweat, the sharp tine of urine just before a crushing blow to her sternum collapsed her lungs.

"G'uh!"

"You heard the man, didn't you, miss? No need to be so standoffish."

The train yard spun around her, she saw stars, the tracks, cars, the train rolled slowly beside them, a boxcar gaped open and one of them jumped onboard.

"Toss her up here!"

They threw her into the car, she struck the floor hard - a breath sucked into her lungs with a long wheeze.

"Nuh!" A large hand slammed her head sideways to the wood and steel floor, a feeling like ice striking her temple. She blacked out, *her senses flooded back.*

Hands everywhere, tearing at her clothes, tearing them from her.

She kicked, punched them away and they forced her limbs to the floor.

Rancid breath, decay, the smell of cheap liquor as they forced her jaws open and her teeth rattled against the throat of a bottle – the liquor was acid in her throat, burned its way as she helplessly chugged it down.

Demon eyes. The dark world around them shrank then expanded, her temples throbbed.

"Yeah! Baby! *That's it! Just like that."*

The ragged sound of jeans yanked down – a horrible new stench as the bottle was yanked from her mouth – and rancid flesh took its place, she gagged.

"Oh yeah, choke on this! Come on ch--"

"My turn!"

"Flip her over!"

She fought, but there was no traction, and no leverage, they lifted her into the air and flopped her onto her chest, her bare breasts raked against splintered wood. She screamed.

But the scream she heard wasn't hers – it couldn't have been.

A roar like a giant wave crashed behind her and the clawing fingers released her, the weight of the horrid men lifted suddenly away.

A splintering sound like the snap of an old branch and another scream, over the grind and clack of the tracks beneath them, *an awful ripping – tearing.*

Deanne rolled onto her back just in time to see a headless man flying backwards into the night.

Snap!

A one-armed man followed him spraying black ink across the moon from an empty sleeve.

As this nightmare spun around her, blue eyes glowed from a face cut from ice, impossibly muscled arms wrapped like pythons around her, lifting her high into the fresh, clean air of the night.

But the train was moving fast now, and the ground was far below them – way too far, moving way too fast!

Barely conscious, she saw that ground rise up. She braced for bone-crunching impact, *for death...*

Death felt like easing into a warm, shallow lake...

-=-=-=-=-=-=-

The midnight train rumbled noisily behind him as Barney swayed toward his tiny house.

He'd move out of this shit-hole someday.

Sure he would.

"Fuck it." His keys dropped to the small patch of Saint Augustine grass he'd cultivated between the Barrel Cacti and Prickly Pear guarding his front door. Squinting through the pain in his forehead, he let the glint of the keys guide his fingers through the few healthy blades of grass.

"Gotcha, *you bastards."*

His door was open.

Not just open, *broken, the frame was splintered, snapped at the lock plate.*

Sobriety struck hard and fast.

He moved surely and silently back to his truck. He recovered his snub-nose .38 from its makeshift harness beneath the driver's seat and returned to his front door.

The break-in was anything but subtle, and any window would have been easier game for a robber - *someone was sending a message.*

He waited until the train had passed, then pressed his ear close to the door to listen. Not a sound from inside.

Barney held the revolver close, slowly pushed the door open. But for the familiar, flickering lights in his den. The house was dark.

But someone *was* there. He heard...

A soft but tortured...*snoring.*

He gripped the revolver in both hands now, moving quickly through the kitchen to his bedroom. He flicked the light switch with his elbow.

"What the fuck?"

The woman in his bed woke and screamed,

"Who are you! Where...am I?"

"I *live* here! Face the window!"

His heart beat fast, way-too fast. *He was fucked!*

Barney scooped up the clothing piled on his desk chair, and dropped it onto the shaking woman's lap. *"For God's sake put your clothes on.* I'm not...I don't *want* to hurt you – *but I will."*

"How did I get here?"

Deanne buttoned up what was left of her blouse. She gingerly slid her jacket on over the bloody, crusted lump on her right temple. Her head pounded, she wanted to throw up.

Pulling on her slacks made her head spin, but somehow she managed.

This is a nightmare. This can't be happening.

But it was. She stared at the dirty, shuttered window of a sad, dilapidated room, *somewhere.* A train blasted its air horn not far off. She shuddered.

She'd been on a train...something awful had happened.

Vapors of hard alcohol...she recognized gin, Jack Daniels, vodka...and something else, cloying and sweet, not alcohol, but familiar – she fought against her nausea. Her chest ached, her stomach ached.

A foul taste...

She had asked the man how she'd gotten here. Finally, he answered her.

"I don't know how you got here. But you're gonna leave now."

"You didn't bring me here?"

"Hell no!"

Had she walked here?

"Can...can I use your phone?" She heard herself croak. Her tongue felt too big for her dry mouth, "Can I call a cab?"

"A cab from *here?* Your night's gonna go from *shit* to *fucked* in no time flat."

"I can't take a cab, I can't stay here – *what do you want me to do?"*

"Call a friend. You tell them to pick you up at The Big Apple on Van Buren. Tell them to do it half an hour from right now."

That little place she kept her heart and soul went suddenly empty.

She had no friends. No one to call.

The brother she never spoke to was in California. Her cousin Patrick was at some retreat back east. Patrick was her only friend. She wanted to cry like a little girl, and almost did.

And then she remembered there was *someone.*

She reached into her slacks pocket and withdrew a torn, crushed corner of paper.

“I've got...someone I can call.”

-=-=-=-=-=-=-=-

The threadbare, sweat-infused pillowcase had been yanked over her head the moment she'd finished her call. *Song birds go to sleep,* she thought, dully...*when you put the cover over their cage...songbirds just go to sleep*...maybe she could too.

But that hadn't happened. She was in shock, she knew that, and she thanked God for the small favor. Shock kept her from screaming like a lunatic, and she was drunk. *Still drunk.* How long had she been that way?

The truck jounced, and her back thumped the dash. Blind except for the occasional flash of light along the road, huddled on the floor, her face rested on the passenger seat of his truck. At least she knew it was a truck - she'd added one more bruise, this one to her right shin, climbing up into the vehicle and, once inside, the suspension was as smooth as any you'd find on a covered wagon. It was a truck alright. An old one.

Through the pillowcase, she felt the frayed weave of the seat cushion against her cheek, smelled foam rubber made rough, cracked and powdered in places by countless Phoenix summers. There were acrid smells of fuel and oil, and then that sweet *cloying, and strangely familiar scent again.*

And suddenly it all came clear.

Dead flowers. More importantly, *dead lilies.*

“What do they mean?” She heard the drunken journalist inside her ask before her all-too-sober lizard-brain, that part invested in survival, could stop her.

Her captor said nothing, but she heard a sharp intake of breath in his throat.

"The flowers you bring me? What do they mean?"

Another breath, and then.

"They mean *shut the fuck up."*

She did.

"You're behind the restaurant. You're going to keep this hood on and count to one hundred. Then you're going to take it off and wait for your friend. Play it smart, stay put in the shadows until you know exactly who it is. It's no picnic out here at night."

Comforting smells from not so long ago, barbecue beef, sawdust, memory brought images of a big longhorn steer on the swinging doors, her hand in her father's as they pushed through those doors, her leather dress shoes swiping the sawdust from the concrete floor.

She knew this place well – at least the inside of it. But behind the restaurant was sour milk, the stink of that *other* side of comforting food, the refuse. All that mixed with raw fear and exhaustion.

He ripped the tape from the bottom of her makeshift, pillowcase blindfold, and finally, from her wrists. The raw sting of losing what fine little hairs had been there was almost a comfort. It told her she was alive.

She was shaking now, couldn't stop shaking. It had nothing to do at all with the coolness of the night. If it had been 110 she'd be shaking now.

"*No picnic out here at night," he'd said.*

No, nothing about this night had been a picnic. She wondered if anything would ever be a picnic for her now.

He'd kept the truck running and over its rumble she heard his rough steps in the dirt, moving away from her now, the crack and whine of his door as he climbed in. *A moment of relief, and then the steps quickly approached her again. She ducked reflexively.*

"I don't *want* to hurt you."

She felt him push cold steel into her hands.

"You might need this. Don't get any ideas. There's another one pointed at your head."

She nodded. Nearly thanked him out of one more mindless reflex.

His steps receded.

She knew a revolver was in her hands, likely a .38. She knew exactly how to use it. Her dad had made sure of that. She had to fight the impulse to pull off the pillowcase and shoot, *center mass.*

Even her lizard-brain had sense enough to know that was a bad idea.

She counted to twenty after she heard him pull away, then she tugged the pillowcase off her head.

West. He was headed west. He blew past three red lights before turning left.

West, then south.

No cops out here to worry about now. Not this late. But running those lights was still careless. He'd done all of this on the fly. He was as scared as *she* was.

No. *Not that scared.*

Her knees buckled, she barely caught herself before she hit the ground. She stumbled toward the front entrance. High overhead a huge sign featuring that same longhorn steer she remembered read, "Bill Johnson's Big Apple. "Let's Eat."

She pushed the release on the revolver. She was right, a .38 Special. She swung the cylinder out. Fully loaded. She snapped it back in place.

He had taken a chance alright. And there had been no "other" gun pointed at her head. She'd felt both of his hands press this gun into hers.

Up above the restaurant's old-west facade, a glassed-in marquee featured a statue of a cowboy cook roasting a pig on spit. A big control button was situated at child level.

Headlights swept her, approaching slowly, coming east on Van Buren Street. The car picked up speed when Deanne stepped out into the parking lot. The car, a Chevy with California plates, pulled quickly into the lot with a young woman behind the wheel.

"Deanne Mulhenney?"

"Sara Poole?"

The woman's eyes moved from Deanne to the big, longhorn steer sign glaring "Let's Eat," and then to the odd roasting pig tableau over Deanne's head.

Welcome to Phoenix.

Then she swung open her door and jumped out to help Deanne in.

"Wait..." Deanne said, "I can't help it. I *have* to do this..."

Deanne pushed the big button beneath the tableau.

Up above them the cook began slowly turning the pig on the spit.

Deanne smiled before she collapsed.

Deanne woke to the smell of motel coffee, *and the awful pulsing of a screaming migraine.*

"What...?"

She was wrapped in a cheap, stiff white robe that smelled like bleach. She sat up from the rock hard bed - and that hurt. Somehow, she had bathed.

The blinds were shut, but once day hits, Phoenix sunlight always seemed to make its presence known. She heard cars passing quickly by outside.

Her torn and dirty clothes sat folded neatly inside a paper Bayless Grocery bag beside the bed. When she pulled them out, flakes of sawdust dropped to the floor. *A nice memento of the evening* – courtesy The Big Apple.

It was nearly ten AM.

The young woman who had saved her from who knows what, emerged from the bathroom in man's pajamas. She set a white cup of coffee and a glass of water beside her.

"Sorry for the robe. That's all they had. Your gun's in the nightstand drawer - next to the Bible."

"It's not mine, but thank you."

The girl seemed barely old enough to be a woman, her aquiline face had no lines, her body was streamlined and smooth as the hull of a speedboat beneath the pajamas. Intense, bright eyes, looked at Deanne expectantly as she sipped her coffee.

"I'm...sorting out what happened," Deanne said.

"I want to hear it, when you're ready. I'm certain you have a concussion. You wouldn't let me take you to the hospital last night. But I'll take you there now."

Deanne started to shake her head, "no," and immediately regretted that move.

"No time. I've got to get my car and get some answers. How...did I...wind up in bed...and clean?"

"I washed you in the shower. You weren't steady on your feet, you'd have fallen."

Deanne wasn't sure what she'd expected with her own question. So many violations last night, what was one more? Perhaps nothing would be private for her again.

"Don't worry. It wasn't personal. I'm used to washing...*people.*"

That she'd almost said "bodies," wasn't lost on Deanne. The girl was a Medical Examiner after all.

"Okay," she said because she really didn't know what else to say about it.

Deanne rose unsteadily to her feet.

"I'll buy us some breakfast. Then I'll take a cab to my car."

"I'll take you there. But...let's get you home first, I don't think the clothes in that bag are really...*serviceable* at this point."

"You've already gone *way* above and beyond -"

"I drove all the way out here on my vacation time. If you want to think of it as a favor, Miss Mulhenney, that's fine. The truth is I need your help."

"Deanne, *please.* Can I call you, Sara?"

"Sure, yes...Deanne."

The drive to her house had cleared her head somewhat, she'd rolled her window down, taken in as much clean spring desert air as possible. Sara's jaw dropped when she pulled up the drive to Deanne's little eagle's nest on the shoulder of Camelback Mountain.

"You live here?"

"Yeah, I know..." Deanne said. "Long story...and no, my career in reporting didn't pay for any of it."

She managed to keep scrambled eggs and toast down. Despite everything that had happened, despite her raging headache, the sting of sunshine in her eyes as they headed back to the ice-house, more than anything, she craved a Bloody Mary right now.

Sara believed there was a connection between the deaths of two men she'd autopsied in Los Angeles and two deaths in Phoenix, Deanne had caught that much, but now Sara was much more interested in Deanne's recollection of last night.

"He gave you his gun?"

"Yes. Nothing he did was thought out. I'm pretty sure he was as frightened and surprised as I was."

"You're certain he wasn't one of the men who attacked you?"

"Yes...as gruff as he was, he wasn't trying to hurt me."

"And you're sure he isn't the Indian guy you think fought them off."

"I'm sure of that. I caught a quick glimpse of him when I woke up. After that all I had was feel and smell. You know what I mean."

"Touch and scent are good identifiers."

"Different scents, different men. *All of them.* This man was slight, not powerfully built, at least compared to Red Hawk."

"And you're sure it was Red Hawk who attacked those men?"

Thinking of him brought back as much of the horror of those moments in the boxcar as Deanne could stomach, but there was a blankness there too, a blind spot.

"I am. I saw his eyes, but – that part of it was wrong. They were blue and his eyes are...very dark. But I can't trust anything I saw at that point. I could feel his arms, the power; the *violence.* But...I still don't know what happened – how we got out of there, and how I got to that house..."

"You were in shock. Your senses would shut down at some point to protect you."

"In shock – *and drunk*, they poured some rank swill down my throat, it still burns. But some things – were, I don't know, *up front and very, very real* – to the point of...I don't know, some super, *hyper*-reality..."

"Violent trauma will do that. But no scent from Red Hawk?"

"None. None at all."

She'd had enough for now. It was too much.

This girl had taken time off from her job only to do what she did every day – her job. She had driven all the way out here. As dedicated as Deanne was – this girl was off the charts.

"So...how can I help you? What's my connection to your murders?"

"I've hit a roadblock using the normal channels. The Medical Examiner here seems to think I'm too young and too female to matter."

"And you think publicity could free up the log jam?"

"Precisely. You've already talked about one of the victims, Ross Tennet, in a story."

"That was a story about a political campaign for a Senator. Tennet was barely a footnote – and how did a copy of *The Tucson Gazette* even wind up at the LA County Crime Lab?"

"I like research. I'm a nerd that way...okay, I'm a nerd in other ways too. But when a story involves politics and connects to a murder I've investigated – you'd be *surprised* what I'll read."

"Politics I get – but what's the connection? Ross Tennet wasn't murdered."

"We don't *know* that. I mentioned his death and another one in Phoenix, Charles Webb, are similar to two deaths I've worked in Los Angeles. All four involved choking or drowning. All four men are from Phoenix and nearly the same age. Your Medical Examiner doesn't see the connection, he won't even consider it."

"I can understand why they won't open a murder investigation into Tennet's death. Exhuming a local big shot on a whim is a big deal here. Phoenix takes up a lot of territory – but it's got a *small town* mentality."

"Yes. I'm already seeing that. You know...a freeway or two wouldn't hurt either – not complaining about the company, but this is a long drive."

"Hah! Try getting *that one* through the City Council. So what's the connection?"

"The two men murdered in LA – on the surface, they led very different lives – one was a wealthy businessman in Hollywood. The other ran a strip club near the airport."

They'd come to the edge of the city, it came with a feeling of dread for Deanne.

"Turn right on Van Buren."

"So here are the connections. Both of the men in Los Angeles drowned with zero proximity to a large water source. Their lungs were filled with a fluid that looks and acts like water for the most part, but *isn't.* Whatever it is, it *does* seem to be carried by water."

"What's it made of?"

"We couldn't keep a sample to test. Not even a trace from the containers."

"How does *that* happen in a crime lab?"

"Every sample we had literally expanded until our collection bottles reached the breaking point. It's non-compressible like water, other than that it doesn't obey the same physics. It's *non-Newtonian.*"

"You're way past me there."

"Did you ever play with an Oobleck?"

"Not...*knowingly*...what is it?"

"It's just a mix of water and cornstarch – when you hold it tight in your fist it's solid as a brick. But relax your fingers just a little bit...and it turns liquid and slips right between them. The name comes from a Dr. Seuss story, *Bartholomew and the Oobleck.*"

"You're kidding."

"No – really. It's about a king who wants something to fall from the sky that *isn't* snow or rain. I forget why he wanted it."

"I'd like to see that."

"If we get some time I'll make it." Then, without skipping a beat, she said. "You said you thought someone was following you yesterday. Dark blue – maybe black sedan?"

A sudden tug in Deanne's chest.

"Yes."

"Don't turn around, check the mirror. A block back. That the car? Okay...it just turned."

"That could have been it."

"Who might be after you?"

"I figured it was the Secret Service – checking up on me because of my campaign coverage. Todd Worwick is tight with President Johnson, there's talk he might have bigger plans."

"Maybe...but I'd expect the Secret Service to be more direct."

"I don't know who else."

"I'll keep my eye out."

Deanne took a deep breath. She *wanted* it to be the Secret Service, as unsettling as an investigation by them might be, there was a certain safety in that. She had already made enemies, and any veneer of toughness she'd carried with her press pass had been torn from her last night.

"Are we still good in this direction?"

"Yes. Those tracks will be crossing the road soon – you'll see the station...and the ice house."

"So let me ask you," Sara said. "Why would two Phoenix men the same age show up drowned in LA only a week apart?"

"There have to be a heck of a lot of *Zonies* from Phoenix in LA. Phoenix is the biggest city in Arizona."

"And the two men here – same age, same mode of death, days apart?"

"I guess," Deanne shook her head. It seemed like a terrific stretch, "Maybe, if you can somehow prove Tennet even drowned."

"I'll need to see the autopsy records."

"Oh my God."

Three Phoenix PD, cherries flashing. A Maricopa County Medical Examiner's truck sat not far up the tracks from them.

Half a block the other way, her bright red Starfire with the big white stripe on the sides, wallowed with the wrecks in the dirt parking lot.

"Well, if it's any consolation, you weren't dreaming last night," Sara remarked. "But this may not be the best time to pick up your car."

"They've probably run the plates already. But...they know the car, they'll know I was here."

"Maybe it won't make any difference. This could be an *accident* scene, not a crime scene."

"If you turn around now, it's going to look suspicious."

"Stay in the car, I need to talk to the Medical Examiner anyway, I'll handle it." Sara pulled the car a respectful distance from the police, but the moment she set the brake, Deanne opened the door and walked directly toward the officers.

"Or...you can just walk right up to them..."

Sara grimaced. Then she followed Deanne.

"Hi Bill." Deanne called out to a grizzly bear of a cop. He smiled down at her.

"Deanne. You haven't been listening to the scanner again, have you?"

"I have no life, Bill, you know that. This is my friend, Sara Poole, an assistant Medical Examiner from the LA County Crime Lab. Sara, Sergeant, Bill Henry."

"Bill is more than fine, Miss...Poole, is it?"

"Sara."

"You're a ways from home."

"I've come to talk to the Medical Examiner."

"Well, he's been under the weather lately. Probably holed up back at County. But I'm sure his assistants could use another *hand*. So to speak."

A short way up the tracks, two young men in white jackets struggled with several black bags obviously filled with loose, dead weight.

Sergeant Henry called up to them. "Danny. Mark. Got a medical examiner all the way from LA County who'd like to speak to you.

"There you go, Sara. They're good folks."

"Thank you. So what do you have here?"

"Well...about a half-mile west we have what looks to be 3 to 4 hobos, hard to tell how many just yet, scattered another half-mile along the tracks. Probably were sleeping along the rail bed, or got liquored up and fell out of a car. Easy to get pulled under that way."

She nodded as she made her way briskly to them over the ties.

When she was out of earshot, the big cop turned back to Deanne.

"Mike would be proud of you, Deanne."

An image of her father, Officer Michael Mulhenney, wrapping her fingers around the thick handle of a police special, placing one hand under the other for support.

"I'm not so sure of that," she said.

"I didn't say he'd be *happy...*"

She nodded. "Copy that."

"I'm going to take a wild guess that your car sitting here at Union Station has no connection to this morning's mayhem."

"None. I was here following a lead at the ice house last night – complete dud. Sara met me. It was dark. We drove back together."

"Smart move. This is no place to be after dark."

Deanne's heart didn't beat again until she was a mile down the road, and then it made up for lost time.

Bill Henry was a friend. He was also a cop.

She had lied. *Clearly. Omission or not, she'd told a lie to a cop.*

Who the hell was she protecting, the dead men who'd attacked her? *She* was the victim. She'd done nothing wrong.

Until she'd lied.

The Volkswagen bug directly in front of her stopped short. She barely hit the brakes in time.

A block behind her, she watched Sara's car in her rear view mirror, still following at a distance as Deanne led the way to the Maricopa County Hospital. *County,* as they called it, was swallowing the Medical Examiner's Office. Since the takeover was as much political as it was a logical consolidation, Deanne had followed the story somewhat. The Medical Examiner's generous salary, somewhere in the ballpark of $30K a year, and a number of mishaps, had put the examiner under intense scrutiny. As a result, the examiner's health itself was failing – it was no wonder Sara's calls for the exhumation of a wealthy Phoenix businessman had fallen on unsympathetic, if not completely deaf ears.

Sara was keeping her distance, looking out for Deanne's mysterious tail. So far this morning, the sedan had not shown its dark face.

Deanne pulled into the hospital visitors' lot and parked. Moments later, Sara did the same.

"What did you tell your friend?" Sara asked as they made their way to the lobby.

"As little as possible. I said I was following a lead, you came to meet me after. It was dark, we decided to drive back together."

"Just two helpless girls scared of the dark. That works."

"Do I detect a smirk?"

"Not at all."

But then Sara added a qualified, "*Maybe*...but it was the right thing to say."

"I *lied.*"

"We all do...sometimes." Sara shifted gears, "The Medical Examiner isn't going to help with an exhumation. But his assistants, my new best buddies, called ahead. We'll get to view their records on Tennet and Webb."

"Is that good enough?"

"If they were thorough...maybe."

From the moment they entered the inner sanctum of the morgue, Deanne felt *eyes;* they stared from the hallway, from behind the counter. Curious, suspicious, and ultimately dismissive.

The world of journalism, investigative journalism in particular, was a man's world no doubt about it. There was something even more closed off and rigid here. Deanne was only a passenger on this ride, and the deputies and the staff sensed that. The eyes zeroed in on Sara as she walked straight and sure to the counter; though the unwelcome mat had never been more obvious.

How, Deanne wondered, did someone like Sara exist in this world?

Sara was, behind her no-nonsense, clipped manner, a beauty. Handsome by her own design, but decidedly *feminine.*

And here she was. Here they *both* were.

The bite of harsh cleanser was powerful. The usual medicinal hospital smells she expected, but there was something else down here in the world of the Medical Examiner, another odor on the edge of oppressive, the scent of something no one living should encounter. It brought her back to last night, the boxcar, the filth and violation. The violence. Her head ached.

Only last night, just hours ago...

She pulled herself back.

A call was made to confirm the call they'd already received from Sara's new best buddies; after identification was checked and double checked, two folders were passed to them. The officer behind the desk pointed toward a door across the dingy hallway.

The room was coffin-small, a small desk, two chairs, a light that flickered overhead. As the door clicked behind them, Deanne couldn't help but feel an interrogation would be next.

An interrogation conducted by ghosts.

"These photos can be disturbing, if you're not used to them."

"My dad was a cop. He had folders full of crime scene photos."

She didn't mention that they had made her sick when she'd discovered them, and after the trauma she'd just experienced, hungover from a gut full of cheap booze and wine...

Sara nodded, spreading the photos of Ross Tennet across the table. Black and white images of a corpse slumped over a desk, eyes wide open, an empty water glass near his hand.

And then photos from his autopsy, the naked corpse with a terrible, Y-shaped cut extending shoulder to shoulder and down to his pubis. The same cut shown wide open in another, his insides bared, his trachea had been removed and it lay between his legs.

Deanne had to look away.

Sara opened the folder to the several pages of notes and diagrams. Comparing photos to the descriptions, she quickly scribbled notes on a pad.

"Good. They kept some of the fluid from his throat. *Or tried to...*"

She jotted down an evidence number.

"The Oobleck?"

"Exactly. Except...if I'm right, and I'm willing to bet I am, they don't actually *have* it anymore."

She pointed to some notes – and then to the bare trachea. Deanne couldn't look long.

"No fluid in the lungs, it never reached them. Trachea's distended near the top, epiglottis shut down tight."

"Then he couldn't really have drowned."

"That's where this gets tricky."

She put the contents back precisely as she had found them.

"I do a lot of martial arts now," she said, "but I was a competitive diver as a kid. Hitting water is a shock to your body even when you know it's coming. Your body reacts to it. In rare cases that reaction can be deadly."

Deanne tried to picture that; it did make sense, to a point.

"But you just said there wasn't any fluid in his lungs."

"He *dry*-drowned. It's uncommon – but think of what happens when you react to really cold water – especially if you're not expecting it to be cold. You know that feeling when you first hit the water and you can't breathe?"

"Yeah, I've floated down the Salt River in an inner tube in the summer. You bake on top and freeze your butt in the water."

"Picture falling in, not gradually wading in. You suck in a quick, shallow breath – and that's it, your lungs go into lock-down. Your epiglottis – think of it as a little cap over your airway – that cap shuts tight. In rare cases, it never opens again – you take in a little air, but not enough, and that's all she wrote. You drown without a drop of water in your lungs."

"Dry drown... Why didn't your new best friends see that?"

"Because this is a *zebra*...and they were looking for a *horse.*"

"What?"

"That's an old forensic pathology saying – *when you see hoof prints look for a horse not a zebra.* It means look for the obvious explanation first. Normally that works to your advantage, keeps you from wasting time chasing an unlikely answer when the simple one is right in front of you.

"They saw a water glass, saw signs of oxygen deprivation. They were looking for asphyxiation by choking. Ninety-nine times out of one hundred they'd be right. That's their *horse.* Once they've found it they make their notes and go on to the next customer. I probably wouldn't see *drowning* here myself if I weren't looking for it. But that's the connection I needed to all four of these cases."

"But doesn't that make drowning *your* horse now? You could be wrong too."

Sara smiled.

"You are absolutely correct. Forensic pathology is both art *and* science – but this fits a pattern I'm seeing lately – and, because my zebra-horse has very big hooves, I'm looking for something else to back up my theory – signs of force. Tennet's trachea was compressed at the top – which extended it outward to the sides. Unless he was drinking from a fire-hose, water didn't do that."

"The Oobleck wanted him dead," Deanne said.

Sara cocked her head to one side. She frowned.

She quickly noted the time, checking her watch against the clock. They'd been given free but short access to the files.

"Let's take a look at Mr. Webb."

She carefully placed the contents back into the Tennet file, moved it to the top of the table, and spread the Webb file before them.

Charles Webb had once been a mountain of a man...obviously muscular at one point, a mound of fat when he'd met his demise. Splayed on the table, the fat layer over his gut was several inches think. Deanne was reminded of depictions of whaling, cartoons delivered with her study packet of *Moby Dick* in school, slabs of blubber sliced open for their eventual rendering to oil. She couldn't help hoping her death would be of obvious natural causes – she never wanted her own body examined this way.

Sara looked quickly through the photos, comparing diagrams and notes, making her own notes along the way.

“Okay. This one’s a horse at first, obvious drowning. But the lungs show signs of tearing – force beyond the trauma you'd normally see in a drowning victim. Slight, but it is there if you look, and not if you don't. Which makes it a zebra after all.”

Sara glanced quickly at the clock above them as she placed the contents precisely the way she’d found them.

“Holy shit!” She held one photo out.

She flipped through the attached forms until she found the outline of a body, with several scribbled notes and arrows. One arrow pointed to a small circle on the victim's ankle, with the abbreviation “tat” and a reference number. The corresponding photo, the one Sara held, was of the man's thick ankle. Just above his ankle bone there was a tattoo so unevenly executed it might have been a birthmark.

Sara paged back through her notepad until she found her own depiction of a similar tattoo.

Deanne saw a sunburst of long more-or-less straight lines fanning out from the center of both images. Each line was thicker at its base. Each sunburst was built with the same number of lines: *seven.* Suddenly Sara’s connection was *hers* as well.

Seven lines. *Seven lilies.*

...and then there were four.

Chapter 8

Huffing loudly, Donovan forced the pedals down, commanding his exhausted legs to give him just a few more cycles before he stopped to rest again. His bike had one gear, and it wasn't a gear set for an easy ride up a desert mountain.

The long driveway he'd ridden into provided no shade, but at least it was level. Dressed in nothing more than a blue T-shirt and Board shorts, he was already more sun-burnt than he'd been – at least since last summer. He untied the beach towel from his waist and threw it over his head to shade his face and shoulders.

What was he thinking?

It was not quite his 13th birthday – that would be Wednesday. But today was Saturday, no school, so today it would be. *And it would be the best birthday ever.*

He wished he'd brought his canteen with him though, and sunglasses. The bright glare from the pavement was already bleaching the color from his sight.

There was a faucet and a hose on the other end of the driveway. Did he dare ride up to it?

He wouldn't have thought twice about riding up to any of the houses on his block to douse himself in the life-spring of their sprinklers, or to cool his throat with the grassy, rubbery-tasting nectar of their lawn hoses. A kid just did that on his block.

The houses on Camelback Mountain were nice – *really* nice. There was something not-so-welcoming here.

What? Just 'cause these people are rich?

And yes. That was it. What was the word his mom used, "exclusive." The houses on Camelback Mountain and the people who owned these houses were *exclusive.* They excluded middle-class kids like Donovan and his family.

His school, Saint Bartholomew, was the school rich people sent their kids to. His mom didn't want him there – she didn't want him in a Catholic school at all.

"Those kids are mean."

That was her memory from growing up poor in Minnesota, from passing those schools, those kids, on her walk to school. But Dad had worked hard, and his son was going to a private school. It had been a badge of honor with him, Donovan guessed.

But badge of honor or not, his hard work had somehow placed Donovan close to Cassandra. If Donovan had been in public school he'd have never been invited to her birthday, and never *ever* would have been invited to her house to celebrate his!

Crud. It was a long, open ride up this driveway to the faucet.

The drive was gated, but those gates were wide open, and a cool drink was just down that red sandstone drive.

He pushed off and cycled up the driveway.

Inside the front yard, the drive broke off to a horseshoe in front of the long, two-story stucco house. Twin blue Mercedes Benz sedans sat baking in the Arizona sun, flanked by small, nicely kept islands of Barrel Cactus, Palo Verde trees, and a number of large Saguaros.

He rode up to the faucet, twisted the handle and waited for the hot water trapped in the hose to gurgle out.

Windows, like eyes, watched him from above.

When the water finally ran cool he squirted it over his head and shoulders knowing he'd be dry by the time he reached Cassandra's house, heck by the time he'd gone another two blocks. The water up here had more of a mineral taste maybe, but rubbery, like hose water anywhere.

Above him, around him, the big house and the grounds surrounding it, were quiet.

The windows looked freshly washed and squeaky clean. The same with the cars, squeaky clean and well-kept, not a spot of dust on them – even with nothing but desert landscaping around them.

He turned off the water.

Silence.

People *had* to be inside. A big house like this had to have a family inside. Especially with two cars parked out front and the open gate.

An odd prickly feeling ran over his shoulders.

He didn't belong here. He knew that. This wasn't his neighborhood. He'd known that going in. He was only here because of the sun raining down from above, radiating up from the asphalt.

The sun must have baked his brain, because, for a moment a very, very strange thought made its way to him:

I'm not here at all.

It doesn't matter what I do. I'm a ghost.

To this house, to whoever was inside it, he literally didn't exist.

And then he saw her.

The little girl stood a few feet back from the nearest window. White-skinned, dark-haired. Black eyes looked directly at him.

Donovan stepped back, just catching himself before he toppled over his bike.

No. She wasn't looking at him. She was looking *past* him.

I'm not here.

He dropped the hose, circled the bike back toward the road and peddled out fast.

He pushed himself hard, continued up the hill as fast as he could. Cassandra, the girl he couldn't stop thinking about, had invited him to her house to swim. *He wasn't a ghost.* Cassandra had invited him, *he was headed to his best birthday ever.*

He pushed himself up the hill past other gates, some of them open, some shut. And beyond those gates, more silent houses.

By the time he reached the Worwick gate, the creepiness had evaporated in the Phoenix sun; a crazy excitement was all he felt.

Cassandra's house was huge. Donovan figured just cutting the rock from the mountain to make a place for it had cost a fortune. Three stories tall, the design was what Mom would call, "mod," the upper slabs sat off-center, overhanging the bottom floor with large panoramic windows to give a clear view of the Valley of the Sun below. Donovan heard Janis Joplin singing, begging someone to take a little piece of her heart.

He rode up to the gate and pressed the button beneath the speaker.

"I'm, uh, Donovan O' Malley – I'm here to see -"

Cassandra's laugh crackled through the speaker.

"I know. Happy birthday! Just go through the gate and come around back."

The gate slowly opened before him, and Donovan pedaled inside, the lead in his legs gone, he floated on a cloud of possibilities.

What if her dad wasn't home? *What if it was just the two of them?*

He'd never really been alone with a girl before. *What would that be like?*

Jesus, what would they even talk about? School?

Why hadn't he thought about any of this before?

As he coasted over the stone, past the urns filled with sweet rosemary, the entire valley seemed to open to him – the wide tracks of small houses in neat rows, the orange groves as yet untapped as he knew they would be, to be cut into ever more subdivisions, Tovrea castle, the Papago Mountains, the Phoenix Zoo and Legend City, to the west he saw the small cluster of buildings that comprised their "downtown," the train tracks and South Mountain beyond.

Here on Camelback Mountain, he was literally on top of his world looking down.

A cool breeze brought the scent of chlorine as he cruised onto the terrazzo past a corner of the building that was all tinted glass.

The pool was tiled in deep blue, with stone lions pouring water from their mouths at each end. It was a T-shape with its trunk actually *inside* the Worwick house. He'd never seen anything like it.

And if that weren't amazing enough – another realization, *her father wasn't home.* If her father was here, if *any* adult was here, they'd come out to greet him, to set the rules. At least that's how it was down in the valley. Once the parent took the measure of you, once you were passed in and the rules had been established, you generally had the run of the place – you didn't even knock after that, whatever the refrigerator held was generally yours.

But the parent *always* set the rules, at least the first time you came over – and it wasn't a well-stocked refrigerator Donovan had in mind.

It was Cassandra on his mind, and here she came, all shiny golden hair down to her shoulders, tan in her tiny bikini, her only other clothing a thin gold bracelet on her left ankle as she walked out to greet him.

The sight of her like this literally took his breath away.

"Go ahead and drop your towel over by the umbrella. We have something for you first!"

He parked the bike. Extremely self-conscious about where he should be looking. More than ever he wished he'd brought sunglasses.

And then it hit him, she'd said, *we.* That took him down a notch or two. Maybe her dad was home after all. It made sense. Every time he'd seen him at Cassandra's birthday, there had been an unspoken warning when their eyes met – it was obvious her dad was very protective of her – and what dad wouldn't be.

There was something a little scary about Mr. Worwick anyway. Donovan guessed a big part of that came with his importance – he was likely going to be their next Senator. And, it was likely obvious to Mr. Worwick that Donovan liked his daughter...*a lot.* The guy was imposing – confident and tall – he'd been a college football star headed for the NFL.

Donovan was a tall but scrawny *nobody* from a "*nobody"* family.

But Cassandra had invited him to her birthday and now to her home.

And just as Donovan's eyes adjusted to the tinted shade of their den, Cindy Tapper appeared, she held his birthday cake aloft, ablaze with 13 candles.

"Happy Birthday, Donovan!" The girls shouted at once.

"Come on – come on, we have to hurry!" Cindy was practically squealing.

The two girls ushered him to a seat beside a table next to the pool – and Cassandra drew a knife nearly the size of the sword she'd used to attack her own birthday cake at Green Gables. She handed it to Donovan.

Just like that Donovan's day, his world, had turned upside down, blown out, healed, and righted itself. It faced in a very different direction now.

The sensory overload made him laugh.

"Okay - ! Here we go!"

But as he began to slice into the frosting – the knife hit resistance, something hard.

"What the heck? It has a shell?"

"It's a *Baked Alaska,"* Cindy said.

"Yeah – I've never had one, but it sounded cool," Cassandra said.

"And I never made one before." Cindy laughed, "It's got chocolate ice-cream in the middle."

"What?"

"Go for it."

"Here goes -"

He pushed the knife down hard, just past the whip cream skin, the crust cracked beneath with the sound of chicken bones snapping.

Chocolate spurted from the side and oozed across the plate.

"Ew..." Donovan said.

"Oh my, God!" Cassandra laughed.

"It's bleeding!" Cindy said.

"Is it supposed to?"

"I wasn't expecting that," Cindy remarked, "but I guess I should have…"

"I'll grab the plates!" Cassandra rushed across the kitchen.

The long crack in the cake split, it frothed with bubbles of molten chocolate popping, trickling over the side of the cake platter.

"Quick – I think I hit an artery!"

And then they were all laughing, sitting near the pool, stuffing the sweet, chocolaty mess in their mouths with their fingers.

"God...*this is so good!"* Cassandra squealed.

"It really is!" Cindy crowed proudly.

He'd been too excited for breakfast, he'd had a hot, dehydrating bike ride up a desert mountain, filled with the wild anticipation only puberty can bring...*and now a major sugar rush.* Donovan suddenly melted back into a full sugar-coma.

"Oh...man. How do we swim now?" He moaned.

"Easy!" Cassie said. She and Cindy both pulled him toward the water.

"Jesus – you guys, I got to wash my hands!"

“What do you think the pool's for, silly?” Cassandra laughed impishly. He had the feeling that was the exact opposite of what her parents had told her many times.

His resistance was easily overcome.

And then they were all doused in the cool heaven of Cassie's pool, the sweet muck floating from them as they laughed and moaned, sugar-happy and gut-swelled.

“You've still got some on you.” Cindy laughed, but it was a different laugh than before. “Right there...” she reached up from the water and her fingers touched his lips.

A spark at the touch. Not a shock. *A spark.* It was something he'd never felt before and it caught him completely by surprise.

With a sweep of her arms, Cindy backed away from him through the water, her toes pushing off the floor as she went. Once she reached the back wall of the pool she seemed to melt against it.

Donovan swam to her, reeled in as though hooked on some cosmic fishing line.

Suddenly, their faces, their bodies were close, they breathed together as one. Her eyes looked directly into his, not *past* him, not at all like that strange otherworldly girl in the window, but *directly* into his eyes, into *him.* She smiled with confident expectation...and then something that *wasn't* confident at all, *a sense of the unknown.*

Her lips parted. Donovan felt his own lips do the same...and then, a sudden awareness...

Behind them, the splashing had stopped.

Silence.

Donovan was aware of Cassandra's eyes as he had never been aware of *anything* before.

Slowly he turned to see Cassandra, perfectly still, watching them.

And when he turned back to Cindy, Cindy frowned. Then she smiled sadly and turned away.

With no idea of what had just happened, the true depth of the abyss over which he now stood, Donovan felt himself sink. In that moment Donovan knew only that he had missed something, *lost* something, very, very important.

That lost moment would haunt him, he knew that much right then. He had no idea just how long it would. *No idea at all.*

Without a word between any of them, Donovan collected his shirt and towel. He righted his bike and rode back down the mountain.

Halfway to his small house in the valley he felt a terrible tightness in his chest, and then the first tears he could remember since his father died came in a torrent. He rode faster and harder, dangerously so, hoping to dry them under the scorching sun. But they wouldn't dry and they wouldn't stop.

Chapter 9

"You're coming for *me* one of these days, I know."

Barney stood overlooking her grave as he had so many times before.

He swept the other flowers to the side as he knelt, and placed another stolen bouquet at the base of the stone. Then he made the Sign of the Cross, feeling the stiffness in his knees more than ever as he forced his way upright again. The grave was dappled with deep shadows and bright sunlight from the trees. His temples ached.

One nice feature had appeared since he'd been here last, a concrete bench squatted just a few feet from the grave.

"You put this here? Much appreciated." He sat on the bench, twisted the cap from a brand new bottle of Jack Daniels and took a long swallow. He tipped the bottle, watching the stream snake its way to the little creek beyond.

"One favor. *Only one I'm ever gonna ask you."*

Beyond the stone, a raft of dead leaves and algae lay quietly over the surface of the creek. Then a tremble and ripples, not the simple rings of a pebble dropped in a pool but a series of small waves, traversed the surface until a shiny ribbon of wetness snaked up the parched earth and met the stream of bourbon.

Barney nodded.

"Alright, here it is. Take *them* out before me. *Let me see them all dead.* After that, fuck it. I could give a shit."

Barney looked back to the small cross. The inscription read, Haseya Avery, September 8, 1939 – 1953.

She hadn't even reached fourteen.

"I know she's not here. And I know I don't deserve a favor."

The sparse grass rustled softly as a shiny wave moved swiftly through and over it. Thickening and growing, it traced its way up the concrete bench.

Barney took a deep breath and closed his eyes as he set the empty bottle beside him on the bench. His lay his open hand beside it.

A powerful hand squeezed his own.

Barney *knew* it was there, could *feel* it, but he couldn't bring himself to open his eyes, *to actually see it.*

“Thanks, Tommy.”

A few minutes later Barney popped the clutch and he was on his way to his favorite, lonely table at The Big Apple.

He'd drink his coffee, plow through his bacon and eggs, and read all about how Todd Worwick was plowing his way toward the Senate and beyond.

He was still rattled from Tommy Red Hawk dropping that reporter at his house – *in his own bed for God sakes!*

“Not working fast enough for you, that it?” he mumbled.

Barney was a small man; a nobody. It wasn't like him to be direct. He'd left *clues;* that was his way. He couldn't help it if that woman couldn't figure it out. He just wanted to be alone, to fade away in peace and die that way; hopefully drunk enough not to feel the end come.

He knew that wasn't going to happen now. Not after she had shown up at his place. *He had to be direct now.*

Tommy Red Hawk was impatient. But at least Barney knew he’d let him see the rest of them die first.

A good breakfast would calm his nerves, then a few more shots. Then he'd put *Plan B* into effect...only problem was hadn’t built up enough nerve for plan B yet. Didn't have the gut for it. Food in that gut would help.

Too much to deal with. So much in fact, he didn't notice the dark sedan that had followed him ever since he'd pulled onto Van Buren.

Not an hour later, breakfast to steady him, he was ready for Plan B.

It wasn't a long ride from The Big Apple to Barney's *palatial estate* near the tracks. Plan B was, *Plan Barney.* It was time to take the dive and implicate himself.

He could have just dropped a letter on that reporter's doorstep any day. He could have spelled everything out sweet and clear. Maybe he should have done that long ago – it was all going to come back on him anyway. *It had too.*

In the end he was a coward – just like they said he was that night. They may have been wrong about his sexual preferences – but they did have that coward bit right.

If he hadn't been frightened to death right there from the beginning, if he'd stepped up and stopped them back then none of this would be necessary. *None of this would have happened.*

Water under the bridge. *Literally.*

Instead, he'd left a simple riddle for the reporter; one straight from Haseya's empty grave.

Seven lilies...*one for each of us. Seven was always our number.*

The lily that was meant for him, and his letter, would complete the puzzle. That was Part B of his great plan. The part he'd hoped he'd never actually have to do.

But now it was time. Red Hawk had made that clear.

What cosmic event had pulled Red Hawk back into the picture, Barney had no idea. Red Hawk wasn't much for the spoken word.

He pulled onto the oily gravel patch beside his broken down shack of a house, set the brake and shut his old junker down. He looked at that shack, *really* looked at it now. What stood in front of him was his life in a nutshell. Greasy windows half-blind with embedded dust and sand. Grey cinder-block, the blue paint mostly stripped from countless dust and sandstorms, and continuous neglect. A good quarter of the shingles had left his roof, never to return. The only bit of greenery, a few patches of Saint Augustine grass that never looked quite alive any part of year, and some cactus, itself scarred-over and wrinkled from God-knew-what-animal actually chewed into it when nothing else was available.

This was his doing. He hadn't come from wealth, but he hadn't come from this either.

You put yourself here.

Everything could have been different. Should have been. His dad had been hard-working, a man who'd survived The Great Depression with a strong sense of right and wrong, a true belief that you made your bed and in the end you got what you deserved.

This house, *this life,* was exactly what Barney deserved.

He felt the rumble of the approaching train before he even heard it clacking up the tracks. Then the damn familiar whistle blew, followed by the obliterating roar and screech that took all of your senses away. He opened his door to escape it.

And was yanked roughly inside.

A plastic hood slipped over his head; it cinched immediately around his throat.

"Gaah!" He spit and clenched his teeth, spun and kicked, threw his head back and struck bone.

"Fuck!" Someone shouted behind him.

The man's grip released, just enough for Barney to drop and reach-

"Gun! Hold him still!"

His pistol fell uselessly to the floor. The belt around Barney's throat yanked tight again; stars flashed and the belt released. A rush of blood exploded in his temples, his lungs expanded, sucking nothing but plastic into his mouth and nostrils.

"This doesn't have to be this hard, does it Frank?"

"No, it doesn't, Guy. Barney here could make this very, very easy."

Barney's legs kicked out, or tried to, there was no kick left in them.

"Did he just try to kick you, Guy?"

"Yes. I believe he did. But he's dying."

"Did you hear that, Barney? *You're dying."*

"What's that like, Barney? *Knowing you're dying?"*

"Get his pants down."

Barney's gut convulsed, every fiber in him screamed, faded to black, then stars, then screamed again. The scream was in his ears, and a ring louder than the roaring train, more painful than -

"There it is."

"Okay. I got him. Go ahead get that burner on. Get that good and red."

"Barney...did you draw that ugly thing yourself? That is one nasty tattoo. A nasty place to put it too."

"No wonder he wants to *burn it off.*"

"I would too."

Unable to move, unable to resist, he felt them manipulate his nearly dead fingers, felt the heat of the knife handle... and then the flesh on his thigh seared. His teeth clenched, his arms flew out.

"Ow! Ow, shit fuck! Hold him!"

"Okay. Okay, that's it."

Barney floated upward, up and out of himself. He hovered above the three men in his kitchen. Two of them, big men, were dressed in painters coveralls with gloves and masks.

A small man slumped half-naked between them, a black hood covered his head, belted around his neck. The big men stood his limp body up and pulled the hood from his head.

Barney watched them place the knife near the burner, saw them carefully manipulate his fingers around his pistol.

"Guy. Let's paint that wall over there."

"Good choice, Frank. I think it could use a little paint."

An explosion deep inside his head. And then there was only light.

Chapter 10

Deanne had never felt happier to be home.

"You don't need to stay at that motel," she said, "It's not like I have a full house – I don't even have a pet."

I sound just like Pat, Jesus!

"Well..." Sara laughed, "...as much as I'd like to fulfill *that* need - I don't want to impose." She set the phone back on the receiver, not sure what to do.

"Just cancel the room and bring your bags here."

"It *would* be a heck of a lot more convenient than running back and forth."

"How much time do you have?"

"I can take up to three weeks - but at LA County our business is bodies and business is *booming*. I haven't taken a day off since I started."

"Nice vacation for you."

"Sure," she smiled ruefully. Sara's entire life had consisted of study, work, swimming, and martial arts. No "love life" to speak of, only occasional trysts, little more than explosive spasms of relief. And now, Sara's first idea of a good time had been to take time off just to work somewhere else.

"Your beach is nice here..." Sara mused, "Surf sucks eggs though."

"But we have year-round sun – try finding *that* in Southern California."

"Hah! Frickin' *Zonie.*" Arizonan tourists had their own insulting nickname in California, and Sara was happy to use it.

"Whoa – careful, *snowbird.*"

"I don't think *snowbird* is technically correct in this case, Deanne."

Deanne produced a pitcher of orange juice from the fridge, she dropped ice in two glasses, poured a generous helping in each and handed one to Sara. The first sip nearly made Sara choke.

"This isn't orange juice."

"You think it needs Triple Sec? Drink it down and relax for once. I'll mix a batch of Margaritas in a minute."

"Jesus...*how do you function?"*

"Smooth as a well-tuned Ferrari. Take another sip and a deep breath. There...doesn't that feel better?"

As the warmth spread through her, Sara *did* feel better. It definitely beat the pants off of her White Russians – but she only did those at night, and only on occasion...

Deanne refilled their glasses.

"Grab your bag and join me on the veranda."

Sara floated through Deanne's airy southwest nook of curved adobe arches and bare wood beams. The dark wood mantel was lined with pottery of all sizes and shapes, with stone artifacts positioned in between. A grand, feathered and colorful Kachina doll lorded over two smaller ones at the far end.

"Go head and drop your things in here," Deanne slid open what looked to be a barn door, revealing a large bed neatly covered in Navajo blankets that matched the carpets, a large window opened to a spectacular view of clear sky and desert.

There were two bedrooms, they passed through the master with its king bed and hardwood floor similarly adorned with blankets and carpets of bright, angular designs. Through the sliding glass bedroom door, they came to a paradise of stone fountains, succulents, and flowering vines.

Deanne set their glasses atop a white, wrought iron table shaded under the protective branches of a large Palo Verde.

Through a slit in the mountain behind the house, the sun revealed a breathtakingly vast golden valley of desert dotted with blue-gray peaks of rock. Tall Saguaros stood in islands of Barrel Cactus and Prickly Pear. A cool breeze mixed the sweet scents of the morning desert with the heady scent of Honeysuckle.

Sara let herself sink into the cushions of the chair, the soft weave gently massaged her bare thighs. For the first time in, she couldn't say *how* long, she felt something at once alien, and wonderful.

Peace.

For several minutes they looked over the valley, saying nothing. It was Deanne who finally broke the silence.

"Four murders. Four drownings connected by Phoenix, tats, and lilies."

Sara nodded. "And *age* - no more than a year separates any of them."

"Four murders and four lilies."

"After a one-time special delivery of *seven* right to your doorstep," Sara noted.

"Which likely means three more murders will happen if someone doesn't figure this out in time." Deanne took another sip. "We can't do this alone."

"You saw how they treated us at Maricopa County."

The stern eyes, the male condescension and distrust had been palpable.

"We don't have enough evidence to push us past 'accidental death' on the Phoenix incidents. As far as the Medical Examiner is concerned, we don't have a murder, not yet. But we *do* have a crime – you were kidnapped, that's a federal offense which means we can work with the FBI. If we can tie your kidnapping to those deaths we have something."

"The guy that kidnapped me is our Mister Lily, the florist, I'm sure of it. The smell of flowers in his truck was unmistakable. We have his gun. Can you trace it?"

"It can be a longer process than you might think. Faster, if it was used in a previous crime and made its way out of evidence – but that's a stretch. That was my first call this morning, but, like I say, it can take a while. What do you remember about him – even little things?"

"Smells mostly. Those dead lilies. Jack Daniels, vodka... He pulled a pillowcase over my head before I got a good look at his face. White, skinny guy with dark hair – that's about it. Everything was blurry. When he pulled me through the house I saw flickering lights in one room, I smelled burning wicks, hot wax. I'm Catholic, it made me think of votive candles. Two of the lights were higher than the others, big candles, one to each side."

"Like a shrine."

"Exactly. Like he had a shrine."

"Flowers and candles. Maybe he stages funerals for his victims."

"I was terrified and he was rough. But as scared as I was, I got the feeling he was just as shocked to find me there. Kidnapping me wasn't his idea. Once I was out of his hair his first instinct was to protect me. He *gave* me his gun. I could have shot him right then – even by mistake. He had to know that."

"Maybe you're not his type. I'm not being flippant – murderers who kill multiple people over time often pick their victims for a reason, a type. Blondes. Fat. Skinny..."

"Sawdust," Deanne said.

"Not following you there."

"The restaurant where you found me – The Big Apple has sawdust on the floor. There was sawdust stuck to the knees of my slacks when I pulled them out of the bag."

"If that's where he left you it makes sense you'd have it on your clothes."

"But I was never *inside* the restaurant – and even if they had a pile of it outside I wasn't on my knees *except* in his truck. That sawdust had to come from the floor of his cab."

"Maybe he works in a lumberyard."

"Maybe," Deanne said, "but the restaurant's close to his house. A mile away at most. He might work there."

"At least he may go there a lot. If he's a regular, someone will know him."

Sara reached for her glass. The ice, the orange juice that was really just a delivery mechanism for something else, something strong and addictive, the glass was like a syringe...

"I think I need some water."

"Great, I'll make coffee."

"Not *exactly* what I was thinking...but sure."

A cup of coffee...and they were back on the road with Deanne at the wheel and the top up to protect them from the morning sun.

"We can swing by your hotel on the way and pick up the rest of your things."

"Thank you...do they serve alcohol at the restaurant?"

"I *should* know that – but honestly, I haven't been there since I was a kid. It's a family restaurant – mostly barbecue – but my dad and I usually went there for breakfast."

"Just thinking a guy who smells like alcohol might spend his evenings in bars, not a restaurant – we should talk to the morning crew if we can."

"Good point. We'll hit up The Big Apple first. But we don't have much of a description to go on."

"Skinny, short, dark hair, smells like alcohol – drives an old, noisy, rattletrap of a truck – that's something."

"Something else about the truck," Deanne said, "It smelled like oil and fuel...but not like gasoline – like a semi."

"Diesel? That would narrow it down."

Deanne checked her mirrors, as she realized she had been for several blocks now. She could see Sara doing the same.

"No sign of our tail yet."

"Not yet." Sara frowned.

"Disappointed?"

"Not with that."

"Then what?"

"You haven't said much about Red Hawk. What is it you don't want to tell me?"

The question took Deanne by surprise, and yet, she knew exactly what Sara meant. If Mister Lily was connected to Sara's murders, so was Tommy Red Hawk. Mister Lily had delivered the flowers to Deanne, if Deanne were to trust any of her senses, as hazy and broken as they had been that night, Red Hawk had delivered Deanne to Mister Lily. No stretch of her imagination placed Mister Lily at the ice house. He'd been genuinely shocked to find her in his house, let alone in his bed.

"I don't really know what happened after...those men attacked me."

"You didn't throw those men under the train. You said Red Hawk came back."

"I was in shock, I was drunk out of my mind...I'd just -"

"*...been raped.* I understand what that means...what that does to you."

Deanne's grip tightened on the wheel. She suddenly felt herself stifling the urge to scream at this bright, capable and yes, powerful-*looking* but naive girl.

But Sara hadn't just said she knew what it means to *"someone,"* she'd said "to *you."* It didn't take more than a glance between them for Deanne to understand. Sara was pretty, under her bookish, only-the-facts facade, she was more than pretty – she was a knock-out. She had been a competitive swimmer, at some point she'd added martial arts to her repertoire.

Deanne realized now that Sara hadn't added that particular skill on a whim, at some point, it had become a *necessity.*

Deanne nodded.

Sara took a breath.

"You made a point of saying Mister Lily *protected* you. This is someone who covered your face, bound you, forced you into his truck, and after all that, after everything you'd been through that night, *feeling protected is* the *important* part you *want* to remember.

"If anything you remember about the boxcar is true – Red Hawk *rescued* you. *He* protected you too. But that was *after* he *put* you in a position to be raped or worse. *Don't protect him."*

"I'm not -"

Part of her, the little kid part of her, almost said, *"What do you know!"* Deanne shook her head. What Sara said was true.

"Why did you need to talk to him?"

"Part of the same story that brought you here. The Arizona senatorial race."

"Or at least Todd Worwick's side of it from what I've read."

"Everyone else is covering Barry Goldwater."

"The fact that Worwick is tall and drop-dead gorgeous didn't influence you I'm sure."

Her snicker broke the tension at last, and they both guffawed.

"Yeah, he *is* that. But a big part of his campaign is the Central Arizona Water Project. Bringing more water to the reservoir, Lake Pleasant, is part of it. It's about agriculture, urban growth."

"We know all about diverting water for political reasons in California. They've been doing it for decades. Mono Lake is likely going to dry up before they're finished."

"Todd Worwick is trying to prevent that here – CAP will bring more water into Lake Pleasant – he'll make it even bigger."

"Same game – *diverting. I'*m sure there's a political reason. My guess is he's bringing federal money in to do it, right? Everybody gains – mostly the politicians. So where does Red Hawk fit in to all of that?"

"I still don't know if he does. He's a side-story to a side-story in Todd Worwick's background. When I interviewed Worwick's wife, Susan, she gave me the name. She wasn't even sure he was real. But she thinks overfilling Lake Pleasant is more *personal* than political for her husband. Red Hawk's tied into that."

"Personal?"

"Worwick's brother drowned there when they were kids. Tommy Red Hawk might have been there when it happened. The way Susan put it, Todd wants to d*rown the lake*."

"Drown the lake? What?"

"We're here."

The Big Apple sign, the longhorn steer and the Let's Eat logo, the old west facade, the perpetually roasting pig – there it all was, right before her again.

The parking lot was filled with cars, dressed-for-church families just done with mass, getting ready to gorge themselves on breakfast barbecue, their favorite Sunday late morning treat. *Deanne saw her patent leather black shoes kicking up sawdust beneath her best dress, running past the other families waiting along the benches, trying not to trip and slide over the sawdust into the big longhorn face on the swinging door, always wanting to be the one to push them open, as her father laughed behind her...*

...and she saw that same sawdust falling from the knees of her slacks as she pulled them from the grocery sack Sara had used to store her soiled and torn clothes.

She pulled past the big sign out front and parked.

"I'm sure drowning was just her way of putting it."

"You talked to her, not me – but look at what we're doing, why I'm even here. Drownings."

They walked together to the restaurant. Deanne wished she were just a kid being rewarded with a roast beef sandwich for staying quiet and putting up with another Sunday mass.

"Are you trying to pin your murders on Worwick?"

"I'm saying we can't ignore the connection – he was a close friend, a colleague of one of the victims who drowned. His own brother drowned. His wife thinks he's 'drowning' the lake that killed his brother, like he's settling a vendetta."

"Everyone you're looking at died in the last few weeks. I know Worwick's schedule. Outside of one trip to DC, he's campaigned all over the state that entire time."

"Deanne, I'm not saying he's the *killer*. I'm saying he's connected through Tennet and Red Hawk. He could be the next victim."

With that little nugget in her already swirling head, Deanne pulled her press credential and asked the greeter, a young lady in a western-style button down shirt and jeans, a large holstered Colt on her hip, to take them to the manager.

Todd could be next.

Todd Worwick had been next in line for partner at the advertising agency where he had worked with Tennet. Tennet's murder, if that's what it was, had become part of Sara's investigation into two murders in Los Angeles and another here in Phoenix. And then there was Mister Lily, her demented florist and kidnapper. Tommy Red Hawk had certainly delivered her to Mister Lily who marked each victim's passing with a flower.

That was four victims connected to Todd Worwick.

No. Not *four* victims. *Seven.* Three more to go...and maybe Todd was next.

What did she do with that information? Warn a US Senatorial Candidate she thought someone wanted to kill him? With no hard evidence they'd lock her up. She was already being followed by someone suspiciously "governmental."

She took a deep breath as she and Sara walked with the young lady passed the recording booth to meet the manager. She was getting way too far ahead of herself.

She reminded herself of what Sara had said, that the only true crime, so far, had been against *her. There isn't even a provable murder...yet.*

"Why is there a recording booth in the middle of a barbecue restaurant?" Sara asked.

Deanne almost answered – but their armed hostess beat her to it.

"Bill Johnson, the owner, runs his own radio show out of here."

"BBQ radio show," Sara mused, "Only in Phoenix."

"Oh...you're from out of town? Welcome to Phoenix! You'll likely be saying 'Only in Phoenix,' a lot out here. We're a testing ground for every new modern convenience, every new fast-food franchise in the country."

"You might want to try that new *freeway thing* one of these days." Sara quipped.

"We don't want to be LA." The girl said completely straight-faced.

Deanne could only smile.

The day manager was a crusty but amiable enough man who offered them breakfast as he welcomed them. The familiar smoky scents of barbecue, grilled potatoes and onions that had filled the air from the moment they'd stepped from her car made Deanne's stomach cry, "Yes!" but they both declined. The two took turns describing the man they were trying to find as part of a "Flavor of Phoenix Story" Deanne was writing.

"Well sure, we have our regulars, some real characters. Bess would know best – she always does," He winked. "She's waited mornings here forever. Pretty much runs the place...if you ask *her.*"

He called to an older waitress chatting up a group of old men at a table near the back of the restaurant. Deanne was sure she'd seen a much younger version of that woman back in the days her father brought her here.

"Well...that could be a few folks," Bess said after Deanne did her best to describe him. "That man sounds older than who I'm thinking."

"That's Barney," said another, younger waitress. "He's not old – he's an 'old soul' if you know what I mean. Like he's had a hard life."

"Hardly *sober,* if you ask me," the older woman said. "I don't like to say nothing bad about no one, but Barney *carries the air,* if you know what I mean."

Deanne and Sara exchanged a glance.

"Does Barney drive an old truck? Really noisy?" Deanne asked.

"Beat up, '53 International Harvester," said one of the old men Bess had been chatting up. "Tried everything I could to buy that old diesel off Barney."

"Diesel..." Deanne said.

"Do you know where he lives?" Sara asked.

"Real close by. Went over there for a closer look a few months back. Even offered cash."

"Could you take us there – it's important we talk to him. We'll drive."

The old man looked them over. The other men at the table laughed.

"Well. As much as I like the *sound* of that. I'm a married man...more important, I have a tee-time at Encanto a half hour from now. Give you this though." He pulled out the oily remains of a leather wallet, fished around the wadded up bills and notes until he found a tattered napkin with an address and directions scribbled across it.

"Just head west on Van Buren, turn left and another right. Not more than a mile from here."

The crumbling adobe and cinder-block structures they passed made Sara think she was in a third-world country. A few houses had battered cyclone fences, half of those has lost the original wire somewhere along the line and were patched with chicken wire.

Cactus, sand and sun-leached desert soil wherever she looked. A few chickens roamed freely, pecking at nothing in the potholed road. That explained the chicken-wire patches anyway.

A sunbaked boy with short black hair eyed them vacantly from his perch on a broken swing.

As they made a final turn just before the railroad tracks, they saw a small dilapidated cinder-block structure that may have been painted blue once. Sara heard Deanne draw a quick breath.

"This is it."

A boxy National Harvester truck, its oxidized green paint chipped and peeling over several rusty dents, sat in a gravel patch near a porch that barely seemed attached to the house behind it.

"I don't expect he'll be happy to see you."

Deanne turned to the side of the road. She pulled the .38 from her purse, quickly checking it before she slid it back. She looped the purse over her shoulder.

"No. I don't expect he will."

The sun was high enough now to give its full attention to the valley, and Sara could feel it grasp her shoulders with heat, felt it radiating up through the soles of her sneakers. Every drop of moisture in her eyes and nose had evaporated.

For a moment all color seemed to drain away. She pulled on her sunglasses.

"And I thought the San Fernando Valley was hot."

"You get used to it. In a way...."

A swamp cooler rattled noisily from the roof as they approached the porch.

Deanne took a quick look in the cab of the truck.

"Sawdust on the floor."

Sara nodded.

"We have our man. *And he's home.*"

They stood to each side of the door. Deanne knocked.

No answer.

"Barney? It's Deanne Mulhenney, from *The Tucson Gazette.* I just want to talk."

She knocked louder. She rang the doorbell. Nothing. They looked at each other.

"Barney, I'm not angry. I want to know what happened. I'm here with a friend. We just want to talk to you."

Sara looked through the window. She saw a small living space, a couch, and next to the east wall of the room...a small table with candles, a photo she couldn't make out and -

"No!"

She caught Deanne's forearm as Deanne reached for the doorknob.

"Do you smell that?" Sara quickly pulled a pair of gloves from her purse and slid them on. "Step back. Way back."

Sara grasped the knob and it turned easily in her hand, Deanne's face blanched as the door opened and a cloud of houseflies battered them.

The stench of death was overpowering.

"It's a crime scene, Deanne. I have to close this door and call it in."

Deanne coughed.

"We *have* to go in."

"It would be a severe breech of protocol."

"You'll never know the real story. They'll *never* tell you."

Sara looked up and down the street. No one on the streets, but there were *other houses...windows.* She thought of that little boy on the swing only a few blocks away…

"Crap."

She pulled a small vial from her purse, spun off the cap. The smell of peppermint cut through, she dabbed it under Deanne's nostrils and her own.

"Peppermint oil. Breathe through your mouth. Don't touch anything. Make notes with your eyes, we don't have long – and put these on."

She handed Deanne another pair of gloves.

They shut the door behind them. Deanne's mouth locked shut, tears welled in her eyes.

Sara recognized her condition immediately - it was everyone's first reaction to the stench – not to breathe at all. She'd swoon if she didn't catch a breath soon.

"*You have to breathe,* Deanne. Like I say – through your mouth. You can't pass out. You can't disturb anything."

Deanne nodded painfully. She began to retch.

"Don't throw up! If you do, we're here. *And we are definitely NOT here."*

The man lay face down and bare-legged on the floor, shoulders toward the wall. A good part of Barney's head was splattered on that wall. The gun was still in the swollen fingers of his right hand.

My new buds at Maricopa County are gonna have a hell of a time prying that out.

Heat had spun the hands of the decomposition clock forward at a rapid pace, the Petri dish of bacteria inside him had already bloated his gut near the tearing point of his T-shirt. His pants lay beside him. She noted the holster on his right ankle, and on the inner thigh of his left leg, *a gruesome, blade-shaped burn teaming with life from the gorged, happily fornicating flies gathered there.*

A kitchen knife sat close to a burner on the stove. Sara noted its position, pointing toward the victim, gauged the size and shape of the blade relative to the wound on his inner thigh. There was a crust of burnt skin glued to the upturned side.

"See that burn?"

Deanne nodded, but Sara could tell she wouldn't last long in here. The windows were shut tight, but cob webs blew from a cooler vent in the living area.

And up against one wall in that area...a small table lined with candles.

The *shrine* Deanne must have seen through the pillowcase.

"Go toward that vent, but stay in the center of the room. The worst of the smell will pool in the corners. Keep your feet clear of the kitchen floor. The bloodstains won't be obvious. Blood will mist with a contact shot and settle everywhere. Step several feet past the spatter you can see. Go have a look at that shrine, note everything you see, but don't touch it."

Deanne backed away from the blood, from the horror.

She moved with deliberate, if slightly woozy steps toward the vent, happy to take in the moldy air from the swamp-cooler, careful to stay in the middle of the room as Sara had instructed her. She was in Sara's world now.

How the hell could anyone function in this world?

The makeshift shrine she'd seen only as flickering lights before was no longer lit. But the pattern of the candles was exactly as she remembered. The large photo frame those candles had honored was *empty.* Three decaying lilies sat beneath that frame and even through the powerful peppermint oil burning the tender membranes of her nostrils, the cloying perfume of their death wafted up to her, mixed with the noxious smell of spoiled human meat and mold. A vague thought, the kind that save the mind from absolute destruction in horrible times: she wondered if she could ever tolerate a flower in her own home again – *or a pork roast.*

Whose photo had that frame held? His mother? A girlfriend? One person or a group of people? If Mister Lily, Barney, was the killer, had he taken his final victims before taking his own life? Were there three more bodies out there?

Or was Barney one of the final three?

"We have to leave now." Sara called.

Deanne stepped past Sara, past the kitchen, taking as wide a birth, as long a stride as possible around the gruesome tableau.

"Deanne! Stop!"

And then Deanne was in the bedroom. A tremor swept from her shoulders down her spine as she saw the bed she'd awoken in. The chair that served as a nightstand, the lamp, the grimy window. She'd woken from her boxcar nightmare to the rattling and thunder of yet another train, to a burst of light and a flash of Barney's surprised, *no horrified,* face, terrified to find her there *in his house, in his bed.* He had known exactly who she was. And yes, Tommy Red Hawk had brought her to him for a purpose. Tommy had known who she was when he saw her too.

But she was the last person Barney wanted to see.

No. *Not the last. Obviously not the last. W*hoever the person or persons who frightened him the most were - they had finally come.

"Deanne!"

The nearby tracks rumbled, sending another shiver through her as the house began to shake with the weight and thunder of the passing train.

The empty bottles beneath Barney's bed shook and clanked to life. One rolled out and a corner of newsprint poked out beneath the metal frame at the head of his bed.

"Don't touch it!"

But before Sara could stop her, Deanne had tugged the corner of the paper. It slid partway from beneath the bed. A page from an old *Arizona Tribune,* yellow-brown and bone dry. A large section had been torn from the middle. The masthead date read June 4, 1953.

"Good find."

Sara looked it over quickly then slid it carefully back beneath the bed.

Sara swirled her index finger in the air. "Take one last 360. Remember every surface, what's out of the ordinary and everything that *seems* perfectly normal."

The rattling swamp cooler had done a better job than Sara realized. Now she stepped outside to an oven of white blindness. The heat nearly threw her backwards. She dumped her gloves back in her purse and quickly slid her sun glasses back in place.

A desolate encampment of low, sad houses came back into view, a world where nothing but sparse patches of desert-hardened plants clung to life.

She saw the last car of the train move past as they quickly made their way back to Deanne's car. She judged the traces their shoes made in the mostly gravel and hard earth as minimal. Deanne hadn't moved the car off the asphalt, tread-marks would be difficult to trace...unless the tar had melted into the treads...

A hot breeze fanned her cheeks. One decent dust-devil would remove *most* traces of their transgression.

One decent sandstorm would remove this entire community.

How the hell were people strong enough to survive here in summer?

As they made their way back to the now familiar drab features of Van Buren, and after they'd replaced as much of the peppermint oil with a dab of Coppertone from Deanne's glove compartment, Deanne sighed.

"I need a drink," she said.

Sara didn't hesitate this time. "I'm buyin'."

"Good girl."

"I need to make a call before we do anything." Sara said.

Two blocks down Van Buren, Deanne pulled next to a bus stop. Sara made an anonymous call to the Phoenix PD.

"Okay," She said as she slid carefully back into the car, trying not to stick to the hot upholstery, even with the air-conditioner blasting, her legs were sweating. "We were first on that scene. What do you remember about it?"

"Nothing I care to right now."

"You need to cement it in. Fifteen minutes from now you'll have lost 90% of it."

"Sara...let's get you checked out of that fine establishment you're in and *take a break.*"

Sara frowned, they were smack in the middle of the most exciting case she'd ever worked.

But she had violated crime scene protocol, contaminated the scene with their presence, worst of all – she had allowed evidence to be touched and moved.

She was in serious trouble if she were found out. But rather than be disgusted with herself and frightened for her future, she found herself *oddly exhilarated.*

This was no time for a break.

And that, my friend, is why you're alone.

Deanne smiled at her.

How the hell could this woman...

Deanne's smile became a grin. Finally, Sara nodded. She sighed.

"Got it."

-=-=-=-=-=-=-=-

What had been one patrol car in Guy's view had quickly become a hive of flashing lights and blaring sirens, joined now by a Maricopa County Medical Examiner's van.

"Well, we're certainly done there *now,* Frank."

"I was betting on two more days." Guy set down the binoculars.

Frank shook his head. "Are we compromised here?"

"No," Guy assured him. "We are never compromised. Because we never *can* be."

Chapter 11

Four Corners, New Mexico, June, 1953

"And what *were* you, my little one?"

His grandmother's eyes were milky, barely functioning, but they saw him as he woke, *saw deep inside him.* He dared not disappoint her.

"I...was...a wolf."

"A wolf..."

"Yes. I chased the dogs...and I ate the white-man's sheep."

"The rancher who lives in the valley? You ate his sheep."

"Yes."

"How many dogs did you chase? How many sheep."

"Five black dogs. Two white sheep."

The old woman nodded.

"You possess a gift," she said. "But deception is not your gift."

When she left him, her disappointment stayed with him.

He would *never* be what she wanted him to be, no matter how much he wanted to please his grandmother. Her chants, the sweet smoke of the leaves she swept through his room. *He would never be the wolf.*

Suddenly, he felt it. The wetness beneath him. And yes, he had felt it in his dreams.

Had she touched the mattress as she knelt beside him? Had she noticed his legs?

Another ten-year-old boy, in any town or city in America, would have felt a very different shame than what Tahoma felt now. He had not "wet the bed" as other boys often did.

He slowly lifted the blanket, seeing the familiar rise of his hips past his flat stomach, and beyond his hips, the sharp slope downwards to...*nothing but the soaked mattress beneath him.*

The boy took a deep breath and closed his eyes, until the dream came again – not of chasing dogs and eating sheep. Instead, he dreamed of cool waters, of a spring rising from the desert stone. He dreamed not of wolves, but of creatures more fierce than wolves, more powerful; *more noble.*

The *true creatures* of the world mother.

And when he woke to the sounds of an argument in their small house, his long legs were with him once again.

It was an argument he had heard building for several months.

"There's nothing for him here."

"His *world* is here. His *way* is to remain here. To *become.*"

"To become what? A rooster among frightened hens? This is a world of hens afraid to leave the hen house."

"You break my heart. He has so much to learn."

"I will work in California. Tahoma will go to a *real* school there."

"White man's school? And *they* will teach him the way?"

"They will teach him mathematics. They will teach him the way of the *real* world."

"You know that is not his path."

Away from the only world he'd really known, over a long road that seemed never to end, Tahoma and his father traveled mostly in silence, their poor, sun-bleached truck was passed by shiny new ones, by long cars filled with families, with children who sometimes waved, sometimes took pictures. Roofless cars passed with blonde people wearing dark glasses, looking past them to the great California beyond.

He slept with no dreams and woke, suddenly to the smell of nighttime in a new desert. The truck had stopped. The air was cool and the moon was full.

A broad, bare lake lay before them, surrounded by boulders and rocky hills. His father held a flashlight to a map. He ran his strong fingers through his hair, his eyes narrow in his broad, deeply creased face.

"We'll stay here tonight and fish, build a fire. We have a long way to California."

Tahoma stretched life into his limbs and back. He pushed the door open, its familiar creak seemed to echo forever in this empty place. He quickly found a pile of rocks and happily relieved himself over them.

"Tahoma, collect wood." His father tossed him the canvas sling from the truck bed. "Only go as far as you can see the truck. Be mindful of the land *and who owns it."*

Tahoma nodded.

This was not *their* desert, but it was a desert after all. He knew snakes would be on the move in the night and could be anywhere. Coyotes and desert cats, lizards with strong, locking jaws and poisonous bites. Cholla stood defiantly between the boulders.

There would be little wood to be gathered from the scrub trees here. He would rely mostly on the skeletons of dead cactus.

Tahoma climbed a small hill and looked back when he heard the shriek from the hood of their truck as his father lifted it. Tahoma knew collecting fuel was only part of the reason his father had sent him away. His father had been worried their truck might not have the heart to carry them to California, and those worries gripped his father now.

It hadn't taken long for Tahoma to lose site of the truck despite his father's orders. But Tahoma kept the lake nearby and the lake was the only bearing he really needed. He crested a group of boulders, and a long, tall span of concrete stretched before him, he heard water cascading behind it. The gentle slope to the lake ended near the dam in a sheer wall of rock.

He trotted down for a closer look at the structure.

He heard the far off rumble of cars. Tahoma set down the sling and moved further from the path, as headlights broke, suddenly, over the hill. Gravel flew, and a group of cars and trucks fishtailed over a curving path between the rocks. Hoots and laughter. One of the trucks passed dangerously close, and Tahoma fell backwards on his butt.

A big white face appeared from the open window on the passenger side. The big face screamed, "Whoa, Chief! Watch your shit!"

A young girl sitting between *big face* and the driver laughed.

Moments after they'd passed him the smell of drunkenness still hung in the air.

Tahoma knew that smell all too well. It was the smell of his uncles and cousins laughing and crying and fighting. The smell of long, slow death. It made his eyes water.

The cars disappeared down a gully beside the dam. The trucks slid to a stop near a pile of scrub and cactus at the edge of the cliff.

A scrawny boy and the massive, white-faced one stumbled out from the cab of the truck that had nearly hit him. The girl laughed, nearly falling on her head as the boys pulled her from the truck. Bottles swung by their necks from every free hand, a flat one flashed from the back pocket of the scrawny boy's jeans. A dangling cigarette glowed at the corner of his mouth.

A tall boy and another girl slid from the other truck. They unsteadily found their feet. Happily drunk as the others they joined, the revelers didn't give Tahoma another glance as they made their wobbly, raucous way down the gully.

Tahoma shook his head as he picked up his nearly empty sling. The scrub near the trucks looked to have a wealth of dead branches and the bones of a nearby Saguaro shone blue in the moonlight. He picked his way there around Cholla and wide patches of Prickly Pear, the raucous sounds of a party rising in the night.

He looked toward the din; an odd pang in his heart that was something like loneliness.

The laughing girl had been very pretty, and not much older than he was.

And she was *Navajo.* Fair-skinned, part white perhaps, but Navajo nevertheless, he was sure of it.

He'd found himself thinking of girls as something *other* than annoying lately, although most of those thoughts were as jumbled and pointless as his dreams of the desert spring.

A sudden flash of movement startled him, and the scrape of fabric. Something shifted in the nearby truck bed. A canvas tarp lifted and a boy's head emerged.

"Aaii!" He exclaimed.

"Aggh!" The boy screamed back.

The boy was very slight, younger than Tahoma. For a moment they simply looked at each other, getting over their initial fright.

"Joey." The boy said, finally.

"Tahoma."

"Tomahawk? That's *cool."*

"No. *Tahoma."*

The boy parsed that, nodding as he trotted excitedly backwards toward the sounds of the party behind the dam.

"*Tommy Red Hawk* – now *that's* a *real cool* Indian name. I gotta go now." The boy turned and was halfway up the hill before Tahoma could tell him he still had it wrong.

He was definitely off the Reservation now. This was a different world.

Once he'd filled the sling with as much deadwood as he could carry, Tahoma began the trek back to his father's truck. He stopped after only a few steps.

The sounds of the drunken party beckoned.

He set down the sling. *What would it hurt to look?*

Tahoma kept out of sight behind the boulders, though once he'd crested the hill it was clear the revelers below wouldn't have noticed a giant running toward them.

A large bonfire raged – and around it half-naked, drunken teenagers wrestled each other. The laughter had died to taunts and hoots.

He counted eight in all, two girls and six boys. Little Joey wasn't one of them.

Tahoma scanned the shadows and rocks until he found the boy. Far down the hillside, but clearly out of sight of the others, Joey watched the others play with keen interest.

Clearly Tahoma wasn't the only uninvited guest.

A scream sliced the night wide open.

Tahoma's eyes flew back to the fire.

What Tahoma saw froze his heart.

The laughing girl from the truck ran away from the others, screaming.

The big white-faced boy caught her arm. He yanked her backwards. She slammed headlong to the boulder-strewn ground, *and her scream went silent.*

"Shit, Chuck..."

It was the tall boy who said it. He stumbled toward the still figure as flames jumped and danced behind him.

With each beat of his heart, the thump of drums hammered Tahoma's ears, heat flushed his throat and face. His limbs felt useless as stones.

Joey stood and began to run back up the hill. He fell hard.

"Who the fuck is that!"

Chuck, the white-faced boy who'd flung the girl into the rocks, stepped away from the fire-lit circle. His jeans, halfway down to his ankles, tripped him. He fell to his knees and swore.

The others, too drunk and shocked to believe or comprehend what had just happened, began to stir now, to find their feet.

The tall boy knelt beside the motionless girl, he pushed her shoulder.

"God..." He said, backing away now.

Joey was on his feet again but limping as he threw himself up the steep hill, and Chuck, his pants up now but open, chased him.

"It's your fucking brother!" Chuck bellowed.

"God damn it, Joey!"

Joey ran fast as a frightened rabbit now – straight toward a stand of Cholla with no clear way through and boulders on either side. Chuck, the size of a bear, was amazingly fast, he closed on him as Joey fell again.

"This way!" Tahoma called, he waved his arms. "Joey, this way!"

Chuck spun toward Tahoma and his pants fell again. He pitched into the rocks and cursed.

Tahoma's feet were sure and swift beneath him now. He bent and scooped up a stone without breaking stride.

Chuck angled around a boulder just ahead of Joey; he swung his arm out and struck the boy in the chest as Joey tried to run past. He collared the boy.

Tahoma let the stone fly. Not at Chuck, but into a stand of Cholla that clung to the rocks above him.

The spiny cactus shattered and a fusillade of barbed pain flew into the air. The needle-covered balls rebounded off the boulders and half a dozen struck the boy's wide back and stuck.

The effect was immediate. Chuck bleated like a wounded goat, released the boy, and Joey sprinted away.

"This way!" Tahoma called.

Chuck flailed barehanded at the balls of fire on his back; each swipe drove their barbs deeper into his hands and back. He cried, screamed in agony, and shit his pants before they dropped to the ground beneath him.

Tahoma could see Joey's eyes now as the boy ran; those terrified eyes saw only escape, *not the danger ahead.*

There, where the hillside met the dam, was nothing but a long, terrifying drop to the water on the other side.

"No, Joey! This way! *This way!"* Tahoma shouted.

Joey's brother screamed from behind them.

"Joey, she's okay! Joey stop! She's okay!"

At the very top of the hill, Joey turned with the sound of his brother's voice. Then, to Tahoma's horror, the boy's momentum carried him backwards over the edge.

Tahoma ran until his feet felt nothing beneath him. He shut his eyes.

And then he floated silently over a stone in the sun baked desert. He dove down and when he struck the stone it split wide; a great spring shot upward to catch him.

Tahoma's eyes opened to the dark water just as he struck it, he saw his fingers, hands, then his arms disappear into it, leaving little more than a ripple behind him as he entered the lake.

Became the lake.

The current carried his spirit down with it toward the spillway. Moonlight filtered through the water revealing several large-mouth bass that careened around him, through him. Far below, catfish lazily probed the flat rocks and debris at the bottom of the lake.

Tahoma breathed the water as he had the air above it, pushing himself ever deeper.

No, grandmother, I will never *be the wolf, I will only be the water.*

He found the boy pinned by the current to massive steel bars that guarded the spillway. He saw him just as the boy's terrified struggles ceased; as Joey's eyes and mouth flung wide open with terror.

All fight gone now, the boy's arms flew to the bars and stayed there, his back bent awkwardly with the current.

Tahoma enveloped him, bending the tide now as he might his own elbow, he carried the boy toward the sky until Joey's head shattered the blue-silver plane above, scattering a thousand moons over its surface.

Chapter 12

Donovan trudged behind the mower, his head in a cloud of choking blue-white smoke.

The needle on the big thermometer mounted near their door pointed just shy of 105 degrees in the shade of the porch. Even Yertle, his tortoise, had retreated to a hollow deep between the roots of their mulberry trees.

No shade where Donovan was now, smack in the center of their backyard.

The heat didn't matter to him now. Nothing did.

Shirtless and sunburned, his own sweat stung him as it broke through. That was fine; just one more affirmation that he was indeed, in Hell.

He'd mowed the yards of two other houses today before starting on his own.

The money he'd been saving from mowing lawns and his paper route had been intended for a Remington .22 rifle, but now buying a ticket out of Phoenix was his focus.

He'd entertained a lot of escape ideas lately. He'd read a book called, *Beau Geste,* by PC Wren, where three brothers joined the French Foreign Legion only to fight someone else's suicidal battle for a doomed fort. Joining the French Foreign Legion wasn't out of the question.

Of course, there was always Vietnam. He was thirteen now – but if that mess was still going on in a few years -

"Donnie!"

He hated being called that. Mom and his aunts were the only ones who used it.

"Yes, Mom?"

"You've had enough sun."

"I know."

"You didn't *need* to mow our neighbors' lawns today."

Yes, I did. I need the money. I need to get away.

"Almost done."

He looked down at his mom, at the pink, ever-widening bald part in her hair. Barely five feet tall and small-boned, he'd been watching that part since he was eleven. She'd been nearly forty-five when she'd had him, his birth either a *miracle* or a *terrible surprise* depending on her mood or Donovan's latest achievements or transgressions. The eyes behind her horned-rim glasses were a piercing blue-gray, a much harsher version of Donovan's own. Her hair had been a mix of peppered black with gray streaks for as long as he remembered, and other than at Mass when she pinned it beneath her hat, always hung limply just below her shoulders.

"Come in!"

"I *will.* I'm almost done here."

She shook her head.

"You're not hurting her. She's a pretty girl. She doesn't care about you."

He shut the mower down, scorched by a mixture of pain and raw anger hotter than the afternoon sun. His fingers bit into the handlebar, he imagined himself lifting the entire machine over his head – *bringing it down swiftly on that bald spot on her cranium.*

"The car is squealing again."

He grit his teeth.

God, where had that image come from? That anger. That isn't me.

"The brakes need work. I'll do that when I'm done here."

How did she do it? No matter how bad he hurt, how did she always find a way to make it worse, to take that nail and drive it deeper?

She turned and, with her customary clipped stride, crossed the yard and disappeared into their house; her work done here.

She was right of course. That was the worst part of it. Cassandra was pretty, and she didn't care about him; might as well throw in rich - from a different class entirely.

Cindy was pretty too, and she likely *had* cared about him, at least a little bit, but not anymore. He'd been given one chance, one choice, and he chose wrong. He blew it. He was too stupid to even *know* what was happening until it was all over.

The two didn't exactly ignore him at school, even worse they acted *polite,* said “Hi” like he was just any kid they might pass in the hallway, a kid they hadn’t previously met and didn't much care to.

When he finished the back yard, Donovan finally took a break. He'd checked their Chevy's brakes and purchased new pads last week. Jacking up the car and installing them could wait until the cool of the evening. He'd punished himself enough for one day.

The haunted eyes of martyred saints stared through him as he passed down the narrow hall to the bathroom. He knew what *they* had to say about his pain. He was already damned for masturbating. Even *thinking* about a naked girl was a sin. As a nun-trained Catholic boy, once puberty hit, every time you so much as *looked* at a girl, you did so with the threat of eternal damnation in mind. Even the choice he'd made to ride his bike to Cassandra's house with the ever-so-slight possibility no adults would be around had been a flagrant violation.

As awful as burning in Hell had to be, eternal damnation wasn't the *only* bad thing about sex; the sex-act was only one twist of the barbed-wire cage his upbringing had built. His mother had informed him that girls were, at best, “pretty traps” meant to ensnare his life, heart, and soul. Having no father to talk to about his feelings, and hearing only the rudest descriptions from male friends of what females actually looked like under their clothes, in a fit of desperate frustration and guilt he'd finally asked his mother for the honest truth. She'd given that answer firmly and without hesitation.

“S*ex is rape. Never* do that to someone you love.”

Once in the shower, under the lukewarm flow of water, he soaped himself up, trying not to think of Cindy and Cassandra the way they’d been that day, mostly naked in their bikinis.

-=-=-=-=-=-=-=-

"They're calling it suicide."

"We both know it *wasn't.*" The sweet Manhattan Sara sipped was going down far too easily. A week ago she wouldn't have known it *was* a Manhattan. She wasn't sure how long she could survive her visit with Deanne.

Happily gorged and slow from a dinner of take-out tacos from the TeePee restaurant down in the valley, they wallowed at the table on Deanne's back porch, Deanne's "thinking nook." It was evening and the sunset painted everything in pale reds.

"He burned himself then shot himself. Who does that?"

"Buddhist monk?" Deanne was referring to an incident in Saigon a few years earlier – a monk had set himself on fire to protest oppression in Vietnam.

"That monk probably *wished* he could shoot himself." Sara was feeling lightheaded. It wasn't an unwelcome feeling. Given what they'd been through, not unwelcome at all. "We're going to need to see the photos they took."

"Great, another trip to County." Deanne shuddered at the thought.

"I *would* like to have your eyes on them – but I completely understand -"

"*God* you're formal."

Sara sighed, so she'd been told, *often.* "Maybe we don't have to see the photos. Let's do a quick rundown of what we saw. And then, we'll do something fun. I promise."

"Hah!"

"Seriously; I do fun things sometimes." Sara retrieved her notepad and flipped through a few pages of notes. She sketched a quick line drawing, a birds-eye layout of Barney's kitchen, den, and bedroom.

"Close your eyes and remember yourself walking in, what you saw."

"One second."

Deanne poured herself a refill from the shaker. She took a deep gulp from her martini glass. Sara shook her head.

"Okay. I'm ready." Deanne closed her eyes.

Sara quickly drew what she remembered of Barney, his body on the kitchen floor, gun in hand; the knife on the stove. In the den, she marked the location of the shrine. She scratched a quick diagram of the bedroom, the placement of the window, chair and bed with the corner of newsprint protruding from beneath.

"What are you seeing?" Sara inquired.

"Ughh. He's lying face down on the kitchen floor. His pants are next to him. Part of his head is gone."

"Which part?"

"Jesus, Sara."

"It's important."

"Okay, the front, left side – what looks like gray popcorn and ketchup on the wall. Blood beneath his head. Gun in his hand."

"Which hand?"

"Right."

"What do you see on his legs?"

"Nasty, fresh burn on his upper left thigh. A holster strapped to his right ankle."

"Your dad was a cop, right? You know guns and holsters."

"Pretty much."

"How is that holster oriented? Inside ankle or out?"

"Outside."

"Front or rear draw?"

Deanne opened her eyes.

"Front draw. I'm definitely seeing it *front."*

"What's it like drawing a weapon with your right hand in that position?"

"Awkward. More than awkward." She considered that for a moment.

"He's *left-handed."* She said, finally.

Sara showed her the drawing.

"I remember it the same way. With the left side of his face shot out that gives us a lefty shooting himself toward the back of his right temple. How likely is that?"

"Not likely at all."

"That gun was *placed* in his hand," Sara said. "The wall spatter shows he was upright when it happened. Even if he'd been unconscious – holding him up to shoot him like that wouldn't be easy for one person to pull off. We're talking two killers at least. One to hold him steady, one to control the gun."

"What about the knife?"

"If I burned myself that badly – even if I did it on purpose – that knife would be across the room, not lying next to the burner."

"Even if you set it down, I'm guessing the blade would be facing away from you," Deanne added.

Sara nodded. "Whoever did this gave the Medical Examiner just enough to call it suicide if he didn't *care* to look for anything else."

"Or if he was *told* not to."

"Which makes this even more disturbing. What do you remember about the shrine?"

Deanne looked out over the valley, at gold veins of sunlight between the dark red clouds. She closed her eyes.

"There had been a frame on the wall surrounded by candles, the real frame was gone, but the dust shadow around it looked like a standard size, maybe eight by ten. The picture could have been matted so it might be smaller than that. Whatever was missing from that newspaper could have fit either way."

"It could have been a photo of his mom."

"Who knows? I can go to the archive – heck I can just go the library - they have them on microfiche."

"See. That's more fun than a trip back to County."

"Are you kidding me? You said you do fun things sometimes - *that* was the *fun* you were talking about?"

"Not even." Sara stood, maybe too quickly; definitely feeling the liquor now. "Whoa," She said, steadying herself.

"You okay?"

"Sure – just getting used to...your lifestyle."

"Lightweight."

"To your kitchen! You *do* have cornstarch, right?" Despite herself, Sara took another sip, and carried the glass with her back through the house.

Deanne followed right behind her – after scooping up the pitcher.

"Well, yeah...in Phoenix? Kitchen, bathroom, got cornstarch everywhere. It's the best thing yet for heat rash."

"Well – this is even more fun than heat rash – *we're making an Oobleck!"*

"Ah – that's right. You're non-Newtonian...stuff."

"Exactly."

Sara took a quick look around the kitchen; she collected a large plastic bowl, a smaller one, a mixing spoon, and a tablespoon.

"Measuring cup?" She asked.

"Right side cabinet. Over the percolator." Deanne pulled a big yellow box of Argo cornstarch, the front panel emblazoned with a large corncob adorned with the head of an Indian girl.

"Perfect." Sara neatly lined up the implements near the sink.

"Okay – we have to get this just right for it to work. If you really want to do it right, we could throw in some food-coloring and make it green like it is in the Seuss story."

"I'll pass on that."

"Okay – white it is."

She measured out two cups of cornstarch, dumping it into the smaller bowl. She rinsed the cup, then precisely measured one cup of water.

"Will bourbon help?"

"No! That would completely throw off the properties!"

"I wasn't talking about the Oobleck." Deanne tipped two fingers of bourbon into each of their glasses.

"Ah!"

"To Oobleck!" They toasted and threw it back. Sara felt *this* one all through her – her lungs were on fire.

"Wow!" But it was a good sweet fire. "Okay. My chances of getting this right are greatly diminithed." *Had she actually said that?*

"Hah!"

"Diminished. Oh man. This is *serious* business."

"Of *courth."* Deanne chided.

"Jesus; 'kay. I'm gonna pour some water and cornstarch in. Stir it up. Have to get it mixed just right."

Deanne stirred quickly, but the more she mixed it – the tougher it got to keep it from lumping up.

"Go ahead and use your hands."

She dove in.

"Ewww..."

"That's it. Good! Try to form it into a ball."

"Grodie. I's squishy. I can't – it's just...*stuff."*

"It's affected by humidity and air pressure. We're pretty much sea-level here right?"

"Far as I know..."

"No humidity though. Hmm..."

Sara shook a teaspoon more of water over the bowl while Deanne's fingers squelched through it.

"Yeah! Yeah, there it is. Form it up!"

Deanne scooped as much into the middle as she could.

"Squeeze it! *Tight!* Real tight fist. Just go for it!"

Deanne did – *the Oobleck stopped running.* Just like that, she held a solid ball of...*whatever it was* in her hand.

"Okay, keep it there – now relax your grip."

Deanne did...and it ran between her fingers like water...*but not exactly like water.*

"Oh...that is...*weird.*"

"Grip it!"

She did. *Solid again.*

"Wow...."

"Okay – okay. A plate – we need a plate!"

"Cabinet behind me – right side."

Sara pulled one from the cabinet and set it next to the bowl.

"Okay – drop the Oobleck in the middle of it."

She did; it slid outward all the way to the edges.

"Slap it."

"What?"

"Slap the surface!"

"It'll go everywhere!"

"Try it."

Deanne did, she slapped it, soundly – it rippled...and stayed put. None of it so much as slipped over the rim.

"Oh...that is just...*odd.*"

"Non-Newtonian. It doesn't obey the normal laws of physics. Solid, but not solid. Like water...*but not water.*"

Deanne cocked her head to one side. She scooped the Oobleck from the plate, squeezed it into a hard, solid ball; let it slip through her fingers again.

"Okay. Infuse intelligence into this stuff. Say it *wants* to change. Fluid when it needs to move – or *escape.* Solid as a rock when it wants to *strike."*

For a few moments they stood silently in the kitchen, watching the last of the white goo run through Deanne's fingers and into the bowl.

"But how can it *think?* Where are the brains?"

"We've already seen something that doesn't obey the rules of physics; maybe it breaks other rules too."

Deanne's eyes moved from the bowl to her fingers, and directly into Sara's eyes.

Sara took a deep breath.

Before she even realized what she was doing, Sara kissed her, *fully* on the lips.

Deanne stepped away. Surprised, but not shocked.

Sara blinked. *Had she really...?*

"I'm sorry; I...shouldn't have done that."

"Don't be sorry."

Deanne pulled her in, kissed her lips, her cheeks, her eyes. A heat, an energy swept through them both, drew them together, until it seemed everything else was far, far away, and completely unimportant.

"My hands...are all -" Deanne sighed.

"Don't worry..." Sara scooped up a handful of the warm, semi-solid goop. She smeared it over the small of Deanne's back. *"...now we're even."*

-=-=-=-=-=-=-=-

Deanne woke to the sweet smells of talcum and bourbon, the purr of soft breathing beside her.

With a feeling of wonder and content, she watched the rise and fall of Sara's breasts as the girl slept.

She should question those feelings, *maybe.*

Right now it was just good to be.

The girl's body was a wonder, lithe and toned. Feminine the way a panther is thought to be, the embodiment of smooth feminine power. Swimming, martial arts, whatever – this girl took her training seriously. Deanne was zaftig by comparison, downright Rubenesque, *not that she was comparing.*

Of course I am. How can I help it?

God. I'm a terrible influence.

She pulled herself to Sara, softly kissed her nipple and Sara moaned luxuriously in her sleep, turned to her, and smiled.

And then a solid *rat-tat-tat* from her front door. Deanne sat straight.

Pat! God! Timing is everything.

Sara quickly pulled the sheet to her shoulders, just as quickly her hand went to her head.

"Hey, cuz!" Pat called. The front door cracked open.

Sara glanced quickly at Deanne, eyes wide. Then she grimaced, her fingers worked her temples.

"Don't worry. It's just my cousin, Pat."

"The priest?"

Deanne smiled, wryly.

"Pat. Stay put, I'll be right there!"

"No lilies today!" Pat called from the kitchen.

"I'll get you some water." She said to Sara, "Coffee? Orange juice?"

"All three..." Sara moaned. "Heck...no...I'll settle for water."

"All three it is."

"You're horrible," Sara said. "You know that?"

"So I've been told."

Deanne slid from the bed oddly surprised at her own nakedness. When was the last time she'd been naked in her own bed? When was the last time she'd had *naked company* there?

Sara smiled approvingly at her.

For no reason at all, they began chuckling. Deanne quickly pulled on her robe, cinching the waist as she left her bedroom to greet her cousin.

"Go ahead and get the coffee started, Pat."

"Is someone *else* here?" Pat inquired sheepishly from the kitchen. *"I'm so sorry."* She heard him gasp. *"Oh my gosh!"*

"Is that *really* such a...surprise?" Her voice trailed off when she saw the white-Oobleck spattered walls, counter, and floor of her own kitchen. There were clear palm prints on the floor tiles. Pat stood stunned.

"So!" She greeted her cousin with exaggerated cheer. "How was Barcelona?"

"It was...*priests.* Lots...of priests."

"Well...that's fun."

There was no use cleaning up now. She took the coffee pot out of his hands and filled it. Sara appeared from the hallway, dark hair beautifully mussed. The tightly cinched robe did little more than accentuate her figure. Pat's jaw may have bruised his sternum when it dropped.

"Good morning, Father." Sara pointed to the pot. "I could...definitely use some of that."

"Won't take long."

"Sara Poole. My cousin, Father Pat Mulhenney."

"*Pat's* fine. Good to meet you...young lady."

"*Sara's* good." She extended her hand confidently and shook his firmly when he finally took it.

"Sara's a Medical Examiner from Los Angeles."

"*Assistant* Medical Examiner, anyway." Sara corrected. "You two probably have a lot to...I'll go take a shower while you two catch up."

Deanne took a breath. She retrieved two juice glasses, pulled her ever-ready pitcher from the refrigerator, and poured a healthy shot for herself, and Pat. They both swallowed readily.

"You always say I should have company."

"I was thinking a cat." Pat said.

She laughed.

"Deanne, I just...I had no idea."

Deanne frowned.

"Believe me, *neither did I.*"

"It does..." Pat stopped himself, not sure exactly where he meant to go with that himself.

"Explain my divorce?"

"Well..."

"It happened. I don't know. I feel good right now. I'm not going to analyze it." She changed the subject. "We know where the lilies came from."

Then she looked at the Oobleck mayhem around the kitchen and nearly laughed again. No use even starting a serious conversation here. Finally, the sweet miracle of percolation did its magic. The comforting aroma of coffee filled the air. She took their glasses, added another and the pitcher.

"Grab the pot and mugs. Let's take this to the nook."

In the cool gold of the morning desert, Deanne brought Pat up to speed. She left out a great deal. She'd only been "hassled" by rough men near the ice house. Tommy Red Hawk had broken that up – and *introduced* her to Barney.

Lying to her cousin was a first. But he *couldn't* know the truth, not just yet anyway. Even the white-washed story left Pat slack-jawed.

"Do you have *any* idea how much danger you're in?" He said.

"More than you know, Pat." She sipped her coffee, high above the desert floor, but nearly level with her mountain nook, three vultures circled something or someone unfortunate in the valley below that she couldn't see.

Sara, now in shorts, a beach shirt and deck shoes, joined them at the table. She waved off the juice glass and gulped the hot coffee and water.

"Okay. There's more. But before I say anything else. Father, we need to make a confession."

Sara straightened.

"What are you doing?"

Deanne shook her head.

"Trust me on this, Sara."

Pat nodded, "I was afraid this was coming. You *know* it's irregular."

"Of course it is. But you need to know exactly what we've done. It protects *you* as much as it does us."

"Okay. When you're both ready."

Deanne took Sara's hand.

"Sara, I need you to repeat *exactly* what I say."

Sara took a deep breath. She nodded.

"Bless me Father, for I have sinned..."

-=-=-=-=-=-=-=-

Pure gold. Marble stones, concrete crosses. The Arizona sunrise had gilded them all. In the dappled shade of the olive and mulberry trees, water-sprites skipped, floated, and took flight from the still surface of the creek behind the lily-covered grave of Haseya Avery.

The stone bench sat empty before it, as empty as the grave itself.

Warren Perkins pulled a dirty rag from his pocket and wiped his forehead. It was a cool spring morning by Phoenix standards, as long as you were in the shadows, as long as you had a good breeze going to cool your sweat.

But wherever that gold light hit you straight on it baked you. Made you sweat like a damn pig. Warren had maintained this cemetery for more years than he cared to count. It had grown, and he'd grown old. There were parts of it he rarely got to anymore. Parts no one else got to either – those places where the long forgotten slept.

"God damn it!"

Kids. God damn thieves.

One thing he really couldn't stand for – was flower robbing. Most folks left a bouquet and were done with it. Once those flowers had passed – and it didn't take long in this heat, Warren cleared them out to the incinerator. But the folks who just couldn't let go, the ones who actually tended the graves of their dearly beloved – that was a different story altogether. Removing those flowers was an affront, a very personal attack.

Who the hell was Haseya Avery anyway? He'd been to this area a couple weeks back to find a few stolen bouquets near the stone that bore her name. Now her grave lay beneath a moldering, sickly sweet heap of flowers high as his hip – all robbed from the suddenly bare "rich" sections several hundred yards from here.

And how the hell had a bench, a god damn concrete bench, been moved in front of it?

"God damn..." He cursed again.

That bench belonged under a mulberry over thirty feet away.

He'd had to clean up after sick teens who came out here to cause mischief – or *make-out*, yeah, he'd had to dump condoms in the trash. *Sick little shits.*

Sometimes they'd vandalize, knock over stones. Setting those stones upright was no easy chore.

But how the Hell?

His eyes moved from the mulberry, where the base of the bench had left its footprint sunk a good three inches into the hard earth, to its new resting place facing Haseya Avery's grave.

There were no drag marks.

How was that even possible?

Come to think of it...how would *dragging* it be possible? That damn thing had been placed with a crane maybe fifteen years ago, the mulberry sapling planted next to it the same day.

He pulled a flask from his overalls and took a good, long, pondering drink. A thin cloud of flies and sprites rose from the lazy creek just beyond the row of graves.

He saw only muddy, moss covered rocks there. Not that it ever held that much...but there was barely a skin of water over those rocks now.

And then…*the flowers rose slowly up from the grave.*

"Ah!"

The flask slipped from his hand as Warren stepped quickly backwards. His heel struck a stone and he fell, roughly on his butt.

He'd seen things in this cemetery before – when he was nearly blind drunk he'd seen things that *couldn't* be there.

But Warren had never seen anything like this.

The shape of a man, a very, very big man, a man formed of dead flowers, mud, and water rose to its knees then stood. The flowers and mud sluiced away, dropping back onto the grave as the *creature* faced him.

Warren crossed his arms in front of him, kicked his heels into the ground, pushing backwards and away from it.

"No! No-no-no!"

Its face crinkled into a grimace, its jaws opened and a piercing scream turned the cemetery into a mirage, a wavy smear of color.

There was a "pop" in Warren's ears...and a high, static-filled whine.

A silent explosion of water, mud and flowers, sent Warren rolling halfway to the mulberry.

-=-=-=-=-=-=-=-

Deanne cranked the wheels on the big microfiche machine, sending page after page of black and gray newsprint images sliding across the big screen where she sat.

Not quite up to braving the hostile cave dwellers at Maricopa County only to see Barney's mutilated body in detailed crime-scene photos, Deanne had let Sara tackle that particular chore.

Deanne opted instead for a date at the Phoenix Public Library. *Persona non gratis* at *The Arizona Tribune* these days and happily avoiding the drive to Tucson where questions about three unwritten features were sure to rise, the easy drive downtown to the air-conditioned quiet of the library was a welcome choice.

Why did it suddenly seem strange to be alone?

God, what was she doing? Maybe Pat's arrival had been Providence, a necessary interruption. What would she have told Sara if they'd simply woken in each other's arms, *"I love you?" Aggghh.*

She pushed the thought aside. It did make her smile on the way out though, what was she a teenager?

Had she been attracted to *girls* before? Maybe.

It was one night. It didn't mean anything. *Probably.*

Finally, June 4, 1953 appeared in all its gray glory. A Sunday – big news day too. The front page headline read, *"Truce Agreement Reported in Korea."* She rolled the dial, more images and print flew by. *So which one was Barney's favorite article, the one he'd enshrined?*

You remembered the date; the page number would have helped.

Whatever had been in that hole Barney had clipped from this paper would need to fit the frame shadow in his den. Just as easily, it could have nothing at all to do with that frame.

Not much to go on – but "not much" was all they had.

And then...she found something. An article entitled, *"Tragedy at Lake Pleasant."* A photo of the Waddell Dam beneath that carried the cutline, "A ten-year-old boy clings to life after a fall from the Waddell Dam."

Clings to life?

No photo of the boy, only of the dam itself and the lake beneath it.

"A ten-year-old boy was pulled unconscious from the water by his older brother and a group of teens camping near the dam and rushed to St. Joseph's Hospital where he remains in critical condition." The story went on to credit the quick thinking and actions of the teens.

The boy wasn't named, he was a minor, but it *had* to be Todd's brother.

He hadn't drowned as Susan and Todd said. But was that really so strange? Deanne put herself in Todd's place; if her own brother had died of complications shortly after being "pulled unconscious" from a lake, would she have said he drowned? Maybe.

Had Barney been with them at the lake? Was he one of the rescuers?

But really, a shrine to Todd's little brother? Did Barney blame himself for the boy's death? Did he blame Todd?

Camping? 1953. That would have made Todd and Barney seventeen. How many seventeen year olds wanted a little brother tagging along when they "camped" with their friends? Partying was more like it. One of those get-drunk-quick desert parties the kids called a "Boondocker" these days.

What actually happened that night?

-=-=-=-=-=-=-=-

A few short miles away, Sara sat alone in the dingy room at County with a folder of crime scene and autopsy photographs, feeling more like a prisoner today than an examiner. This place made the LA County Crime Lab seem like Main Street Disneyland. She found herself actually missing Ben.

Out of nowhere, the faintest scent of Deanne's perfume made her smile. She shook her head.

What the hell is wrong with you?

She took a deep breath, and spread the gruesome photos of Barney's last stand out before her on the table. She pulled her diagrams from her bag, and quickly compared them. The images matched her diagrams in all ways but *one.*

The placement of the ankle holster was wrong...

A light knock on the door made her jump.

"Hi, Sara."

It was Mark, one of the Assistants she'd met on the train tracks – one of her new "best friends." A little taller than she was, uncertain and bookish, but actually not bad looking – if he'd buy new glasses and grow his hair out, right now it looked like his dad still buzzed his head with an electric razor, and the only thing his glasses needed was tape on the frame to complete the look.

"Thank you, for these," she held up the folder.

"Oh," he pushed the glasses back up onto his forehead, "no problem at all."

He stood there awkwardly for a moment.

"You think there's a connection with the others?" He asked, mostly to humor her, she knew.

"There might be."

"But...this one didn't choke or drown."

"Yes. I'd say with the powder burns and large exit wound we can rule that one out. While we're on drowning though – did you keep samples of the fluid from Ross Tennet's airway?"

She could see the gears turning in his head as he suddenly brightened. *If you get what the pretty girl wants, you'll please her. Pleasing the pretty girl is good.*

"Yes, we did. Would you like to examine the vials?"

She reached out to him, careful to touch his wrist.

"If you can, Mark. I would *really* like that."

"Uh...okay. I can do that."

Men. If he *only* knew…"One quick question."

"Sure."

"How much do you know about guns and holsters?"

"Well...enough, I guess. I mean, I don't like to brag. I'm not exactly a "quick-draw" artist, but I'm pretty good with a gun."

"I'll bet you are. Did you take these photos?"

"No – that was Donald, he's a real pro – he has a Hasselblad."

"But you were with him, right?"

"Well, yes."

"Just wondering. Looks like this holster is set up for a right-handed draw doesn't it?"

"Let's see – on the inside of the ankle, handle facing front – that would put it right where you want it. I mean, you could still cross-draw with your left. A little awkward. But if you're right-handed, you could just, you know, pretend you were tying your shoes." Mark knelt to show her. "Then it's right there. Your hand's in position, you grab it and BANG!"

"So this guy was a righty?"

"Sure – you can see in those other shots that the gun was still in his right hand when we got to him. I'm in the NRA by the way."

"That's really great. Do we know why he shot himself? Did he leave a note?"

"No. But he was a drunk. Say, you know they recreate the shootout at the OK Corral in Tombstone every year on Helldorado Days! Quickdraw contests, *beer,* all sorts of stuff. If you ever happen to be here in the fall. I could show you around."

"Sounds like a date, then."

He actually blushed. "Oh...I didn't mean it...that way."

"No, I mean it, Mark. It sounds like fun. *Really.* Do you think I could have a look at those samples?"

"Uh. Yeah. Oh sure, sorry. Do you want to come with? I can give you the tour -"

"You know, I'd like to come back and do that...*sometime.* But right now, just having a look at the samples would be great."

"Okay. No problem. Any time. I'll be right back."

Sara's heartbeat tripled as he left her. She took a deep breath, calmed herself as she had done so many times standing high above the surface of the water, feeling that solid connection her toes made with the platform as she prepared for lift off.

Like many holsters, the one Barney had worn was generic, built with straps on either side to accommodate left or right-hand use. She checked her diagrams against the photos one more time, they confirmed what she'd suspected: at some point between the time she and Deanne had left the scene and the time these photos had been taken, Barney's holster had been re-oriented and replaced.

The murderers had slipped up when they'd placed the gun in his right hand and shot him. Barney was already unconscious or dead, and Barney was a lefty.

She held another photo to the dim light, this one a wide shot of the crime scene that included the living room beyond the kitchen.

In this photo a framed portrait now hung on the wall where only the dust shadow had been.

She found a close-up shot of the candle-filled stand and the portrait enshrined there. The portrait was that of a young woman, her dark hair wavy and full in a style popular in the forties; most likely Barney's mother.

Sara slid the photos back as the door opened quickly behind her. She nearly hit the ceiling.

"I don't know what happened!" Mark said, his face flushed. "The samples are gone. *Someone smashed the vials!"*

-=-=-=-=-=-=-=-

"Hey, Deanne. I'm glad you called. I didn't like the way we left things the other night."

Phones were ringing off the hook in the background, a dozen conversations at once. The Worwick campaign was obviously in full press donations mode.

"That was on me. It was a family night. I'm sure I pressed harder than I should have."

"Heck," Todd laughed, "I invited a reporter to a birthday party, what did I expect?"

And that was the question, wasn't it? What had he expected or *wanted* from her.

"Yeah. Guess that one was on you. You did say you'd make time for a real interview."

"Yeah, I did – and I want to do that. I'm at the campaign office now."

"On Camelback? I can meet you there."

"It's going to be a little crazy here for a while."

"Even a few minutes on the phone would be good. Just give me a time."

"Excuse me a second -"

"No problem," But he was already talking to someone else. She could hear Sondra's voice over the rest, but she couldn't make out the words. Muffled now, Worwick had obviously covered the receiver.

He came back on.

"Tell you what. Do you like a good steak?"

"Sure, who doesn't?"

"Monti's – 8:30 tonight. Meet me. Sorry for the late dinner. Lenny'll make it worth your while."

He was referring to the owner, Leonard Monti, former boxer, now local celebrity – he'd been the proprietor of the steakhouse, Monti's La Casa Vieja for as long as Deanne could remember. The building that housed the restaurant had been the childhood home of Carl Hayden, once Arizona Governor and now retiring Senator – the man Todd Worwick was working hard to replace.

"Big things happening. You'll want to hear it first. An exclusive – a scoop! Just for you. Will I see you there?"

She'd attended his daughter's birthday party…and now what was this? A date? She took a deep breath.

"Steak and a *scoop* – what girl could resist?"

"Outstanding."

Deanne placed the phone back on the receiver, feeling exhilarated and steamrolled at the same time.

She thanked the librarian for the use of her office and the phone. But now she needed air.

-=-=-=-=-=-=-=-

Ten minutes later Deanne sat in the palm-shaded grass near the stone bridge at the Encanto Park lagoon, with a burger and a Dr. Pepper. An oasis of shade trees, grass and man-made lakes, Encanto Park was a welcome refuge from the brutal summer heat for man and fowl alike. Ducks and geese paddled lazily across the lagoon, no doubt with great relief. Not far away, kids laughed and screamed as they rode the hills and valleys of the park's roller coaster.

A cool breeze brought the scent of fresh-cut grass from the nearby golf-course.

Peace and contentment.

In the midst of politics, mayhem, and murder.

She took a smoky, meaty bite of the burger, washed it down with sweet bubbles sucked from a straw. She closed her eyes and saw herself riding that very same roller coaster, her dad watching with feigned confidence from below.

It was the first time he'd let her ride alone...

What would he think of her now? She always felt him, always knew he was there. His death had left her heartbroken and scared, but it had never broken that connection.

She thought of Sara. How good it had felt to be with her, to be *with someone.*

You barely know her.

That was true.

You barely know yourself.

She guessed that was every bit as true.

And you like men, very much. Their touch, their scent. Their presence.

Jesus. She'd never questioned those things. She still didn't, not really. So how had it happened? And what the hell was she doing with Worwick?

Maybe things weren't so black and white after all.

"Deanne."

She straightened, searched for the source. No one nearby.

A cold shiver in her shoulders and back.

In the lagoon a snapping turtle pushed aside a group of lily pads then disappeared beneath the surface. A duck flapped its wings, shook its tail and sidled up the bank. Not far away, a family of ducks made their quacking way across the lagoon.

The roller coaster creaked, rattled and roared and the kids laughed and screamed with it.

The nearest people were a man and his boy fishing for blue-gill – all the way on the other side of the lagoon.

She had heard her name distinctly, a voice – a man's voice, low and desperately sad. She had heard it. *Felt it. She'd heard the voice before. Where?*

The shiver returned. She felt the hair rising at the back of her neck, as she stood.

Nothing had changed.

No. T*hat wasn't entirely true.*

Water no longer cascaded from the big rock pile a short distance away. The waterfall had been shut off.

The turtle climbed up the bank and out of the water; she saw several other turtles doing the same. The ducks flapped their wings and they too left the water.

A rippling over the surface – not the concentric rings drops of water or a stone dropped in the center would make, but long, straight waves.

It wasn't the breeze; the air was still now, silent.

"Deanne."

There in the waist-deep watery shadows beneath the stone bridge stood a tall naked man.

"Tommy!" She gasped.

And then he was gone.

-=-=-=-=-=-=-=-

An oasis! Sara felt like a little kid at Disneyland.

It was no more than a park with a swimming pool surrounded by baseball diamonds under the shade of cottonwood trees and palms – but to Sara, who had been driving through air so dry bugs didn't splatter so much as shatter against her windshield, their component parts rolling away without so much as a trace, the rubber of her wheels ripping over asphalt so hot the heat waves rising from it tormented her with wavy images of her own Hermosa Beach – this city park and its swimming pool looked like heaven.

She parked and found a shaded bench close enough to the pool to taste chlorine, the tang of mustard and franks being served from the concession stand across the water.

Watching the slim lifeguard whistling at kids roughhousing in the shallow end, Sara had to smile. The kids immediately stopped their splashing, the boys no doubt seeing this fifteen-year-old in her red bodysuit and shades, the white zinc oxide cream slathered over the bridge of her freckled nose, as both the height of authority and ultimate object of nascent desire.

That had been Sara...*and not that long ago.*

Those hot dogs smell good.

Her stomach rumbled. *Careful girl.* No way she was going to drive around that odd Jack in the Box thing on the corner and order food, she'd stop at the Bayless grocery store on the way back to Deanne's – pick up some greens. She could already feel the unaccustomed effects of alcohol and rich comfort food in the growing tightness of her clothes; an unfamiliar and unwelcome pooch in her belly. She couldn't let herself get used to this.

In the buoyed-off deep end, a girl climbed cautiously up to the high dive, her friends egging her on from the deck. The lifeguard turned a casually watchful eye on the girl and her friends.

Sara closed her eyes. She could feel the cool platform beneath the balls of her feet, *in a few heartbeats she would take that backwards leap of faith, leave the security of concrete and steel and fling herself into the unknown of thin air.* You knew the water was still right there where you'd left it. You knew it was waiting to catch you if only you kept to your routine, tucked and released and sprang toward it in time. The water was there before, it would be there when you reached for it. *And yet...there was always that doubt...*

And that doubt, that excitement, was why you did it in the first place.

A calming breath and the decision was made, the pull of her calves, and the lift...and Sara was ten years old again, leaping backwards up toward the sun high above, the exhilaration of weightlessness, then the tuck, the spring toward the surface, her fingers knifing through the surface, the cool water taking her in, enveloping her, protecting her. The happy bubbles and spin of success, the dolphin kick back to the side of the pool and the hiss of water and applause of her teammates and the approval of her coach.

And as he helped her up the pool ladder, his hand slipped down from her upper arm, and briefly touched her breast.

It had been a slip, hadn't it?

But it wasn't the first time. And not the last.

Sara blinked. The breeze brought something other than chlorine, mustard and dogs. It brought the stink of standing water from the nearest baseball diamond. From the dank shadowy pools at the edge of right field, near the tall stands of oleander, the smell of a primordial soup, a Petri dish of expanding biology. *And dead fish.*

It made sense – to grow grass in a desert you needed water and lots of it. The good people of Phoenix were draining nearby lakes to do that. No doubt many lake dwellers were sucked right along with their watery home only to find themselves choking to death on someone's thirsty Bermuda lawn a few hours later.

That was Todd Worwick's big project right? The Central Arizona Water Project. His plan to bring the rivers and lakes to the ranches and farms, not to mention the completely alien St. Augustine and Bermuda thatched lawns and ballparks of the young and growing metropolis affectionately known as *The Valley of the Sun.*

And just like that she was back in the present. Back to *why* she was here in the first place: connections between seemingly unrelated murders.

Two in LA, two in Phoenix…and now one more – different, but surely connected. And no matter how many back flips you took trying to find another way – all paths led to water and Todd Worwick.

She was pretty sure she'd be meeting Deanne's favorite investigative reporting project, senatorial hopeful, Todd Worwick, soon. Somehow she suspected it would not be a happy encounter. At least not as happy as Deanne's seemed to be.

A twinge at that. Jealousy, perhaps. *Oh Christ, yeah, I am jealous...a little.* Might as well admit it. *God, they'd had one night.* That was all it was.

Deanne had obviously never been with another woman. As far as Sara knew she could be nothing more than an experiment for Deanne, a "one-off."

It wouldn't be the first time.

A loud splash in the pool beside her. *Ow!* Sara could feel that belly-flop in her bones.

The girl's friends were laughing hysterically. The lifeguard looked concerned, but couldn't help a wry smile when the girl burst to the surface, laughing and crying in pain at the same time.

Sara shook her head. Man, did that ever bring her back. But it was time to go. She smoothed her skirt, collected her bag and sunglasses.

There in the shadowy stands of oleander beneath the palms, a squat cylindrical structure caught her eye. That thing likely held the irrigation controls for the baseball diamonds. The structure reminded her of that *Time Machine* movie – the one with the scary *Morlocks,* snow-white, evil creatures who lived underground and emerged through holes like this one to capture and feast on the cattle-like Eloy living in the city above them.

The shadows in the oleander hedge beyond brought an image she had never been able to shake.

She'd stayed late to practice on her own, and now, she danced on the rubber mat with her eyes closed, her feet stomping hidden controls that shot cool, fresh water over her, washing the chlorine away. She hadn't bothered turning on the lights, there was still enough sunset filtering through the locker windows high above her for her to shower, towel off and change.

She reached for her towel, and couldn't find it right away. She opened her eyes and was startled to see a tall silhouette in the short hallway between the showers and the lockers beyond...he held the towel out to her.

"Coach?"

Sara caught a scream before it left her throat.

A tall man stood in the shadows near the Morlock hole.

"Sara..." He said.

The warmth of the sun drained down through her heels. She nearly ran away like a frightened little girl.

But no one was there; only shadows.

She'd seen a man, she'd heard him. He'd been right there near the Morlock hole.

So where had he gone?

Irrigation water lapped up to her feet and withdrew, surely, suddenly back to the field before her.

The grass at her feet was completely dry.

As dry as the table had been once the water pulled to the gutters, burst the collection jugs, and slithered down the drain.

It was here. The same substance, like water but not water, a non-Newtonian semi-fluid, *her Oobleck; it had seen her at LA County, and it had found her here.*

She took a deep breath, her fists clenched.

She pulled off her sandals and carried them with her as she crossed the sun-drenched field into the enveloping shade of the cottonwoods and palms, feeling the cool jelly of life between her toes, the odors of life mixed with the all-too-familiar stench of death.

Finally, she stood at the concrete base of the Morlock hole. She hoisted herself up on her elbows for a look down into it. There was a steel Captain's wheel connected to heavy plates that would, no doubt, open or close the channels far below. A small ladder, not unlike those you'd find at the sides of a pool, led deep into it.

"What are you?" She whispered down into the hole.

Nothing.

And even with no one in the immediate area, she found herself unable to escape the embarrassment of speaking to no one at the bottom of a flow control pipe.

What did you expect? An answer?

Chapter 13

"I was expecting to see Carl..."

"Carl sends his regards and regrets."

Todd had entered the deep wood and leather sanctum of Monti's, La Casa Vieja – loosely translated as, "the old lady's house," the very house Senator Carl Hayden's parents had built, where they'd lived and conducted business for decades before moving on.

But Carl hadn't moved on, not completely. The building was a steak house now, but you wouldn't know that in here.

This was *Carl's* place of business, *the keep of Carl's castle.*

But Carl clearly wasn't going to be with them tonight.

Todd extended his hand. He took the seat offered him when he saw there would be no reciprocal gesture. The white-gloved black man who offered that seat stepped quietly away into the darkness.

The man who sat across from Todd had a face resembling a skull Todd once had seen in the Museum of Natural History. Unnaturally large bones protected small, keen eyes like the wooden frame of a frontier stockade.

"You've invited the press."

"A friend."

The man nodded, "That sort of friend can be good to have...if properly handled."

And now Todd understood: he *had indeed reached the upper echelon.* With that feeling came an unaccustomed one, just there at the edge of elation...*dread.* The man before him moved mountains – out of your way, or *over* you.

"You're, Mr. G."

Half of the man's face grinned, "*Mr. G?" The man considered the nickname.* "Carl does have a sense of humor."

"I'm honored. But why now?"

"That's only half the question you should be asking, the full question is, 'why *you,* why now?'"

"Fair enough."

"Change is coming. Not everyone is onboard with several projects that will be *key* going forward."

Todd considered his answer carefully.

"My focus is the same as Carl's. My stand on CAP, that won't shift."

Senator Hayden, nearly 90 now, was the "father of the Grand Coulee Dam" a project that tapped the biggest natural cash cow in the southwest, the Colorado River. Hayden had left his mark on every agricultural project in the southwest. Not only had he spawned Arizona's agricultural boom, the tax on water allotments negotiated with California and Nevada created the sort of political clout that made even Washington D.C. prick up its ears and take notice.

"Yes. That's where your focus needs to be for now. Make sure *both* heads are aligned on that – the big one *and the little one.* America still likes to believe its heroes are family men. There are bigger projects ahead if you play this correctly."

"The pressure is too much for Susan, right now."

"I can assure you, that pressure is only going to build from here."

"She's tougher than you know. She'll get her head together. She just needs a little time away."

"Understandable, *to a point.* And that point is *Sondra Tucker*."

"She's my *campaign manager."*

"And right now you and Sondra make a darling couple. That may be a problem."

"You've really come all the way here to tell me to fire Sondra?"

"I'm saying you and Sondra look good together; voters will see a triangle unless you pull her back, *way back.*

"We're all men here. We know the score. John Kennedy? Of course we knew about Marilyn and a dozen others...and I don't think we even *have* to mention Teddy's exploits. Even Lyndon has his little sideshow going.

"It's up to you to control the story. As long as the press is with you, we can count on a certain, *polite ignorance* from them. Give them a reason to keep the blinders on. If you don't, no *insurance policy* is going to cover that damage. The press won't claim ignorance forever. An *unfriendly* Press won't be ignorant at all."

Todd set his glass down, another pair of gloved hands took the glass away, wiped the ice sweat from the dark wood, and set another whiskey in its place.

"Focus on what's important. Lyndon has put a lot of leverage into this – but he's on his way out. Without him, and without Carl, we need to make sure our stars stay aligned.

"Like it or not – *and we know you do like it,* you are one of those stars, Candidate Worwick. That is *why you, why now."*

Todd took a healthy sip; the heady feel of raw power rising in him. *But was he getting too far ahead of himself?*

"I'd say Robert Kennedy's star is on the rise," he said, "and Chicago's not far off."

The Democratic National Convention would be in August, and time was flying toward it. With Lyndon and Carl out, the assassination of Martin Luther King, Jr. only weeks behind them, and racial tensions worse than they'd been in decades, this convention was going to resemble the Wild West. But Bobby Kennedy was in position to pull all of those horses in line.

The shadows over Mr. G's eyes were deep and dark. Only the candles on the table gave them any light at all, their only spark.

"The last thing Bobby Kennedy wants is *anything* Lyndon wants," Mr. G said, flatly.

Todd took a bigger sip than he should have. The burn nearly choked him. He held it.

Mister G. rose.

"Your *date* is here."

The waiter opened a door at the back of the room Todd hadn't even noticed before, seamlessly hidden in the rough, dark wood.

"How do you like your meat?" Mister G. asked. "They tell me the filet is *especially tender* tonight."

The waiter finally spoke, "What will the lady be drinking?"

"Manhattan."

The nameless waiter was gone. So was Mister G.

When Deanne entered, the drink was already in her hand.

"I remember the old movieolas in the lobby – but...I never knew this room was here."

"Nobody does," Todd said, still processing what had just taken place here, and what *could be* taking place behind the scenes. He'd always known he was meant for big things...*for real power.*

"Is something wrong?" She asked.

Deanne had chosen a blue dress, cut low in the front, the hem mid-thigh, the fabric embraced every curve of her.

"Not at all. Do you like filet mignon, rare?"

"Who doesn't?"

"It's coming. Drink that."

She did.

"Set the glass on the stand and come here."

She swallowed, set the glass down and took a hesitant step toward him.

He swept her into his arms and kissed her fully on the lips, she tasted sweet, and warm. Her resistance was slight...and gone, *and then there was only her mouth full on his, and the warm softness of her as he pulled up her dress and drove himself deep inside her.*

Chapter 14

"I'll get it!" Donovan tripped but caught himself, taking the short hallway from his room to the kitchen in two quick strides. He pounced on the phone.

He needn't have rushed. His mother rarely did anything quickly anyway, and, as soon as he lifted the receiver to his ear he knew it was only Terry. Terry suffered from every allergy known to man, and during the hot months – pretty much every month between March and November - Terry sounded like he was breathing through a straw.

He knew it *wouldn't* be Cassandra, but he'd hoped. *He always hoped.*

"Hey, Donnie."

"Hey, Terry."

"Whatcha' doin'?"

"Nothin,'"

"Wanna come over and swim?"

"Sure."

It was pretty much the same phone conversation they'd have every day once school was finally out - until they started high school in the fall. Not much time before they'd graduate elementary and start that familiar summer routine. Some days *golf* would replace *swim*, sometimes *watch a movie.* A science fiction movie called *Planet of Apes* was out. That looked good; they'd likely see that one pretty soon.

When he put the phone down, he saw his mother leaning in the doorway of the den, the TV was playing some soap opera behind her.

"You didn't think that was *her,* did you?"

"It was Terry, I'm going swimming."

"Your chores done?"

"Yes."

"Be back before the streetlights come on."

He went outside, retrieved his board shorts and a towel from the line. He dropped his pants and pulled on the shorts.

"You're better off *without* girls, Donnie." He hadn't realized Mom had followed him outside. "They're nothing but pretty traps. They'll trick you into putting a baby in them and you'll be with them forever."

"Yeah, Mom, I get it. I love you."

"I love you too, Donnie. You're meant for better things."

-=-=-=-=-=-=-=-

A minute later he was flying his bike down the street toward Terry's house. He pedaled fast and hard, the way he always did, but there was something more to it now, as though he were running away.

What he was running away from now was any clear thought.

The soreness in his muscles, the aches in his growing bones, the exhaustion, that stuff they called endorphins – what he needed more than anything right now was something to keep him from thinking.

Something had changed in him during that one moment at Cassandra's. A switch had flipped deep in his heart, a vital piece of him had been shut off – or *wanted* to be. These days, he wasn't thinking so much about cars and *fixing* things. *These days his thoughts had become very, very dark.*

Oddly, he'd thought a lot about *Spider-Man* – superheroes in general – but Spider-Man in particular. Spider-Man usually wound up winning in the long run, but he was very different than most of them. Peter Parker, the kid beneath the mask, was a few years older than Donovan, and he was *very* human. He could beat up bad guys, sure, but he took some heavy shots himself. Sometimes, you weren't quite sure he'd make it to the last panel.

Some comic book heroes were more like gods – impervious, maybe even immortal – but not *Spidey*. He actually got hurt a lot. You got the feeling he just might die.

And now, if Donovan thought too much, if he didn't distract himself, he wondered if he might die too.

Was this what happens when your heart breaks?

There would be other girls out there, *right?*

Cindy had been right under his nose all along. She might have been *the one* for him if there was such a thing.

So why did Cassandra's face come up whenever he didn't occupy himself with something else?

He rode past the stables on back streets shaded by cottonwoods and maple-leafed mulberry trees without even glancing their way. A year ago, even a few weeks ago, he would have stopped along the road to pet the horses, he'd have listened to the cackle of the chickens, reveled in the cool breeze as he weaved his way to Terry's. Now, head down, he pedaled fast and hard, seeing little more than the blur of asphalt passing beneath him.

One depressing *truth* about Spider-Man came to him then: Peter Parker *never got the girl.*

Peter Parker was meant for better things.

It didn't take long until Donovan found himself gliding up Terry's driveway.

He leaned the bike near the front door and let himself in as always.

Terry's older sister, Jenny, was practicing piano in the living room, she nodded to him without missing a note. Jenny was sixteen, she was cute, *really* cute, and already dating a sophomore at Arizona State University.

Donovan pulled sliced meat and cheese from the fridge like he always did at Terry's and fixed a sandwich.

Terry's pool was literally located right outside their sliding back door. One long step and you were in it.

Terry floated flaming red belly up on the raft. He wore blue and white board shorts like Donovan's. Terry himself went through several color changes in summer, white, red, or dappled white, brown and red once the peel started. It had already been a hot summer, and dappled would likely be his next stage.

For an Irish kid, Donovan was lucky. His mom was Italian and his skin tanned to a deep olive by mid-summer.

"You could make me a sandwich too, you know."

"Figured you'd already had two by now," Donovan said between bites.

"I had a bowl of cereal too, so what?"

Donovan waded in and sat on the steps in the shallow end, already halfway through with the sandwich.

Terry paddled lazily over.

"Something *special* in the pool-house."

"Alright." Donovan knew exactly what that meant. Terry was part of a very large family with lots of aunts, uncles and cousins. There was a party just about every Friday, and just about every Friday night, a bottle went missing. Not *missing* exactly since his parents never really seemed to keep track of them.

The pool house was nice, the rooms were actually bigger than Terry's bedroom, and furnished with whatever had been in the den or living room the last time Mrs. Denon refurnished. That happened every two or three years so the chairs and couches were new. The little house had its own swamp cooler, and a little kitchenette with a refrigerator.

Terry poured them both a plastic juice-glass full of vodka. They definitely wouldn't be golfing or even *leaving* Terry's today.

Ten minutes later, lightheaded, his throat and stomach burning, Donovan floated on his own raft a couple feet away from Terry's.

"You're still going camping at Lake Pleasant, right?"

It was an event with their Boy Scout troop. Since they'd both be in high school next year, it would likely be their last such outing. Being in the Boy Scouts wouldn't be cool in High School.

"Yeah, I'm going." Donovan said, without much enthusiasm.

"Cassie's dad is going to be there."

"I know."

"Do you think she'll be there?"

"It's *Boy* Scouts, *doofus.*"

They both laughed. It felt good. He and Terry told each other everything. Terry knew as much about that day at Cassandra's pool as Donovan did himself. Not that Donovan could really wrap his head around all of it. All he could be sure of was the experience had hurt him deeply.

It would be tough seeing her dad, but it wasn't like he really knew her dad anyway, and he'd have to get used to seeing his face a lot in the papers and on the news. The guy was likely to be their next Senator. The overnight at Lake Pleasant was just one more chance for the guy to get his picture taken for his campaign. There would be cameras and news people around, and Cassandra's dad probably wouldn't recognize Donovan from her birthday. Why would she say anything about him?

That thought made Donovan hurt even more inside. He wished he hadn't drunk the stupid vodka. He felt worse than ever now. He'd tried drinking beer once – he'd spit it out the second it hit his tongue. That stuff was gross.

"Man...you are...like completely gone," Terry said.

The sun baked Donovan's skin, his forehead was burning up, he rolled off the raft into the cool water, the chlorine stung his eyes a little, but it was good to be sealed off from the outside. He sank down into the water world, feeling the bubbles, watching the dance of bright diamonds and shadows made by the ripples above him, all the way down to the aqua floor. He pushed off and burst through the surface.

The sliding door opened and there was Jenny in a striped bikini, her hair pulled back and tied into a ponytail. He pulled himself onto the raft, careful to stay belly down.

"Remember...*she's my sister.*" Terry said, without so much as moving his head.

"You're such a dork," Jenny said, "Hi, Donovan."

"Hi, Jenny."

She sat at the side of the pool, splashed her legs and chest with water. She had been one of those untouchable objects of every boy's fantasy in their class for as long as Donovan could remember. He felt that embarrassing twitch down below. As melancholy as he was feeling, she *still* had that effect.

Acclimated to the cool water now, she slid down to the bottom step.

"I saw your friend, Cindy, yesterday," she said.

Donovan's heart leaped, questions quickly racing through his head, *had she asked about him? Was she feeling as bad as he was? Did she want to talk?* But the only question that made its way out was,

"Where?" And he was immediately sorry he'd asked.

"At Jimmy's. Cindy's a friend of his brother, Dave. Dave's the varsity quarterback at Ignatius."

Jimmy, of course, *was* Jenny's sophomore boyfriend from ASU. Donovan didn't know Jimmy or his brother, *Dave.*

"We caught them *kissing. Hot and heavy,"* she laughed. "It was kind of cute."

If Donovan could have dropped then, not just to the bottom of the pool but deep down through its grate to be sucked out to the ocean in pieces, he would have.

Chapter 15

"Did they ever find that donkey?" Sara quipped.

Deanne clacked away at her behemoth of a typewriter.

It had burned Sara. *Stupidly,* it really had.

But what had she expected, really? Todd was a powerful, handsome, manly-man with a little-boy grin. Deanne was, ultimately, a straight woman.

And I'm a lesbian or bisexual...or whatever the hell I am.

I was an experiment for her, nothing more. Let it go.

After meeting with Todd Worwick, Deanne had come home with *that look; that scent.* Deanne didn't need to say anything, *Sara knew what happened.*

Still, for someone used to the dispassionate dissection of the worst things imaginable, going deeply into the how and why of *this*...was…

Fuck...it hurts.

Deanne's house on the mountain was thankfully, large enough for two. Even without saying a word, they'd more or less divided things in half.

But the case they were working *couldn't* be divided in half.

They needed each other to solve it, and with one careless fall Deanne had taken herself out of it. At least from the investigative reporting standpoint. Deanne was *part* of the story now. Anything she wrote about the campaign was suspect from that night on. So she'd quit writing about it. Worse yet...she'd quit investigating it.

He'd done that on purpose, of course. Sara knew that, whether Deanne did or didn't. Todd Worwick, candidate, murder suspect, or potential victim, he had only been a piece in a puzzle before this, not worth hating. That was no longer the case. *Sara despised him now.*

No use telling Deanne the obvious, that she'd been used in more ways than one that night. One more broken heart was one more than that bastard deserved.

For now, Deanne had set up office in her desert nook just outside the master bedroom. Even with the cork mat she'd placed between her typewriter and the wrought-iron picnic table, to Sara the old beast sounded like a machine gun with a serious jamming problem.

"It's not a donkey – it's a white stallion," Deanne said, finally.

"Ah."

Apparently a prized high-school mascot had been abducted near school's end in Tucson. It was a big story...*in some alternate universe.*

Sara wasn't sure which was worse, her stupidity in thinking this relationship could have been something more for both of them, or Deanne's sudden lack of interest in the case.

Either way, it hadn't taken much to pack. All she had was her overnight and camera bags, and a small suitcase.

"You don't have to go, Sara."

"I only have a few more vacation days. It wouldn't hurt to actually take one."

Deanne nodded. Finally, she stopped typing. There was no glass beside her coffee cup. *Sober at last.* A small victory there, Sara thought, though Deanne's new sobriety likely wouldn't last.

"I'll miss you," Deanne said.

Her tears were real.

-=-=-=-=-=-=-=-

It took driving down the steep mountain road and several blocks after that for Sara's own tears to flow, and when they did, they flowed hard.

Before meeting Deanne her life was her job. It hadn't been the *best* way to fill a life, maybe, but it *had* filled it; it had been enough. The emptiness inside her now, was stark and deep.

As she drove toward the heart of the city, a huge window blue banner caught her eye. It nearly covered a half-floor of the windows on a glittering high-rise.

"Worwick's Our Man!"

*Oh, he is **that** all right...*

She nearly vomited.

Move on.

There were faster ways to get to that long freeway which would ultimately take her all the way home to Hermosa Beach. She should just drive straight there and ride out like some heartbroken cowboy galloping off into the sunset, but there was something she *had* to do while she was still here. One bit of unfinished business.

She had to go back to the park with the swimming pool and the Morlock hole one more time.

One good thing about this desert-survival experiment called Phoenix, was that it had been a *well-planned* experiment. The streets were built on an easy, square grid. You drove north-south or east-west. Make enough turns and you'd eventually be wherever you needed to be.

Eventually, she found her way back to the park. She turned down the tree-lined path, drove up to the lot near the swimming pool and set her brake.

No one else here yet, too early to open.

She scoured the baseball field with all of its shadows and light. There were still pools of mud the sun hadn't yet found and baked to hard clay.

W*here are you?*

What are you?

When that fluid had poured off her examination table on its way to freedom, it had *slowed* when she'd touched it, right before it escaped down the drain. It *knew* she was there. That *wasn't* her imagination. *Something drove it, an intelligence, a life-force. She'd felt it then, as impossible as that seemed.*

You came a hell of a long way to find me.

Or was it the other way around? Had she come a hell of a long way to find...it?

She took her shoes off and walked barefoot into the stinky, warm and sodden grass toward that big, upright concrete pipe. Her *Morlock hole.*

Sara stopped. *You're insane. You're heartbroken. Leave this manufactured, unlivable patch of desert and go home.*

But she would never travel this way again.

"Come out..." she said, out loud this time. "If you have something to say to me, say it!"

A movement...coming just beyond the tall oleander hedge beyond the pipe. Her broken heart stopped cold. Through a dead and leafless patch in the oleander, she saw a dark sedan pull to the side of the road. *Once more she'd been followed,* and once more she'd been too deep in her own stupid thoughts to notice.

She glanced toward her own car. No way she could get to it and drive away unseen.

Beyond the hedge, the sedan's doors creaked open and two men, overdressed in dark suits and sunglasses stepped out. One was tall and lanky, the other shorter, but thick as a bear. They approached the ballpark on foot, *not toward the entrance but through the oleander hedge.*

She was in the open, completely unprotected. Only the Morlock hole offered cover.

Three long fast strides and she was there, she set her shoes on the lip, pulled herself up and looked over.

God.

Water was thundering through it today. If she slipped she'd be pulled down and under, she'd drown and no one would ever know.

Twigs snapped off to her right. She caught the ladder with one hand, snatched her shoes from the lip, and threw herself over. She huddled tight against the concrete wall.

There couldn't be more than ten yards between this godforsaken pipe and that hedge, but she couldn't hear the men over the rush of the water. She had no idea how close they were. They could be walking past her hiding place or straight to it. Her heartbeat pulsed in her ears.

The current just beneath her feet slowed to a crawl, *then it stopped completely, the surface smooth as glass.*

In the sudden silence, she heard them picking their way through the branches of the oleander.

To her horror, *the water began to rise...but not straight up and over her as it should have. It climbed quickly up the sides of the tube and flowed over the lip.* A sheet of dark plastic slid with it. *No...not a sheet.*

Rain gear, the sort she associated with deep-sea fishermen.

Behind it, the concrete was completely dry.

The footsteps were close now.

"What the fuck!" She heard one of the men say.

"Are you gentleman lost?" The voice that spoke was deep, measured, and firm.

"What the hell?"

"You'll need to move your car. You're in a no-parking zone."

A long silence, and then one of them said, "...yeah, we didn't see that."

"The park entrance is just a few feet away if you care to drive in and visit."

"Sure...we'll do that."

"This hedge ends right over there. No need to ruin your fine suits on the way out."

Sara inched herself up the wall.

What the hell had just happened? Who was that?

She heard the men moving away, the swish of their suits, the squish of what were likely very expensive leather shoes now destroyed by the mud.

She had to see what was going on. Sara began climbing back to the surface, but self-preservation held her back. She clung to the side.

Creaks and cracks as the sedan's doors opened and shut. She heard the starter catch, the engine roared and the car drove off.

Sara nearly fell from the ladder when a man's head and shoulders appeared over the lip of Morlock hole. He was dressed in the gear she'd just seen rise up the wall.

The man's face was chiseled and handsome, with a hawkish nose and black hair that fell to his shoulders beneath the hood of his rain gear.

"You're safe now, *Sara.*"

He disappeared beyond the concrete lip. The rain gear flew over her head and dropped to the depths below her.

Once again...the water began to flow.

She pulled herself over the top and saw -

No one. No one there at all...

A few feet from the pipe, a large pool of water sank into the grass and was gone.

Sara walked back to her car stepping carefully now, slowly, as though she couldn't quite trust her feet to find solid earth beneath them.

Other cars had pulled in, the pool had opened. The slim lifeguard daubed a white gob of zinc oxide on her nose as she made her way to the chair.

Real kids screamed with laughter as they made their way from the pool house. The sun beat down with *real* heat.

Sara moved through the life around her as a ghost passes through walls, numbly aware, perhaps, that physical laws were no longer important to her, that she was not part of this world at all…

As she slid behind the wheel, she found herself gripping it with all her might, until her knuckles went white, refusing to let her *oh-so-light* head ascend through the roof and into that cloudless sky like a child's balloon, never to return.

She forced herself to breathe slowly, evenly. The temperature was rising inside the car, baking her where she sat. She started it, turned the air conditioning to full blast, until the contrasts of heat and cold shocked her back to life.

Had she died just then, just for a moment?

Yes. Yes, I did.

But now you are alive.

She was alive...and she couldn't leave now. Not after what she'd seen.

Sunlight glared from the squat concrete pipe far across the field.

Sara pulled out, this time winding her way around the pool and through the park until she found a different way out.

She had dissected death, she had leaped backwards from ridiculous heights and found safety below. *She had always done what it took to conquer her fear and she would conquer it now.*

And as much as she didn't want to believe in the supernatural, *the supernatural had touched her today.* She couldn't deny it.

Who are you fooling?

The truth was, she'd *wanted* to believe there was *something more* her whole life. It was the fear there was nothing more than this, no more than what she could see, that had driven her to forensics from the start. It had driven her, literally, to dissect *everything.*

She checked her mirrors for the dark sedan and saw none. They could be further back, they could be anywhere. How much did they know about her and about Deanne? Would the Secret Service *really* care enough about one candidate in Arizona to assign even one agent, let alone two?

In this age of political assassination maybe they did. She really didn't know.

But there had been a malignancy in the air with those two. She trusted her intuition on that. If the Secret Service wanted to talk to her or Deanne they would walk up to the door and do it.

These two were *predatory,* not protective.

Private detectives? Maybe.

How could she contact Tommy Red Hawk again? That had to be *him. Red Hawk was* her *non-Newtonian, her Oobleck.*

And he was real.

But what the hell was he? He'd saved her just now. He'd saved Deanne before. What did he know and why didn't he just come out of the shadows and tell them? He knew how to find them when he wanted to.

Because he's also a killer, Sara. A murderer many times over and you can prove that.

So why didn't he just kill me?

At last, Sara found the building she was looking for.

The high-rise with the big blue banner, the one that now contained Worwick's campaign headquarters, was also emblazoned with the words *Burl & Tennet.* His headquarters were in the agency where Worwick and campaign-manager Sondra had formerly worked.

How kind of his dead friend to offer him that space.

Inside that building, likely an office on that very floor with the banners, Tommy Red Hawk had murdered Ross Bennet.

So how does one get inside?

Sara wasn't likely to get an invitation to the Worwick Campaign Headquarters and even her new best buddies at Maricopa County would never get a search warrant.

Outside, volunteers with Stars & Stripes-emblazoned "*Worwick's Our Man!*" paper hats and shirts, busily hefted boxes of pennants, hats, and pamphlets from a van parked in the adjacent lot.

Sara pulled in and parked. *How do I play this?*

The answer came in the form of a gawky teenage boy who walked past her car, carrying a box of hats and shirts.

In less than two minutes, Sara was dressed in "*Worwick's Our Man!*" regalia, carrying a box filled with the same regalia into the building. The boy back in the van wore a smile and an image he'd never forget – his first glimpse of a twenty-four year old woman's back as she'd quickly changed in front of him. In *his* memory, he'd seen *boobies.*

She followed two chattering teen-aged girls and walked right past the security officers and into the elevator.

"He was actually here yesterday!" One of them chirped.

"No!"

"Yes!"

"You saw him!"

"Yes!!!"

"He's a *dream!*"

"I know!!!"

Sara felt like she was fifty. When they finally noticed her, Sara smiled and nodded, "so *cute!*" She said.

They went back to their chattering as if they'd never seen her.

The elevator opened to a reception desk. She followed the girls into the bedlam beyond.

Banks of desks, chairs, girls and phones ringing off the hook. Stacks of boxes filled with shirts, hats and pennants. Posters of a smiling, "Our Man" Worwick, and American flags everywhere she looked.

"*Worwick's our man, thanks for calling. Keep our water flowing! How much will you pledge?*"

"Worwick's Our Man, thanks -"

And from the few windows not plastered with the bright blue banner, she saw pure, bright, unadulterated desert sunlight.

"Just over here girls..."

A pretty woman not much older than Sara, chin squeezing a phone to her shoulder, waved her hand, barely looking at them as she thrust one finger toward boxes of Worwick paraphernalia stacked near the windows.

The woman turned away quickly, speaking sharply into the phone.

Sondra? Was this Todd Worwick's other woman?

Other than Deanne, of course.

The girls reverently placed their boxes on top of the others.

In the crime scene photos, Tennet's desk had been larger than what she could see through the windows of any offices off the main room - and there was one feature in particular that didn't match at all – his view. In the photos, Tennet's office boasted a panorama of desert and the pointy mountain just north of here – the one they called Squaw Peak. All the offices in this room faced the city.

But a hallway led off the main room.

Sara placed her box atop the others and followed the girls back toward the reception desk. As another group came in, she slipped by them into that hallway.

The offices here had a clear view of Squaw Peak.

And next to the last one, a shiny skin of water flowed down a sandstone water feature built into the wall.

She'd found Tommy Red Hawk's way in.

A sign indicated this was Todd Worwick's campaign office now, but as she reached for the door, something she saw through the window took her breath away.

Two large framed movie posters, one featuring cowboys, the other, men carrying long, straight swords.

The Magnificent Seven. The Seven Samurai.

"Excuse me, volunteers aren't allowed in this area."

It was the woman she'd just seen on the phone.

"Sorry, I'm having a little...female *emergency, you know - where's the ladies' room?"*

"The *public* restrooms are just outside the elevators – before you get to the reception desk -"

"Oh *thank you!"*

"They should have covered that at orientation." The woman said.

"You know – I was just so excited to be part of this, I mean, I must have missed that!"

"I'm sorry...but you don't look familiar."

"Wait...are you, *Sondra Tucker? THE Sondra Tucker?"*

"...yes."

"Oh my gosh, I've heard so much about you! *I can't believe it's actually you!* My name's Sara! I can't believe I really got to meet you!"

"Well, thank you...you need to use the bathrooms just outside -"

Sara grabbed her hand and shook it vigorously.

"Thank you! This is *boss!"*

She moved past Sondra as quickly as she could, down the hall, past the mayhem and reception. She sent a box-carrying volunteer tumbling as she raced to catch the closing elevator door.

-=-=-=-=-=-=-=-

Deanne's red Starfire was still parked at the top of the drive.

Thank god, she hasn't left.

Sara screeched her brakes as she pulled up next to it.

Deanne must have heard her. She'd already run around the outside of the house to greet her. She threw her arms around Sara before Sara was halfway out of her car.

"Don't *ever* do that again!"

"Leave you?"

"Never race up my driveway like that – you nearly hit my car."

"You're an ass."

The hug was warm and strong. It felt like *home.*

Chapter 16

"A story came off the wire you need to hear," Deanne said.

"Another mascot? Did someone *TP* a house?"

"Who's the ass now?" Deanne asked.

"There's a lot *you* need to hear – about Red Hawk, and those goons who have been following us."

"Tell me while we drive. Throw your stuff in the house and grab your camera bag."

Sara dropped her overnight in the kitchen.

"Where's that gun?"

"I've got it."

"Good."

Sara slung her camera pack over her shoulder and slid in beside Deanne, just as Deanne started backing down the hill.

"Our friend, Red Hawk, saved *my ass* today. Those goons following us mean business. They came after me. I don't know what they would have done if Red Hawk hadn't shown up."

"Where were you?"

"At a park down in the valley. Where we going?"

"Cemetery across town – then to the library. I think I missed something in that paper. You went to a park? What park?"

"Perry, or something like that. He showed up there that day you and Worwick…," she stopped herself. "Anyway...I should have told you –

but I wasn't sure I actually saw him, or that I really saw *anything*... But it was him – *and if he hadn't come back today -"*

Deanne gripped the wheel so tightly the car moved to the right. She had to pull it back in line. She took a breath and shook her head.

"*I saw him too.* Probably close to the same time you did. I was at Encanto Park. I thought someone called my name. I looked, and he was there in the water and then he was gone – like a ghost."

"It was the same with me. I had to go back there one more time...just to see if there was any chance he was real."

Sara kept her eyes on the mirrors, checked every intersection, every car they passed. No one following them now; at least, no one she could see.

"But there's more, Deanne, *a hell of a lot more."*

She told Deanne everything – from the park and the men from the sedan...to Worwick's campaign headquarters…and last of all, *the movie posters.*

Deanne was silent through it all.

It wasn't until they'd gone all as far west as Sara figured the civilized part of Arizona went and pulled into what seemed to be an endless field of shade trees and monuments, that Deanne spoke.

"Seven men and seven lilies." She said. "*The Magnificent Seven. The Seven Samurai.*"

She drove into a particularly sad looking section of the cemetery, poorly kept, bald earth where grass should be, even the trees here seemed to be struggling to hold on. Deanne parked, quickly checked a map she'd scrawled on a sheet of typing paper, and they began to walk.

"Whatever bond they have, Worwick's obviously proud to be one of them."

"Even though four of them are dead," Sara noted.

"At *least* four. I'm pretty sure the tattoo is what they burned off his thigh when they killed Barney."

"They burned it off so *we* wouldn't see it. Barney didn't drown so Red Hawk didn't kill him. Those two I saw this morning - they weren't there to question me, I *know* that. Red Hawk knew it too."

"I was such a fool." Deanne shook her head.

Sara fought the urge to agree out loud. But there were much more important things at stake. And now they were walking through the home of the dead, the final destination for their bodies anyway. For some, the most unfortunate of them, after a short stay with someone very much like herself.

"Whatever connects the *seven,* Todd Worwick is likely more than *one* of them. There's a very good possibility he's the ringleader or he'd be dead by now," Sara said. "So who are we looking for?"

Deanne checked her map again, she looked toward a hilly area not far away, she started that way and Sara followed.

"We're looking for that *connection.* I think we're about to find it," Deanne said. "A caretaker was badly injured here yesterday - thrown into the air *by a geyser of water.*"

"If that was Red Hawk, from what I've seen he needs a way in – a water source of some kind. This place is *bone* dry, like this whole town, if you don't mind my saying."

They stopped atop a hill in the shade of a tall, wide tree.

"There's an underground stream that comes out...right there."

"Oh my god."

Below them, a stagnant pool fed the only green spot in this section of the cemetery. Sitting just beyond that pool, one grave was blanketed, foot to headstone, in dead, moldering *lilies.*

They walked down to it in stunned silence.

Deanne cleared the lilies from the stone.

Haseya Avery. September 8, 1939 – *1953.*

"1953? That's all they had?" Deanne asked.

"I'd say they gave up looking for her the same year she disappeared. It shouldn't take more than a bone to pin the time-of-death closer than that – even back then. This girl *vanished.*"

Deanne nodded. "This is the murder Red Hawk wants us to solve."

The trip to the microfiche machines at the Phoenix Public Library confirmed the connection they were looking for. Barney Willis had indeed cut the section from the newspaper that told the story of a boy's drowning, of the brave attempts by his brother and friends to save him, but it was the story on the *back* of that page, the one with the photo of a missing girl, *Haseya Avery,* he'd framed and enshrined.

"Look at these dates," Deanne said. "The paper is from Sunday, June 4, 1953. Joseph Worwick's accident at the lake happened that weekend. The story says Haseya Avery started walking home from school that Friday, June 2, never to be seen again."

"June 2 is *this weekend,*" Sara said, *"Sunday."*

"Todd has a campaign event at Lake Pleasant this weekend - an overnight with the Boy Scouts."

"The *fifteen year anniversary* of her disappearance and he's at Lake Pleasant with the Boy Scouts? Is he *celebrating?"*

Deanne felt the blood drain from her, ice water took its place as she read on. She shook her head. "She went to Saint Bartholomew – my cousin's Parish.

"Sara, it's on the same block as two high schools – *literally* between them."

"Can Pat let us see the school records?"

Deanne nodded, "That's a touchy situation, but I'm pretty sure he can get them."

Sara frowned.

"Where did Worwick go to high school?"

-=-=-=-=-=-=-=-

Donovan forced his fingers between the starched collar and his neck. It was hot, and, as it turned out, he needn't have worn a stupid tie at all. No one else had. His mother had insisted.

Terry sat beside him on the bleachers in the big gym. He too wore a dress shirt and slacks, but no tie. Terry's mom was cool.

With graduation next week, St. Bart's had let the eighth-graders spend this morning at an "open-house." They were in the St. Ignatius gym. It was the biggest and nicest high school gym in the state – the Los Angeles Lakers practiced here when they were in town. It was a major selling point for young athletes to attend the Jesuit-run school. Not like it needed a selling point for Catholics. Donovan really had no choice. It was right next to his elementary school and his mom had already put down most of their savings for him to attend.

The girls' school across the way, St. Augustine's, was the *bigger* interest for Donovan and his male friends. Apparently, after freshman year, you could take classes there. The idea of being the only guy in a class of 40-some girls was the biggest selling point Donovan could think of for being sentenced to four years of a Catholic boys' school run by priests. After this boring presentation was over, the St. Bart's girls would be splitting off and heading through St. Augustine's for a tour. Not like anyone at St. Bart's needed one. At one point or another they'd all slipped into the halls of both schools and explored them thoroughly.

The priest at the microphone in the center of the basketball court droned on.

Donovan had seen Cassandra filing in with the rest of the students today. He was pretty sure she'd seen him too, but she'd looked right past him. That hurt, and maybe it was some stupid game, or maybe she really didn't ever want to see him again.

He'd seen Cindy too – the girls were all in their pleated red skirts and white blouses, the same as always, but somehow she looked prettier than ever today. And, oddly, when she'd looked at him, *he* was the one who looked away.

The Bart girls would be trading in those red skirts for St. Augustine's blue next year.

Terry yawned loudly beside him.

"I'd rather be in Geography class than this."

"No you wouldn't."

"This has to end eventually, right?"

When it eventually did end, they were directed to assemble alphabetically in groups, each assigned to a senior guide from their respective schools.

As Donovan filed out with the others, he looked for a banner with an "O" to assemble beneath. One of the St. Ignatius guides bumped him as he walked past.

"Boondocker at Pleasant, Saturday night," he whispered with a smirk, when Donovan turned.

"What? What's that? What's a *Boondocker?"*

But the kid just kept walking.

Whatever it was, Donovan would be at the lake anyway. He, Terry and the rest of the scouts in his troop were already packed and ready. As soon as this dumb assembly was over, they'd board a bus at St. Bart's for a camping weekend at Lake Pleasant. Great Wave would be open for them all day tomorrow. And, of course, joy of joys, Cassandra's dad would be telling ghost stories and roasting weenies with them tomorrow night.

"Alright eighth-graders, my name is David. Fall in and come with me. We'll go through Gardner Hall first. Stay in the middle of the hall, don't touch anything."

The senior projected that haughty air of authority, even though he was shorter than Donovan, and the boys fell in behind him. To Donovan, he sounded a lot like the hosts at Disneyland's Haunted Mansion – the same spiel they gave as they guided you down the hallway and into the little pods that carried you from room to room.

Black robed priests greeted them as they came through. No matter how much some of them smiled now, four years at this school would be no picnic.

The school had actually been a mission built way back when the Jesuits had first come through to help settle the Indians, and the adobe hall David led them into had been a residence hall built later as "boarders' quarters" when St. Ignatius students actually lived at the school.

Large frames held the senior portraits of past graduating classes – every guy looked to be a grown man, at least from Donovan's point of view.

As he walked quietly past classrooms filled with very serious students, David reverently pointed out the photos of the some of the most famous grads. Near the end of the hall, he stopped the group and pointed to one in particular, that Donovan, and everyone else recognized immediately

"Former Varsity Quarterback, and our next senator, Todd Worwick," David beamed.

If Deanne Mulhenney and Sara Poole had been there, they would have recognized several others in Worwick's class...all of them deceased.

Chapter 17

Deanne's breath whistled through clenched teeth, she gripped her wheel tight as she drove. They hadn't needed Pat's records on this one – a pass through the high school sports pages from the early 'fifties told them everything they needed to know. Todd had been a star quarterback for St. Ignatius. At least three other "samurai," Ross Tennet, Charlie Webb, and Richard Bilken were standout players on the team.

"Todd Worwick *is a monster,"* Deanne said, finally.

Sara nodded as she watched the mirrors, "Have you talked to him since -"

"He won't answer the private line he gave me."

Sara tried not to register her lack of surprise.

"Don't say it."

"I didn't." Sara checked the mirrors again. "Not even think'n it."

Deanne took a breath.

"We need to confront him at the lake – out in the open, in front of the cameras. Any sign of our two friends?"

"Haven't seen them. They're probably scoping out the lake right now."

"I'll call my friends at KPHO, they'll be there tomorrow. They can get us through security as long as Worwick's people haven't gotten to them yet."

"The wildcard in all of this is Red Hawk," Sara said. "We know there was some sort of gathering of the seven simpletons at Lake Pleasant the weekend Haseya disappeared and Worwick's brother had his accident. It doesn't take a genius to place Haseya with them. Red Hawk obviously thinks he's avenging her. This is the same weekend she disappeared. You have to believe Worwick being at the lake tomorrow night is exactly what Red Hawk's waited for."

Deanne nodded. "But it's been so many years. He could have killed Todd and the others a long time ago. Something new set this in motion."

"If Todd Worwick was the ringleader, I'm sure Red Hawk wants him tied to Haseya's death as much as he wants to kill him. He wants you to write the story. My guess is that's why *we're* still alive."

"Tommy Red Hawk's on *our side.*"

Sara shook her head, "no."

"I felt like I'd been saved when he showed up. But he's a killer, Deanne. He's murdered four people we know of – that's not even counting those men on the train."

"He's protected both of us."

"He doesn't want us dead *yet.*" Sara corrected, "That doesn't mean we can trust him."

"Rod Hawk knows what happened to Haseya, he led me to Barney. We know Barney didn't kill himself and his murder doesn't fit the others. Those agents weren't there just to interrogate you – they were *threatening you, maybe worse*, you felt it, so did Red Hawk. What if they were the ones who murdered Barney and set up that scene?"

"We're in way over our heads here." Sara took a deep, calming breath, that didn't calm her at all. "Red Hawk knows who we are, and he knows how to find us. We're all connected by water in one way or another. If he wants us dead or alive he can get to us."

"He knows how to keep a secret too. The men he worked with at the ice house said he was mute."

"I'm sure he had nothing he cared to say to them."

Deanne considered that, it fit what little she really knew of him. That night, throughout the horror of what had happened to her, and what he did to those men, he had said absolutely nothing.

Nothing she could remember, in any case.

"No question Red Hawk was working with Barney. Red Hawk and Barney likely met at that grave. Barney took her flowers and dropped them on my doorstep."

"Barney was giving you the count," Sara said.

"Maybe that was Barney's penance for being one of the seven. The shrine makes me think Barney had real remorse over Haseya. Likely explains the way he lived. He went to an expensive school, had a pretty good shot at a hell of a better life than he wound up with."

"And the "geyser" that blew up on the caretaker – sort of a tantrum by Red Hawk?"

Deanne agreed, "Frustration that Barney was gone, maybe even genuine sorrow. He obviously has feelings. He's carried Haseya's memory with him a long time."

As Deanne drove the car up the long narrow drive up to her house on Camelback Mountain, another thought, a question that had been smoldering beneath all of this for Sara.

"We still don't know the *'why now?'* of all this. There have been plenty of anniversaries before this weekend, but he only started picking off the seven sickos in the past few weeks."

Deanne pulled up beside Sara's car and shut off the engine. She took the keys from the ignition and, for a moment, they sat silently. A red sunset had begun, but the heat remained, and without the constant flow of air it quickly enveloped them in a blanket of heat. Still, neither of them moved a muscle.

"Joey," Deanne said, finally. "Todd's brother. We know he wasn't dead when they pulled him out of that lake... *What if he didn't die at all?"*

A cold tingle ran down the back of Sara's neck despite the heat.

"What if he's been *asleep* all these years...and one month ago *he woke up?"*

Sara could feel Deanne shudder even from where she sat.

Simultaneously, they cracked open their respective doors and got out. Suddenly space had compressed, become unbearably tight and oppressive.

"I've got to check in with the paper and call KPHO. Best to drive out to Lake Pleasant in the evening tomorrow, after the heat breaks. Forget the nice name, there is nothing pleasant out there. No shade to speak of. Nothing but cactus and sun."

"Somehow, that's not a surprise," Sara said.

Deanne dropped her keys on the counter, snatched the receiver off the wall and stretched the cord all the way to the refrigerator. She poured herself a tall glass of water and drank as she dialed.

"Mick," said the gruff voice on the line.

"Mick, it's Deanne."

"Pleasure...you just caught me leaving."

"Are you heading to Lake Pleasant today?"

"You read palms too? Lot of callouses on mine."

"No doubt. I've got a medical examiner with me, any chance we can hitch a ride?"

"As lovely as that sort of company sounds, can't do it. Security's tight on this one."

"She's *really pretty."*

"That's nice. Still, no can do."

"Special favor? Come on, Mick. We'll meet you there. It's important."

"Deanne..." He sighed, *"Zero chance of that happening...so I guess I'll see you there."*

"You're a peach, Mick."

"So you say. Don't thank me yet."

From the back of the house, water ran in the shower. The sound of company. More welcome now than ever.

Sara appeared in the kitchen beside her, toweling her hair, her face flushed and shiny. Even California girls had a tough time in this heat, somehow that made Deanne smile.

"What's the word on your friends?" Sara asked.

"They've been 'gotten to,' but I think we still have a chance with them. If not...we're going in on our own, full cowboy."

Sara nodded.

"*Yippie I Kay Yay."*

Deanne's call to Tricia at The Gazette yielded two messages - one follow-up on the case of *the great mascot-napping,* the other a contact for a story she'd been looking at concerning the homeless in Tucson. She thanked the girl as she mechanically jotted down the numbers.

She tried Todd's line one more time, staring down a bottle of Jack Daniels sitting on the counter. She turned away from it as the phone rang...and rang.

Everything pointed to Todd as being the cause of all of this. But what if he wasn't? He was a target now.

A target either way.

She'd considered calling Sergeant Henry. It was a consideration she'd made and unmade over and over again. In the end she didn't. She was in way too deep. She'd broken too many rules, likely more than one law along the way, Sara too.

Todd was protected. *Well protected.*

She and Sara were the ones headed into the lion's den.

Pat would appreciate that metaphor. They were already meeting for lunch tomorrow. He was the only one who knew the story – at least enough of it that she'd had to buy his silence with the Sacrament of Confession. She'd given him more than a fair share of grief already...

She and Sara were exposed with no one protecting them but each other. Red Hawk would be at the lake, no doubt. If she and Sara got in his way, then what? And if he got to Todd first, who could stop him? No matter what she and Sara did, the future didn't look good.

If only she could talk to Red Hawk first. But Sara was right...he could reach them any time he wanted. The ball was clearly in his court.

She left the Jack where it was, and took a glass of water back to her bed.

After an hour of staring at the veins in the wooden beams overhead, the comfort of Sara slipping under the sheets beside her was a welcome surprise.

They held each other until dreams came at last.

Chapter 18

"Grab something to eat for the drive – I've got a couple thermos bottles for water. I'll make sandwiches. There's -"

"Nothing at the lake, I know. What about that Great Wave thing?"

"Wouldn't chance my life with that food."

They had woken late and driven into the valley for breakfast. They'd met Pat for lunch at the Biltmore Hotel, where Sara had taken advantage of the luxurious, blue-tiled pool. While Deanne and Pat discussed the homeless situation in Tucson and everything *but* Haseya Avery and *The Seven Samurai*, Sara swam like a dolphin and worked on her tan.

They'd made it a perfect day.

Because it could be their last.

Deanne pushed that thought away.

"I need to call the paper."

"Go ahead," Sara, snapped open the fridge, "I'll make the sandwiches."

Moments later, the ever-present, ever-efficient Tricia was on the line.

"You have an urgent call from Susan Worwick."

Deanne felt an odd "click" from somewhere deep in her lizard brain.

"She left her number – she said she has to talk to you immediately."

Of course she did.

"I've got her number – but run it by me again."

Tricia did.

"Did she say anything else?"

"Only that she emphasized 'immediately.'"

"Okay. Thanks, Trish. I'll call her."

"What is it?" Sara asked. She had literally put together an assembly line, bread, sandwich meat, greens, condiments...all in a neat row…

"Susan Worwick wants to talk to me today."

"Well...isn't *that* interesting?"

Deanne nodded. She dialed the number.

"Susan."

"Hi Susan, it's Deanne Mulhenney."

"Deanne, I know you're interested in Haseya Avery. I have something you need to see tonight."

"I can be there tomorrow."

"That won't work. Porter and Aggie are camping at the Arcosanti site tonight. They can't be here when I show you."

Deanne glanced over at Sara and shook her head.

"Can't do it tonight. Tell me what you have."

"I will tonight – you know where I am. I'll be waiting." There was a click, and the line went dead.

Deanne dialed back. The phone rang...and kept ringing.

"What's that all about?" Sara said.

"She wants me there tonight."

"Of course she does."

Deanne took a deep breath.

"Forget her," Sara said. "*If we want to see this through, we have to be at Lake Pleasant tonight.*"

"Susan *knows* we're looking into Haseya Avery now. She didn't even mention her before. *That places them all at the lake that night."*

"They're separating us. It's a set-up."

Deanne nodded, "It is. But what if she really *does* have something. Hard evidence?"

"If it isn't dinnerware made out of Haseya's bones, it's a ruse."

"You haven't seen where she lives. That may not be far off."

"If you really think seeing whatever the hell Susan has is that important, I'm going with you."

"Crap, I want a drink."

"That is *not* the answer."

"What *is?"*

"Come on, Deanne? Do you really think whatever she has is only going to be there one night?"

"What if it is? We don't know if we'll get through security at the lake. Even if KPHO gives us passes, there's no guarantee those goons who've been following us will let us anywhere near him at this point. If we can't get to Todd *and* we miss out on whatever Susan has we miss an opportunity to prove they were all there with Haseya. Like I said – she never mentioned Haseya before. This could be the key."

Sara wanted to scream. Over the mountain, dark storm clouds had begun to form. Finally, she let out a breath she felt she'd been holding all day. She pulled a map from her camera bag.

"Show me where that damn lake is. You make sure you keep that gun close."

The skies were dark now, Sara could feel static electricity building around her. The fine hairs stood straight up on her neck.

Few cars on the highway. No one tailing them now.

Deanne's Starfire followed a short distance behind her. Deanne flashed her turn signal; the next exit would be the one leading Sara to Lake Pleasant.

A creek meandered off to the right of the freeway, and as much as Sara feared Red Hawk, as much as she questioned whether he saw them as anything more than disposable tools of his vengeance now, she wished *and wished hard,* he would rise up from that creek now.

Sara took her foot off the gas, ready to make her turn, feeling very much like the ejected first stage of a rocket as Deanne continued on toward Piñon Rim.

Just past the turn, Deanne slowed too, for a moment it seemed she might stop completely.

Don't do it. Don't turn around. I won't let you go if I see you now.

Deanne flashed her lights and gradually picked up speed. Sara raised her hand; a farewell gesture Deanne couldn't possibly see, but one Sara knew she would *feel.*

An unaccustomed feeling of emptiness and dread as she watched those taillights grow smaller in the night...and an unaccustomed prayer.

God, keep her safe.

Sara looked back to her own road *barely in time to avoid a dark figure standing dead ahead.*

She slammed her brakes and stopped in a cloud of dust.

Tommy Red Hawk stood in her way, a mountain dressed in black rain gear. His long black braids hung to his chest beneath the hooded jacket.

He walked up to her window and tapped it. She rolled it quickly down.

He bent until his big face was even with hers.

"Hitch a ride?" He said softly.

Moments later, Sara was back on her way to a god-forsaken waterhole in the middle of the desert with extreme danger ahead, night falling, and a powerful murderer sitting beside her. The sheer weight of him made the car pull right.

Why the fuck wasn't she terrified?

"Did you really need a ride?" She said, finally, because she had to say something.

"Easier. Faster from here."

"Not enough water?"

He smiled, "That would be a twisting path through a hostile world."

The description nearly made her laugh – at herself. She hadn't *expected* him to be articulate.

"Hostile? What are *you* afraid of?"

"Nothing."

To fear nothing. What could that feel like?

Sara shook her head as they sped through the desert. She, on the other hand, was scared to death of what lay ahead. Even without the brain-baking sun, with the temperature now dropping rapidly and the moonlight fighting its way through the clouds, there was nothing of comfort here. Prickly Pear, Cholla, gigantic, bony Saguaro covered with long needles that were more like little spears, Barrel Cactus also well-armed, even the plant life was built to kill you. She'd lived on or near a beach her entire life. Even with the omnipresent sense of the great mother ocean beside her, the fountain of all life, she had often been afraid. Her first climb up the ladder of a high dive had been frightening, her first backward dive, terrifying. Constant practice had removed much of the uncertainty, but the chance of a miscalculation, a slip...the fear was always there...*and there was always 'that moment,' that hesitation just before you made the decision to push off...*

And then there were the predators – the evil that came to you smiling with praise, a pat on the backside *held just too long...*

Always a danger. Always a fear. Even kumite, practice combat in Karate and Jujitsu, held the danger of crippling blows, permanent injury, even death. The interest she'd developed in martial arts, was her way of fighting back the fear. Forensic pathology was her way of dismantling death, dissecting it – finding courage through understanding.

But even seeing death in its worst forms, often caused by humanity in its worst forms, the realization that the human body was simply a machine that could break down, wreck, be dismantled and crushed for worthless scrap hadn't taken away her fear.

He watched her now, she could feel his eyes.

"I feel pain. I will die like anyone else."

"Then how can you *not* be afraid?"

There was neither humor nor self-pity in his voice when he said.

"Because I don't care."

She didn't want to know how *that* felt. She was more comfortable with her fears. There was a path leading off the main road about a half mile ahead of them.

She'd memorized the map, the few paths leading from the main one all headed to the lake. The Boy Scouts were camped at the dam – not far from the wave machine. Worwick's camp was near a landing across the lake. He'd likely had his evening 'campfire with the scouts' photo shoot. Tomorrow morning he'd be joining them for breakfast and the official opening of *Great Wave.*

The lake wasn't in sight yet, not the barest hint of water but for the building thunderheads above them.

"We will be running into trouble," Red Hawk said.

"Worwick has some nasty people around him."

"Worwick and his people are no trouble."

"You can't just kill them."

There was no assent or denial. Finally, he said, "There are worse things waiting for some than death. I'm not welcome here. My people, the Navajo, are to the north and east. This is mostly Apache land."

"Deanne said Susan Worwick thinks she's safe from you in Piñon Rim."

"My own people would not welcome me there. I've revealed secrets to an outsider. That can't be taken back or forgiven."

"Who's going to mess with *you?"*

He lifted his chin toward the desert beyond.

"*True creatures* like myself...*skinwalkers*."

He wasn't the only one. Of course not. Why would he be?

The moon was being swallowed before her now, only darkness beyond her headlights. God knows whatever else was out there and she didn't even have a gun.

"Are they like you...*water?"*

"Water is *my* way. Their way is over land. They will take the shape of desert beasts."

-=-=-=-=-=-=-=-

Clearly, no one was home in Piñon Rim. The new Porter homestead was dark. Deanne felt a moment of sickening dread. Was it a ruse? Had she truly left Sara alone to face Worwick and his men for nothing?

The clouds here were clearing and the moon behind them had created a landscape of black and silver.

It had been a dangerous enough drive when it was dry and daylight, with Aggie, the perpetually high flower girl, to guide the way. With no light but her headlights revealing the hills of muck and rock, traveling over roads that were barely more than gravel paths, it had been death-defying.

On the way here she'd done exactly what you were never *ever* supposed to do in the desert, she'd driven over a washed-out roadway. For once, luck had been with her.

She took a deep breath.

Susan was here, somewhere. *She could feel it.* But where?

Oh, Jesus, fuck.

Up above the hillside cemetery, at the top of the cross formed by the white stone paths, a campfire flickered near the mouth of the old mine.

"I often come up here to listen to the spirits," Susan said with a whimsical smile, a balloon glass of red wine in one hand, a joint in the other.

"You don't find it creepy?"

She considered that. "Sometimes. How did you find my *husband?"*

"Are you really looking for an answer?"

Susan puffed her joint, Deanne declined when she offered it. Susan gave a '*to each their own'* smile.

"Let me guess...he was rough, you found that erotic. You came."

"Well...*that's* more information than I was going to provide."

Susan gave a laugh that was more of a cough.

"Look at you...you are truly 'screwed.' You wanted a story. Now you're part of that story and you can't use it."

"Not that *part* of it, certainly."

"None of it. You know that as well as I do – as well as Todd does. Whatever ethics your profession pretends to have – you've thrown them away right along with your career. No one will believe anything you write about him now. Todd knew what he was doing. He used you – like he does everyone, and that is exactly why he'll be president one day."

"I seriously doubt that. I know why you're here, Susan. It isn't Todd you're getting away from. *It's Red Hawk.*"

Susan's face seemed to go blank for a moment. She prodded a log closer to the flames with a branch.

"So you found Joey's *imaginary red friend."*

"That's what you wanted isn't it? For me to find him, bring him out in the open?"

"Well." Susan pulled the cork from one of two wine bottles sitting on the Navajo blanket beside her. "You're better at your job than I thought." She filled her half-empty glass to the rim, and nearly emptied it in one long gulp. She withdrew another glass from her picnic basket. "I'm being a terrible hostess, this Cabernet is really, really deep. Would you like a glass?"

"No, thank you, I'm good. Exactly what do you know about Haseya Avery?"

A flicker that had nothing to do with the play of light and darkness the dancing flames cast between them, a flash of very real anger in that pool of perpetual calm Susan Worwick exuded. She set both glasses down.

"I know she was a slut."

"She was only *thirteen* when she disappeared."

"Nearly *fourteen.* And she knew *exactly* what she was doing, *the effect she had on boys.* Don't play naive, Deanne. You're pretty, you remember being that age."

"I must have been sheltered."

"You know as well as I do some girls just have that...*sense.* Or they lack *common* sense, maybe that's a better way to put it. Hassie was one of those."

"Hassie? Like, *Cassie?"*

Susan glared at her now.

"Never, *ever* call Cassandra that."

Your husband does...

"The girl was at least three years younger than you, Susan. Why would you even *know* who she was?"

Susan took a pull from the joint. She eyed Deanne, measured her. Clearly, the conversation had moved into a sensitive area. Despite the elegant facade, Susan had seemed very, very young when they'd first met. She looked much older to Deanne now.

"I didn't really. I just heard the talk. Oh, I saw her flirting with those boys. You couldn't help but see it. Her school, St. Bartholomew, is right between my high school, St. Augustine, and Todd's, Saint Ignatius."

"My cousin is the Pastor at Saint Bartholomew. I know."

"Then you probably know Augustine girls always date Ignatius boys – at least the girls that aren't already dating a college boy."

"So…?"

"Augustine and Ignatius trade classes. The Ignatius boys walk past Bartholomew every day on their way to and from Augustine. Most of them don't pay attention to those little girls."

"Are you saying your husband did?"

Her eyes narrowed.

"Todd...got everything he needed from Augustine. But other boys – if a girl made sure she got their attention..."

"Again...you're putting a lot of blame on a kid."

Susan, shook her head. She raised her chin, literally looked down her nose at Deanne. Deanne had to resist a sudden urge to slap her.

"Are you really that...*inexperienced,* Deanne? Haseya...was *exotic* to the Ignatius boys. Coffee and cream skin, long, black, shiny hair. She was a beautiful young woman."

"Girl," Deanne corrected.

"Whatever you say. She was a lovely half-breed, Irish...and Apache, I think."

"Navajo. Her name means, *She Rises."*

"Does it? Well...this *is* the anniversary of her disappearance isn't it? *Maybe she will."*

"Haseya disappeared the same night Todd's brother had his accident."

Susan said nothing.

The heat of the fire left Deanne entirely. She was sitting only a few feet from the mouth of an old, decrepit mine that itself sat above a creepy cemetery lined with piles of rocks that only barely covered piles of human bones. Just beyond Susan, rusted metal, wooden beams half-eaten by dry rot that only held the tons of rock above them by magic at this point.

This was a place from which anyone could disappear all too easily.

"Was that a coincidence?" Deanne asked.

"Chuck Webb, that dimwitted fool, he had it bad. He skipped classes to watch her. Talked about her all the time. *Nasty comments.* You know, the way boys talk about the girls they can't have. Or maybe you don't know?"

"Did Chuck make her disappear?"

"He was obsessed. He was a stupid boy. Slow. They dropped him two grades in elementary school. They only let him into Ignatius for football."

"Chuck Webb, Ross Tennet, Richard Bilken, Cecil Benson, Barney Willis – did you know them all?"

"I know the names."

"But Todd knew them? They were his friends?"

"Some of them played football. Barney...was a manager, a towel-boy basically. We'd all assumed he was...*you know.* A faggot."

"They're all dead."

Susan uncorked another bottle.

"Thank you for taking my call, Deanne, for coming all the way up here."

"Do you want me to leave?"

"Not at all."

The true story of Haseya Avery. The connection to Todd Worwick and the others. It was all unfolding right here in front of her. There was no reason for Sara to be at Lake Pleasant. None at all. Sara had *asked* to come with her. Why hadn't she said, "yes!" And as this smug, heartless woman poured herself another glass of wine, Deanne saw the last pieces of the puzzle moving into place.

"You were *there* that night. *You're the seventh samurai."*

"You're a Kurosawa fan? I've been since I first saw *Roshomon.* Brilliant work. Todd's a cowboy at heart, he never got *The Seven Samurai.* He prefers *The Magnificent Seven,* but remakes never stand up to the original, do they?"

And now...something worse in Deanne, not unlike the feeling that must come when you realize the nagging ache in your bones, that point of pain in your skull, isn't going away...*until you do.*

"The tattoo was *your* idea."

"You want to see mine, Deanne? My memento of that evening? We made a pact of silence."

"You blame Chuck Webb, but y*ou wanted her there. The party was your idea."*

Was it a smile, *or a snarl* that Deanne saw?

"I wonder. Do you feel *safe* right now, Deanne?"

"The rest of you are *dead.* If you didn't kill them, you and Todd are targets. If you don't turn yourselves in, you're next."

"I'm sorry. Don't you feel safe, Deanne? Because I do."

No. No, she didn't feel safe at all.

She hadn't locked her purse in the trunk this time around. Barney's gun was within arm's reach...if she needed it.

"Things happen, Deanne. Yes, that party was my idea. That idiot Chuck talked her into his truck after school. She'd been playing him for the fool he was all along. A few shots of cheap bourbon and she was the tease we *all* knew she was. But when the time came – she wouldn't put out."

Deanne was stunned, stunned sick.

"You knew he'd bring her. You tried to rape her and you killed her. *It was you all along."*

Susan poured herself another glass.

"Does it really matter who? We were all there."

"Does it really matter? Did Todd's brother see you do it? What about him? Did you kill him too?"

"Joey fell off the dam. Todd revived him. *Todd's a hero."*

"Joey is still alive...?"

"He may as well be dead."

"Where is he?"

"Joey's here; what's left of him. Back at the house. That god-forsaken generator does more than rattle and run the air conditioner. If we had the time I'd introduce you. Not that he'd know you're there. I'm half-hoping that damn thing will just kick off and him with it. Todd refuses to pull the plug and let him go. Porter and Aggie hate having him here. They spend as much time at Arcosanti as they can. Not that Aggie's ever *really here."*

"How do you live with yourself?"

"I drink. *Heavily.* Haven't you noticed?"

More than ever, Deanne wanted to throw up and never, ever drink again. Any parallel between herself and this woman was something she needed to vomit up, out, and away – and then she would drive herself back to reality, get on her knees and beg Sara's forgiveness for hurting her, and worse, f*or letting her face Worwick and those killers alone.*

"Is Haseya here? Buried at Cross Hill?"

Susan waved her glass toward the sad cemetery below them.

"Under one of these rock heaps? God no. Good idea though. Who would think to look? No, it's a long way here from Lake Pleasant...all these years, she's still right where we put her."

"At the lake Todd wants to drown."

"Oh, he *will* drown that lake. Haseya will lie forever at the bottom of a much, much bigger lake."

"Which one of you killed her?"

"She got cold feet. She ran away. Chuck Webb, that stupid moose, grabbed her, spun her right into a boulder. It broke her skull. She wasn't breathing. We were sure she was dead."

"She wasn't?"

"When Joey fell, Todd and Barney ran to the lake to try and rescue him. The rest of us...we were stoned, drunk, and *horrified. We were kids too.* We did...what kids who have done something *very, very wrong* do. We hid it. No one but Joey and the seven of us knew she was there. We buried her."

"How *sure* were you she was dead?"

The superior, chin up, demeanor had vanished. Susan looked like a wax figure of herself now. Beautiful as ever on the outside, dead within.

"We carried her to where she is now...near the dam. We dug a hole the best we could. It wasn't until we began covering her with rocks that *we heard her.* It wasn't a cry, or a moan. It was...a *bleating*...like *an animal.* Haseya was gone. It was clear she'd never be the same. Chuck took a very large rock, and finished what he started."

Deanne blinked, she reached for her purse, felt the weight of the revolver within.

"You and your husband are going to prison."

"No, Deanne. We're not. *We deserve to,* you're right on that. I agree with you absolutely. But life isn't fair, Deanne. Todd will be elected Senator. A new dam will be built and Haseya will be at the bottom of a very large lake. The two of us will reconcile and, eventually, Todd will be President of the United States. I will become First Lady."

Deanne drew the gun from her purse.

"My dad was a cop, I have no problem using this."

"Good for you. Do you really not know why you're here right now?"

"I came to solve a puzzle. *Now I'm here for Haseya,* she deserves justice."

"Justice was Tommy Red Hawk's purpose," Susan said. "But the *Red Hawk* problem is being solved, thanks to you. He's in the open now. Do you know what an *Insurance Policy* is? What it means when someone *very, very high up and important* takes one out?"

She raised the bottle to pour another glass.

"Some very important people have taken out an insurance policy on Todd's future. And they will do *whatever* is necessary."

She glanced to the empty glass.

"I know you like to drink, Deanne. Are you sure?"

Yes, she wanted to drown in that glass, in anything, be anywhere else. More than anything, Deanne wanted to pull the trigger...

"It felt good having you listen to my story. I sincerely thank you for that. But you'll never get to write it. Tell me, do you ever feel like you're being followed?"

The black sedan always in the background, Barney's killers...

The neck of the bottle snapped beneath Susan's hand. The rest of the bottle dropped and rolled, its contents blurted over the sand.

Susan stared down at it, a look of genuine surprise to see the wine mixing with her own blood.

Deanne dove flat on her stomach, clutching the gun. She hadn't heard the rifle shot, *she hadn't heard anything,* not so much as a *pop.*

Susan's hand opened and the bottle's neck slipped, silently into her lap, her head dropped to her chest as if she had simply fallen asleep. She didn't move again.

Deanne crawled frantically toward the cave, so close to the ground she sliced her chin on rocks, sending blood dribbling down her neck, the flesh of her knees and forearms shredded against the packed earth and stone.

There would be another silent bullet coming for her. Just like the one that killed Susan, she wouldn't hear it...*but it would be the last thing she ever felt.*

Her heart pounded, she pulled herself deep into the darkness of the cave, a sharp edge on the rusted rail bit into her palm. Deanne flipped over, kicked her heels into that rail and shoved herself against the wall.

She gripped the gun tightly with both hands, stared into the moonlight beyond the entrance, and waited.

-=-=-=-=-=-=-=-

More than ever, Sara wished Deanne were with them, not just for herself, *but for Deanne.*

They should never have split up.

If it was any comfort at all, it was that Deanne would only have Worwick's wife to deal with in Piñon Rim, not Worwick and the killers protecting him...and Deanne had Barney's gun.

Sara had a gigantic murderer.

Lightning flashed a picture of tragic bleakness, the air around them sizzled with electricity, thunder rolled.

"That was right over our heads." She said.

Red Hawk smiled. "It will rain hard and pass quickly," he said. "The washes will flood. It could give us an advantage, or the skinwalkers will kill us both."

"You have a rotten attitude, my friend."

"I'm a realist."

"Deanne said the scouts will be camped near the Waddell Dam. Worwick and the press have a tent there for show. My guess he's already told a couple ghost stories and shown the scouts how to tie a square knot. Deanne's friends at KPHO said Worwick plans to spend the night across the lake on his boat."

"Unless he's a fool, he won't go anywhere near the dam," Red Hawk said. "*He knows what day tomorrow is.*"

"The day Haseya died. *Worwick's a monster.*"

Red Hawk shook his head, "He's a dead man walking to justice."

"That's why we're here."

"Justice waits at that dam. Your name, Sara, has a meaning to people of your faith whether you follow that faith or not. Navajo names mean exactly what they say. My name, Tahoma, means, *Waters Edge.*"

She blinked. *Tahoma – not Tommy. The Water's Edge was exactly what this man was. A brutally sharp edge. Murderous when it needed to be.*

"What...does *Haseya* mean?"

He looked out into the gathering storm before them.

"It means, *She Rises.*"

Electricity rushed through her. But it wasn't static massing before another strike, it had nothing to do with the storm, nothing to do with anything *natural* at all.

A short distance ahead, a narrow path split from the road.

Another flash – but this one in the rear-view mirror – *headlights.* Someone driving up the road behind them fast. Wildly fast, weaving from one side of the gravel road to the other. It wasn't the press, it wasn't anyone official…

"Jesus!" Sara swerved to the side of the road as a carload of drunken teens shot past. Gravel from the car's tires rattled against her door, bounced from her windshield.

And bright in Sara's headlights, grinning out through the back window of that car, laughing with the others, the unmistakable face of *Cassandra Worwick.*

"Jesus Christ! You stupid little bitch!"

Their car took the other path.

Sara pulled back onto the road, and floored it. Her wheels spun in the gravel, caught and she roared toward them.

"Stop! They're headed toward the scout camp," Red Hawk said.

"I can't let her do this."

"She's in more danger than you know. This way leads to her father. There's *nothing you can do."*

"Those kids are drunk, *she's a stupid kid!"*

"Yes."

And just as suddenly, Sara hit the brakes, the car slid to a stop.

"My God...what is that!?"

Two bright silver orbs in the night, then four. Lightning flashed the silhouettes of two huge coyotes...

...but they stood tall on their hind legs. They weren't coyotes, not like any Sara had ever seen.

They stood nearly as tall as the Saguaros.

Another flash, thunder rolled. Rain pelted down on her car.

Red Hawk threw open the door.

"Get to Worwick. They *will* kill you if they can."

He melted before her eyes, water and rain gear slid out the open door and the door slammed shut behind it.

Sara stomped the gas pedal just as the closest beast struck. The force threw her hard against the wheel, the car fishtailed. A clawed hand swept the windshield with nails like meat-hooks. She fought for control, slammed on the gas and drifted nearly off the road before she righted herself and tore down the path toward the dam.

In the glow of her taillights, Red Hawk seemed to rise up from nowhere. He swung a boulder the size of a suitcase into one creature's ribs as the other tore into him.

They disappeared into a stormy cloud of rain, mud, and darkness behind her.

-=-=-=-=-=-=-=-

The crunch of footsteps on gravel.

Deanne heard something heavy drop to the ground near Susan's body.

She forced herself to breathe slowly, evenly...quietly.

She heard a long zipper being pulled, the scrape of items withdrawn from a canvas bag.

A rustle of clothing.

God. *He's stripping her.*

In a very short time, she'd come to hate Susan, and yet, the stripping of her defenseless, lifeless body, was so disturbing, hit so horribly close and deep.

Finally, a voice. Reedy, thin.

"How does one leave no trace? I know you're wondering, Deanne."

She pulled back the hammer on Barney's gun, the click echoed.

Silence, and then a chuckle.

"You could try that, certainly, any woman in your position would try that. I know your background. I know all about Daddy, the Cop. You're trained with a handgun *to a point.* We could test just where that point is...but I *know* where that point is Deanne."

She heard him stuff Susan's bloody clothes into a bag as he spoke.

"I have other tasks on my mind right now. I could be careless, let my guard down. Maybe that's all the time you'd need to get a shot off."

She heard him unscrew the cap from a bottle, something gurgled and fizzed into the dirt. A terrible, acrid stench floated into the cave.

"I intend to walk away from here without leaving a trace. I really have no quarrel with you, Deanne. When I'm done here – you can walk away too. You don't have to believe me. I doubt I would if I were in your position right now."

A horribly loud snapping, like green branches. Horrible, because she knew it wasn't *tree* limbs being snapped. *It was elbows and knees bent backwards until they separated. It wouldn't be clean, the fabric of life, the tissue would need to be twisted, broken, and cut free.* Bile rose in her throat.

Susan's dead. She can't feel any of this.

"I'm sure that played-out goldmine has more than one entrance. Now *that*, is a variable you might want to consider. I'm out here and armed – that's a given, maybe a *constant*, you don't know. If you come this way, even with your *gun a' blazing,* you have no cover. You already have some idea of *my* training. I hit this woman through the heart. Full metal jacket round. Clean. Well...except for a few bits of glass. I don't want a mess, not here. And, for all you know...I'm not alone. Someone else with the same training I've had might have their cross-hairs trained on that entrance right now."

"Of course, mines have lots of very deep holes in the floor. The wood covering those holes is mostly rotten. And there could be lots of blind dead ends. You see, those miners, they followed a vein...when it ran out, they tried another way, and another. Who knows how many times, how many dead ends they dug before they gave up? One more variable, the further in you go...the less light you'll have, the less oxygen. I don't know if *I'd* be brave enough to go that way...but it *might* be worth a try*...if you're adventurous."*

Susan's fire cast ghosts of light near the entrance, but they were faint at best. From where Deanne sat, her back pressed so hard against the rock her ribs ached, she saw a broken down ore cart on the rails before her, chains and something resembling a large bucket above it… Beyond that, there was only black. Not even the moon to guide her.

No. Her only route to escape was the same way she came in, and *he* was there.

A loud *chop,* one more sickening sound of mutilation, then something heavy dropped into a canvas bag.

Far away, but echoing against the rock walls of the mine now, she heard the howls and yips of coyotes in the night.

"Hear that, Deanne? From death, springs the hope of life. You'd be surprised what a little White-Tail Deer urine can do. Coyotes, wolves, cougars...even those pesky *wildcats,* they love the scent. They already taste blood in the air, but deer urine *and* blood? That's a frightened and wounded rare steak for anyone hungry enough to take it. Oh, if I wanted to spend the time and energy, I could take apart any one of these graves, drop what's left of Susan in, and keep some miner or saloon keeper company throughout eternity. No one would find her.

"But why do that? With so many ravenous mouths to feed, why not just let the hungry creatures who live here fight over this feast...drag this beautiful, tasty meat back to their families?

"Oh, sure, twenty-odd years from now, some hiker will find a piece of bone… so what?"

Deanne could feel the blood from her chin pooling at the base of her throat. Her heart pounded, making her bleed even faster.

She too was giving off the scent of a tasty meal. *And that was exactly his point.*

"I really wish your friend, Sara Poole, was here. But...I imagine she has other concerns right now...*or, let's see; what time is it? She may have no concerns at all anymore."*

Her finger twitched alongside the trigger guard. *God, what had they done to Sara?* Her head went light. She wasn't breathing.

She gasped, and her senses came back.

"Sara...pretty girl. Smart girl. Oh, yes, she's queer. She wouldn't appreciate me the same way she does *you*...but I *know* she would really appreciate the work I'm doing here. *Or would have."*

He's baiting you. Don't take the bait. Don't move.

From somewhere deep in the mine...something dropped, the sound of padded feet, far off, but coming her way now. The blood, the deer urine, whatever sweet cocktail he'd shaken out there had mixed with her own blood, with the scent of fear; a mine was a cave; a cave was shelter to the very things this killer was purposely attracting.

And she was smack between whatever was in here...*and him.*

From outside, a wet explosion like a dropped watermelon. Deanne retched, vomit splattered the tracks.

"A human head presents unique forensic disposal problems. Sara would have loved this."

Just a few feet from where she sat, in the decaying remnants of a bygone industry, Deanne began to see the makings of a killing machine. Rail tracks, a heavy, rusted cart, chains with one band that held a massive, heavy iron bucket above them all. The floor slanted slightly down toward the mouth of the cave. The wheels of the ore cart were rusty themselves, the track too – *but could she set this machine in motion? Was it possible she could get this whole mass moving forward toward the fire and straight down on him?*

The band of metal was all that really held that big bucket to the ceiling. If she shot it, could the chain holding it swing that piece of iron against the cart?

She imagined herself running behind this rolling train of death with her gun, as this killer had said, "a' blazin." She saw the cart mowing him down, felt the pleasure of hearing his skull explode with the force of her bullet.

And then, as your mind will do to shield and protect itself from a shattering fall into complete insanity...it laughed at itself.

Instead of her perfectly simple solution – her mind's eye revealed a ridiculous Rube Goldberg contraption, a machine created to do one simple task through a series of impossibly complex reactions.

If she was James Bond escaping *SPECTRE* it would work. But she wasn't James Bond.

The wheeled cart sitting on the track was, itself, an illusion. Rust had welded all of it into one useless hunk. If she fired this revolver at that metal band holding the bucket to the ceiling one of two things would happen – the ricochet would hit her or the bucket would fall, taking the ceiling and countless tons of rock down on her. She would be crushed and buried forever.

A heavy panting from deep in the cave. Whatever was in there with her was wide awake now, and coming her way, fast.

*Head down, she threw her entire weight at the car*t.

A terrible pain in her shoulder and ribs; her arm went numb.

Rust flaked to the floor. The cart didn't budge.

Deanne fell to the packed earth, frantically crawled, lizard-like, toward the entrance. Behind her, a throaty growl rose in the darkness.

Deanne rolled over in time to see two eyes glowing like embers as the big cat leaped. She fired twice.

The beast took a long, ragged breath and went still beside her.

Deanne's ears rang, her head ached.

She saw the moon. *This isn't over.*

Feeling began traveling slowly back into her arm, but she could barely hear.

What does it matter? A bullet is coming. A silent bullet is coming to end this.

Deanne drew herself back up against the wall. She was at the mouth of the cave now, the last beam between her and that silent bullet with a full metal jacket that would part that beam like a stick of margarine and find her heart.

The smell of wet, burnt mesquite. The killer had put out Susan's fire for good.

From where Deanne sat, pressed against the wall, exhausted, shell-shocked, she could see exactly where she and Susan had been only a short while ago.

Susan's blanket, the wine bottles, the glasses, were gone. No sign at all that either of them had been there. Not a trace.

She sat and pondered that for a long, long while.

Her ears still rang. If the killer walked toward her, if he made any sound at all, would she even hear him?

He was out there, *somewhere*, with his rifle.

Nothing. And then...crickets.

Eventually, daylight would come. *What then?* How long would he wait for her? He was obviously a trained sniper. Hunters could wait for hours perched behind their blinds in the snow...but *snipers?* They were known to crawl silently toward their prey for days if that's what it took.

Deanne's head lifted quickly, her blouse rising with it, tearing the scab from her chin, new blood dribbled down.

She'd fallen asleep!

For how long? *How long had she been out? She could see her watch, but she couldn't read it.*

Deanne allowed herself the first deep breath she'd taken since she'd entered the mine.

She crawled all the way to the fire pit.

No sign of blood or wine. No footprints.

Nothing but a few fire-blackened rocks.

Sure...someone had built a fire up here once. So what?

The cemetery was just below her. She could take her chances, crawl like a spider to the closest pile of rocks, wait, crawl to the next grave, and the next...

Or she could stand up right now and let the silent bullet take all of her cares away.

-=-=-=-=-=-=-=-

Deanne no longer controlled her body. Her feet moved numbly forward beneath her. Exhausted beyond terror, beyond feeling, her being had shrunken into itself, a tiny homunculus that peered through the windows of her eyes as a passenger only.

In the end, she had run headlong to the cemetery, dropping for cover behind the closest grave, waiting for that silent bullet to strike. Finally, her knees ragged, buckling, her arms and hands skinned and bleeding, she had stood as upright as she could, breathed the scent of mesquite and cool night air, and welcomed death.

When the bullet didn't come, her feet began shuffling down the main path through Cross Hill Cemetery and into town.

Piñon Rim was completely dark now, truly a ghost town. Eventually, she reached the old whorehouse and new home to Porter and Aggie Hudson *and the late, Susan Worwick.*

Complete silence. Not even crickets chirped here, the once-noisy rattle of the Hudson generator was gone.

Did she dare go inside? Was Todd's brother, Joey, really there?

The controls of the generator seemed simple enough. *But had the assassin rigged it to explode?*

Curiosity killed the cat...

Would satisfaction bring it back?

What did she care, really?

Her hands moved the switch, and the generator rattled to life. A soft blue glow pulsed to life from a small, painted-over window near her feet.

Leave. Just leave, now...

But she couldn't. Deanne trudged up the steps, and the back door opened all-too-easily.

Deep in the building she saw a steel door that held no kinship at all with the old-west décor. The track of a rolling barn door remained above it. The room it protected had likely been used for stores of liquor and linens in the boom days long ago.

The door wasn't locked; the assassin had taken care of that for her. Whatever lay inside he *wanted* her to see. She held her breath, and pushed the door open.

Hooked by tubes and wires to silent machines once meant to breathe for him, to pump life through him, the body of a man lay motionless on a plastic-covered bed, in a sterile room.

A shelf beneath the window she'd seen near the generator held a baseball glove and a few children's picture books.

The woman inside Deanne finally broke down, melted to the floor. Tears poured down her cheeks.

Eventually, the shell of the reporter she'd once been approached the bed.

This was not a man at all. This was a boy cut off forever from manhood, his limbs grotesquely thin; his face alone was that of a sleeping boy.

Joey Worwick.

Tommy Red Hawk had saved Joey's life, but not Joey.

The Worwicks...for God only knows why...had kept him suspended for years between here and heaven. That likely had ended only hours ago.

This is enough. The puzzle is solved.

She would never be the same.

She had to get back to Sara and Red Hawk, if they had even survived this night. Together, they'd face Worwick and bring him to whatever justice there still was to be had.

But just as Deanne turned away, *something* shifted in the bed.

Joey was moving.

She backed away.

He wasn't moving on his own. He was sinking into the bed... *liquefying.*

Her stomach rolled.

Water seeped over the mattress to the floor and spread. It drew itself into a tight ball and *exploded.*

She threw her arms across her face and screamed.

When she dropped them, finally, a cloud of mist hung motionless before her.

It gathered into the face a boy, his mouth drawn in a silent scream.

A remembered wives' tale, a story told to her long ago... *A soul is leaving! It can't be trapped. Let it out or it will haunt you forever!*

Deanne shattered the window with one shot, and the mist flew away into the night.

Deanne could barely pull herself onto the car seat. She struggled to sit upright. When she turned the key, she thanked God when the car roared to life.

Okay...you can do this. You can find your way out of here.

Sara's alive, she has to be alive!

Something shiny sparkled from her dashboard. Trembling, she reached for it.

A single bullet. Full metal jacket.

-=-=-=-=-=-=-=-

The silver-blue desert opened to a black lake.

Worwick's boat floated beside the pier. The cabin windows glowed warm.

Lightning flashed to reveal four long, curved stripes in Sara's windshield. The skinwalker's nails had bitten deep into the glass.

An unfamiliar shudder rocked Sara as she drove down to the pier. She punched the horn. Security drew their weapons and Sara stopped as they converged.

"Step out of the car. Keep your hands where we can see them!"

She did as they asked. Worwick and Sondra Tucker emerged onto the deck, and a squat, broad-shouldered man stepped quietly behind them.

"Todd Worwick!" Sara called, "Your daughter is here! *Cassandra is here!"*

Worwick ran to the back of the boat. Sondra stood her ground.

"Put your guns down! Bring her here!" He commanded. "Where is she?"

Sara ran to the boat. She could see the concrete wall of the dam far off in the distance, it seemed to glow in the darkness.

"She's headed for that dam with a group of boys – they're drunk."

For a moment, it looked as though some lever inside Worwick had switched to "off" position. The man stood motionless.

The spell broke, he pulled Sara on-board, calling to the security team as he yanked the loops from the gunwale and tossed the ties into the water.

"Marty get to the dam, now!"

He pulled the bumpers onto the deck.

"Frank, get us over there."

They stood at the front of the boat as skeletons of white light burned into the sky and thunder rolled.

The dam was there in front of them...but so far off.

Even as raindrops the size of pebbles struck them, Worwick didn't take his eyes from a pinprick of light near the great wall, likely a campfire from the scouts that would soon be doused by the rain.

"When I told you Cassandra was here," Sara said, "you didn't even question it. Why is that?"

"What were you doing at our campaign headquarters?" Sondra snapped.

Todd waved her off.

"Where did you see Cassie?"

"Just before the turn-off to the landing."

He nodded.

"Let's get out of this rain."

Down in the warm, dry cabin, the unmistakable perfume of recent love-making was in the air. Sondra gave her a look that was likely only a reflection of Sara's own disgust. The woman turned away.

"Why would I expect you to lie about something like that?" Todd answered her, finally.

"Maybe to get you to the dam, back where it all started."

"I don't know what you're talking about."

"Young girl, a bunch of drunk teens near the dam? That's not a familiar story?"

"If you're lying..."

"You'll what? Have me erased? Like Barney, Ross, and the others? Five gone but seven in all, Todd. *The Magnificent Seven. The Seven Samurai.* Five down...two to go. You and who else?"

"Those are serious charges," Sondra snapped, "Deranged charges. Y*ou are talking to the next Senator from Arizona."*

"I'm pretty sure I'm not. Just who is *Captain Frank* at the wheel, *candidate* Worwick?"

The "aw-shucks" all-American quarterback was long gone from him now.

"Someone...*you don't want to mess with."*

"You might want to take note of that, Sondra." Sara said, "We still have one murder target to identify – maybe that's *you.* How well do you know Frank, Sondra? Or *Todd,* for that matter. Enough to bang him, sure – but doesn't that make you one more mess that needs cleaning up?"

"I don't know who you are," Todd said, "but you need to shut it, right now."

"I'm a forensics expert. If Frank's the one who cleaned up Barney for you, he's not perfect. He left a messy trail that leads directly to you."

"What's she talking about?" Sondra looked from Sara to Todd.

"All I care about is my daughter."

"Haseya Avery was someone's daughter too."

The engine cut. They drifted toward shore. The rain had stopped. Sara heard only the lapping of the water outside.

"Who is *Haseya Av-* ?" But before Sondra could finish. Frank called down from above.

"We're here."

At the sound of Frank's voice, Sondra no longer looked disgusted or smug.

She looked terrified.

Donovan O'Malley tugged his weenie free from his shorts and sent a long stream over the trunk of a young acacia tree.

He'd really wanted to let go a big smelly piss into the campfire...and he would have if he was camping with friends...but not with the scouts, not with the group leader and den master sleeping so close by.

Terry stepped up beside him, withdrew his white weenie and did the same.

"Ah…" they said in unison.

"Looks like the rain's already comin' down," Terry laughed.

Donovan laughed too. It had been a good day, all-in-all. They'd turned on the Great Wave early for them and the scouts had gotten in quite a few good rides on the body boards. Tomorrow would be the big day though. It was Great Wave's grand opening, kicked off, unfortunately, with a speech by Cassandra's dad...but it would be followed by a good full day of swimming and body-surfing.

It was fun being with his buddies, and this would really be the last scout outing for most of them. Likely the last time most would really see each other now that high school loomed ahead. Terry, at least, would be with him at St. Ignatius.

Lightning flashed. They both began counting.

"One-"

Boom.

"Crap. We're gonna get hit by lightning standing out here."

"Hey...Donnie..."

They immediately stuffed their things back in their shorts.

Cassandra looked like a beautiful ghost.

"Cassandra?"

Donovan's heart leaped and immediately sank. She'd ignored Donovan since that day at her pool. Seeing her hurt as much as *not* seeing her, but her being here sort of made sense. Her dad was here after all. Mister Worwick told a ghost story they'd all heard before, but they pretended to be scared anyway, and he'd roasted marshmallows in the fire just like one of the scouts. But he hadn't said anything about Cassandra being here...*and girls...weren't allowed.*

"I knew you'd be here," she said. But she sounded...*odd.* Had she been drinking? Sure she had. He'd had enough of those after-party bottles at Terry's to hear it in her voice.

"Well...yeah..." He said. Everyone at school knew about the scout outing with the candidate – *her* dad. Donovan's head was spinning.

"Wanna go for a hike?" She asked.

I'm dreaming. I've fallen asleep...and this is just a stupid, mean dream. But lightning flashed, thunder rolled...and he was wide awake.

Terry just stood there with his mouth open.

"Come on," she turned and walked off.

Without a moment's hesitation the two ran back to their tent and pulled on their uniforms. Neither bothered tying on their scarves.

By the time they'd scampered back to the acacia...she was out of sight.

Donovan's heart sank.

What did you expect?

"Hey, Donnie, come with us."

It was two older boys – one was the kid who'd bumped into him at the open house. A now-familiar pain clamped his chest. *What is she doing with them?*

Terry shook his head.

"I don't know, Donnie. I think we should go back."

Donovan nodded, just as he knew that he couldn't do that, he couldn't possibly go back to the tent now. There was no choice but to go but with them. As bad as his heart was hurting, he had to follow this through.

"Go back. I'll see what's going on. I'll come and get you."

"Okay..." Terry said. But then he shook his head. "No. If you're going, I'm going too."

-=-=-=-=-=-=-=-

The silver-blue glow of moonlight was gone. Lightning flashed a vision of stark death before them. Cactus and sharp rock. As Donovan and Terry crested the hill, the concrete wall of the dam rose beside them.

A white plume of water blasted from a spillway into the valley below. But even that wasn't loud enough to cover the laughter coming from a car parked beside the river.

They'd set up a pup tent nearby and embers flew from a fire that sat way too close to the canvas.

Thunder rolled, echoed against the dam and the nearby boulders.

"What kind of dumb-ass camps *below* a dam?" Terry asked.

The entire mass of Lake Pleasant was above them, untold cubic tons of water, with a big thunderstorm on the way and one spillway already flowing.

"A *drunk* dumb-ass," Donovan said.

"She's a dork, Donnie. Let's go back."

"Yeah..."

And even as they said it, they continued picking their way down toward them.

"Anything could be out here," Terry said.

During the height of a desert day, shadows were the mortal enemies of hands and feet – shadows hid rattlesnakes, Gila Monsters, and other varmints. At night...the deadliest of them didn't need to hide. At night it was your turn to hide.

"I have my scout knife," Donovan said.

"We're saved."

"It's got a *spoon.*"

"Don't make me laugh, I'll slip."

Barely halfway to the valley floor. The huge, but frighteningly thin wall of the dam looming, the plume from the spillway growing, the car's back door opened and pretty Cassandra Worwick vomited into the sand.

One of the boys slid out from behind her, laughing.

Donovan couldn't help himself, needles cut his legs, the boulders scraped his flesh to the bone as he ran now, headlong toward the camp.

"Crap, Donnie!" Terry tried to catch up, slammed into a boulder, limped forward and fell again.

"You asshole!" Donovan yelled at the older boy.

"What's your problem? She likes it, Donnie."

The other boy appeared, shirtless, from the tent. Big as a bear, he brandished a thick-bladed Bowie knife.

"Is there a problem, string bean?"

"My ankle!" Terry howled. He limped forward and fell. When he pulled himself up, his ankle was already swelling.

"Crap. It's broke!"

Donovan looked from Cassandra to the boys coming toward him, then back to Terry. He fought back the tears welling in his eyes.

"Fuck you, Cassandra." He shook his head, "Fuck you." He trotted back to Terry, threw his friend's arm over his shoulder, and lifted him up.

"I'll get you back to camp."

The boy with the knife shouted, "Your friend's a pussy, Cassie!"

Lightning flashed. The thunderclap exploded overhead. The first big drops struck like tiny fists; a few at first, and then a full salvo.

Donnie called over his shoulder to the boy in the car.

"Take her and drive out of the valley, dumb-ass! This place is gonna flood."

The boy stumbled drunkenly, indignantly toward him.

"You're a pussy!"

Donovan ignored him. "Put your weight on me, we need to get to higher ground fast."

Cassandra, shook her head.

"Donovan, don't...*I'm sorry!"*

"Help me! Please, help me!" It was another girl, somewhere. Her voice came from boulders closer to the dam.

Was Cindy with them too? But it wasn't Cindy's voice.

"I'm so...cold. Please...help me."

Now the cry came from all around them...

"What...the...fuck?" The bear-like boy with the big knife said.

"It hurts...and I'm cold!"

Donovan saw her now, sitting atop a boulder closer to the dam. Long black hair completely hid her face.

A shudder ran down Donovan's spine. These idiots hadn't brought *her* here.

Cassandra screamed. So did the bear-like boy, he dropped the knife. It disappeared into the quickly rising water at his feet.

"Cassandra! Run up the hill! Get up here!"

Stone sober now. Cassandra stumbled forward, and a strong current, swept her feet from under her. She splashed down hard.

She scrambled, terrified, toward higher ground, and the current pulled her under.

Donovan shifted Terry's weight to a boulder and tore back down the hill, barely able to keep from falling himself. His momentum nearly carried him past Cassandra into the middle of the stream. He fell, dove and yanked her, screaming, from the water.

The other boy, clearly out-on-his-feet drunk, pointed at the other girl.

"She with you?"

A roar behind Donovan. He turned to see a tall black wall of water racing toward them.

"Run!"

He and Cassandra pounded up the hill to Terry; they snatched up his arms and pulled him with them. Breathless, terrified, and soaked to the bone, the three fought their way as far and fast as adrenaline could take them.

Only when they'd reached safety did Donovan dare to look back.

He saw the black wall take the tent and the car. It snapped the two boys like twigs, and took them down the valley.

The girl still sat atop the boulder. The water hadn't touched her. *It flowed around her.*

Cassandra threw her shaking hands to her face.

"She's not real! She's not real!"

Terry, grimacing in pain, shook his head.

"She's a girl. We all see her!"

"We have to get higher," Donovan said. "The rain's still coming."

They held each other, pushed their way forward and up.

"Please don't leave me! I'm so cold. Come back!"

"You two keep going," Donovan said.

"Donovan!" Cassie sunk her nails into his arm. *"Don't go back there!"*

"I can't just leave her to drown!"

"Look at the water – it won't even touch her! *She's not...real, she can't be real!"*

The girl looked up at them and her hair fell to the side. There was only a shadow where her face should have been.

"I won't let you leave me here again."

Donovan forced them all back up the hill, water coursing around and over their feet.

"Fuck, Donnie! *What is that!?"*

Now Donovan and Cassandra saw them too, silver lights flickered like stars among the boulders and cactus. They moved in pairs.

Not lights. *Eyes...*

We're in Hell, Donovan thought. Just like Mom told me I would be one day...

Gigantic coyotes rose into the night...the creatures stood upright on long, powerful, hind legs.

The trio froze, *the faceless girl behind them, these creatures ahead. There was nowhere to go.*

"I know you!"

Unhindered by cactus, the water, the boulders, the girl walked toward them. With each stride she covered five-yards, *ten; fifteen. Until she stood an arm's reach away.*

But now she had a face. Even more than that, *she was beautiful.*

"You're a ghost!" Cassandra screamed. "Get away from us!"

"It was *you, Susan.* You told him to bring me here. *To you!"*

Cassandra's face pulled into a fist of terror.

"My n-name is Ca- Cassandra. I don't know you! I don't!"

"You left me, Susan, but you came back."

"My mom's name is Susan! *I'm Cassandra, I swear, I don't know you!"*

The girl looked confused…but the anger remained.

"You wanted me, and when you couldn't *have* me, *you crushed my skull and left me for dead."*

The smell of urine cut through the aroma of the desert rain, Terry had let loose once again.

"Please," Donovan said. "*We don't know you.* We don't know…*how you died."*

"Susan." She opened her arms wide. "Come here."

"That's not her name. Listen to her. *Susan is her mom."*

The dead girl cocked her head the way a dog might.

Donovan felt Cassie pull away from him, *but her feet were sliding over nothing but air.*

"No, please! I didn't do anything! I don't know you!"

He tried to pull her back *and his fingers slipped through her arms.*

Donovan threw himself at them with all the force he could muster *and crashed straight through to the boulder behind them.* White hot pain shot through his ribs.

Angry growls; the beasts were coming for them down the hill.

And now we die... Donovan thought, he shut his eyes, they were going to be torn limb-from-limb and there was nothing he could do about it.

A thunderous explosion made his eyes fly wide open. The whistle of a thousand arrows in flight followed closely behind. One of the beasts crashed in a bloody heap at Donovan's feet, then another.

Their bodies shrank, pulled into themselves; fur dropped from them into the water and was quickly carried downhill.

Two naked men lay dead where the creatures had been, bloody cactus spines jutted from their torn flesh.

Behind them, the water coursing down the hillside rose suddenly upwards. Donovan dropped, bracing for the impact.

...but the water took the shape of a man.

A very large Indian man in shredded rain gear stood over them, bleeding from long wounds. The man looked as if he'd come straight from a battle with Lucifer.

"Haseya!" the man shouted. "Let her go!"

The pain returning to Donovan's ribs was a welcome clue that some, tiny bit of the real world with real physical laws was still in control.

Still...he couldn't believe his eyes.

The ghost stories, Navajo legends, stories told around fires at a dozen scout camps - it was all happening in this terrifying nightmare unfolding before them...

The beasts had surrounded them all as if waiting for a sign.

"Haseya. Let her go. She's not the one."

Now the girl looked as perplexed as she was angry.

"She brought me here!"

"No, she didn't. Release the skinwalkers and let her go."

"I don't know these skinwalkers. They are not Navajo."

"Your hate *draws* them. When you sleep, they will sleep. I was here when you died, Haseya."

"You weren't with them."

"I *saw* what they did. I am Tahoma. I've done what I could to avenge your death. These children aren't to blame."

"You were here*...*"

"I thought you had died – another would have if I hadn't left you. I will never be free from that sin."

"This girl…was here last night."

"That night was fifteen years ago, Haseya. You've been tied to this land ever since. One killer remains. I've left him for you. Take him, and sleep."

A look of pure terror on Cassandra's face as Haseya looked her from head to toe.

"Susan...is older…*who are you?"* Haseya's eyes narrowed, pure hatred burned from them now, "You are their daughter…"

"What? What did they do?" Cassandra, pleaded, *"What did my parents do?"*

"They had a life together, a family together...*they made a child..."*

"This girl has nothing to do with what happened," Tahoma said. He raised his hand and a tornado of water arced over and around them, created a swirling wall between them and Haseya.

Haseya's cry bit through the night, straight to the bone.

"I thank you, Tahoma, for this gift!"

"This isn't justice, Haseya!"

"This is *my* justice now."

Cassandra passed through the barrier of water Tahoma had built *as if it weren't there at all.*

"No...please!" she pleaded, "Don't let her take me!"

"Cassandra!" Donovan reached for her, and the water slapped his hands back to his chest.

"You can't let her do this! You can't!"

And then they were gone. Cassandra's scream echoed within the waterspout.

"Why? *How could you let her?"*

Tahoma's face was clenched tight with anger and pain.

Through the top of the spout, the black rain clouds were parting. A full bright moon sent waves of silver shimmering through the spinning wall.

"The skinwalkers cannot pass through moving water. *If I leave, they will tear you apart."*

Terry was white with fear and pain; his waxy skin seemed to glow in the moonlight.

"He needs help! We can't just stay here. *Cassandra needs you!"*

"If I leave, you'll die, the girl too."

Through all of the horror tonight, Donovan had seen *real* magic, *real* ghosts...and now, in this man, Tahoma…a *superhero.*

Real, true-to-life superheroes exist!

It occurred to him then...*my mother is right. She's been right all along.* The *pretty traps of a "normal" life* that held you down and kept you from being what you *could be.* You had to avoid them.

He was meant *to be* something more.

And this was his moment.

"Tahoma, show me *how."*

Tahoma said nothing.

"You have to go after them! You can't stay here with us – *and you know it!"*

One of the beasts swung its great claws toward the water. Tahoma let it through, then instantly swirled the current faster, harder.

The hand dropped to their feet. Before their eyes it shrunk...and became a human hand.

"How do you do it? How do you control the water?"

"A name has a spirit of its own. I am Tahoma, it means *the water's edge."*

Another revelation from Donovan's mother.

"My name is *Donovan. It means, Dark Warrior.*"

Cassandra and the ghost were far away now, fading, *barely there at all.*

"You have to stop her! Show me!"

"When you take the life of water, *you have no life of your own."*

"She'll kill her."

Tahoma grit his teeth. Finally, he cupped Donovan's face with a hand that felt like a steel vise.

"Look at me."

Donovan looked deep into a face that was strong, but whose eyes were filled with nothing but pain. Still, Donovan forced himself not to waver from those eyes.

Tahoma was indeed the water's edge, his other arm not only disappeared into the swirling wall he'd built - *it was part of it.* He let go of Donovan's face and clasped Donovan's forearm so hard that Donovan felt Tahoma's fingers cut into his flesh, deep *into his very soul.*

Fear beyond *anything* he'd ever felt before – and still, Donovan didn't take his eyes away.

A pulse of raw power rushed through him.

"The rainwater at the base of that Saguaro. Direct your spirit there."

Two of the snarling beasts crouched beside the Saguaro, calculating the strength of the water, looking for a weakness in that wall between them.

Donovan concentrated on the stream at its trunk.

Nothing.

Then, the stream moved, it dropped beneath the towering cactus, the giant Saguaro swelled. It burst in a shower of whistling needles that tore through the beasts, killing them instantly.

"Yah!" He shouted. And yet...*something jolted him, tore him deep inside.*

Where Tahoma gripped him...*his own arm ended in Tahoma's arm, a clear, watery bridge between them.* He pulled away, horrified, and his arm and hand were once again his own.

Tahoma took his hand and forced it into the swirling water around them.

Once again, Donovan's hand...*was gone.*

No...it was there, part of the wall as Tahoma's had been - moving that wall now...the strength it took was enormous, he felt exhilarated and completely drained at the same time...

There was only sorrow in Tahoma's eyes when he said,

"You are the water now. Stay where you are."

The man dissolved into the swirling wall, and another flood of power whirled through Donovan, a force that raised him high and dropped him just as quickly to his knees as Tahoma broke away.

Donovan saw Tahoma dive into the fall that cascaded from the spillway. Two of the creatures tried to follow, and were instantly swept away.

Tahoma was gone.

Terry.

Terry hadn't so much as groaned from his pain, hadn't said a word during any of this. But he was staring slack-jawed and wide-eyed at Donovan now.

-=-=-=-=-=-=-=-

"Daddy!"

"Don't move, Cassie! My God, don't move!"

Cassie Worwick stood, terrified, atop an observation tower at the top of the Waddell Dam. From here, she looked the size of a beetle.

How had she managed to get there?

And what kept her from falling? The top of the tower looked barely the width of her shoulders, not a rail beside her, no handle to grip.

Todd leaped to the dock as the boat slid close. He slipped on the wet deck, caught himself and sprinted to the dam, to a frightening ladder of wire rungs. He leaped to the highest he could reach, and frantically pulled himself up.

Sondra and Sara were close behind. The rain had stopped, the moon had broken free, but every surface was slimy and slick.

Frank swore as he threw the bumpers against the dock and secured the boat.

At the bottom of the rusted ladder, Sondra pulled short - horrified at the heights she'd have to reach, at the treacherous landscape of concrete above them, the pilings, debris, and rough water below.

"Move! I've got it."

Sara pushed her aside, it didn't take much. The rungs were as slick and rusty as she knew they would be. But she took them straight, quickly, one after the other, without a glance to the side or below, just as she'd climbed countless platform ladders before.

But it was for glory then, to please yourself, to please your coach. For points, for the sport of the dive, not because someone's life depended on it.

And your own life too...

Frank is a cleaner. She'd known there were such beasts. How many unsolved murders had been their handiwork? *Insufficient forensic evidence.* There had been a cause and a culprit in every murder she'd touched. She hadn't found a perfectly "cleaned" murder yet.

Would hers be?

She pushed that thought aside.

Above her, Worwick had already reached the top of the wall.

"What are you waiting for?"

Sondra turned, quickly.

Frank stood behind her. She had only been able to watch those two brave souls climb to terrible heights. She could feel the spray from the storm-churned waters as waves crashed the dock beneath her feet.

She was petrified.

"Come on – you can do this. *We all need to help,* Sondra."

"There's no way I can help them!"

So very high above them, Todd pulled himself up and onto the walkway. He raced to the tower.

Cassie stood atop that tower staring straight forward, as paralyzed with fear as Sondra.

Sondra was powerless to help...she had to leave it to -

"You *can.* We're all in this together. Come on. One hand up, that's all you need to think about."

She actually tried. As soon as the rusted metal bit the pads of her fingers she yanked her hand away.

"You *need* to help her, Sondra. This is going to take all of us. You need to help her now."

How well do you know Frank?

"There's a radio on the boat, Frank. Did you call this in?"

"Of course I did. Help is on the way. But we're a long way from Phoenix. Just one hand. Then the other. Do it now!"

The KPHO news team camped nearby would be tuned to the emergency frequencies...*if he had called, their boat would be on the way and no other boat was on the water.*

"You go up there, Frank. You can help them. I'll just be in the way."

"You're probably right."

A sharp pain as her hair was yanked backwards; *the concrete wall sped toward her face.*

Static.

Radio silence...

-=-=-=-=-=-=-=-

"Stay right there, honey. Daddy's here."

Cassie stood motionless, completely motionless atop the tower.

Sara's hands were raw and bleeding from dozens of cuts. Her lungs ached as she pulled herself over the edge, she bolted across the top of the dam toward them.

Todd was a man on a mission. He clung to the outside of the concrete housing like Spider-Man. But the tall structure had not been built for easy access or safety, no metal rungs to hold him there. His hands searched the smooth, wet concrete frantically for a handhold, a way up to her.

How the hell had Cassie made her way to the top?

A whirl of frightening vertigo hit Sara like she had never felt it before.

Not so much as a rail along the narrow wall, *who the hell had designed this thing?* To her right, a long drop to crashing water, to logs swept against the dam by the storm. God knew what lay under the surface. To her left, a much, much longer drop to boulders, cactus, and a long plume of white-water blowing from a spillway struggling to release the extra pressure the storm had caused.

What the hell was that?

A few hundred feet from the base of the dam…a small waterspout rose into the air.

Red Hawk is here!

Her excitement was short-lived.

"Thank you for your help, Miss Poole," Frank called to her. "We can handle this from here."

Frank hoisted himself up and onto the walkway, a hulking, brick shit-house of malevolence.

"If that girl falls, the campaign's over! We can talk when she's safe. *Todd, stay where you are!* I'm going to circle around and try the other side."

"Cassie!" Todd pleaded from his perch overhead, "Look at me, baby. Come on, look here at Daddy, you're okay."

Frank quickly closed the gap between them. There was no sense of "helpfulness" in his stride, he didn't even glance toward the tragedy unfolding above Sara; his focus was entirely on *her.*

That familiar exhilaration and fear...the moment of truth that said, "Push off now, take flight...or climb back down...it's not your day..."

A long screech of brakes then shouts from the dock below. The security team Todd sent had finally arrived...*and something else had arrived as well.*

Shots were fired. The skinwalkers were here.

Frank ignored it all.

"Sara. I don't often enjoy my work, but I am going to enjoy this."

The pistol Frank had drawn was pointed center mass. *Her* center mass.

"If you had a *dick* instead of a gun, I might enjoy it too."

He actually started to laugh. "That's not what I've heard -"

The moment.

Her *wheel kick* had been so fast, so unexpected, even Sara was surprised to see the pistol twirling into space. It disappeared soundlessly into the water below. She steadied herself quickly on the slippery concrete, spread her feet just wide enough to deliver another blow.

"Oh...*that* was good. I *did not* expect that from you. So few surprises in this job, anymore." He rubbed life back into his stinging hand. "Yes, I really am going to have some fun tonight."

"I *usually* suck at that kick. If you don't help save that girl, *I'll show you what I'm really good at."*

He dropped into his own stance and with lightning speed threw a straight punch that caught her square in her sternum. A flash of light, pain, *and no breath at all.* She splatted against the concrete like wet clay.

His fingers flew to her throat; she'd never seen anything so fast, felt anything so powerful, s*o deadly!*

The awful realization that her moment, the one real moment of her life that mattered...may have passed forever.

"That wasn't very well done, Sara. It *is* nice to laugh though; rare in this work. Is comedy that thing you're really good at?"

She croaked, "*This*...is what I'm good at..."

Sara yanked her feet up and sprang off his chest with all of her might. She flew blind and backwards into the night.

Her eyes opened to a moon that was full, a huge, silver ball overhead. And then, it flew suddenly away; the sky, the mountains and the desert passed as she pulled her wings together, knifing toward the water below...the sound of Frank's scream faded behind her as the churning water rose up to meet her.

"I've got you!"

Red Hawk enveloped her, pulled her with him deep into the healing cool waters. They rushed quickly back to the silvery surface and burst into the moonlight.

Her lungs filled with the first good breath since Frank's fist had blasted into her sternum. The air was clean and sweet with desert rain; still she choked.

"You know," she said hoarsely. "*I would have nailed that dive."*

Red Hawk's implacable, hawkish face looked down at her. A wry smile broke across it; a look she imagined was not a customary one for him.

"Another time, perhaps."

Now she saw the water crashing against the dam. *All around them...broken logs, jagged concrete and twisted metal... she'd have nailed it alright.*

And something worse near the dock.

Sondra's body floated face-down, a wave pushed it forward; it thudded dully against the pilings, slid back, and thudded into it again. Sara closed her eyes, bile rising in her throat.

You've autopsied floaters. It's nothing you haven't seen before...

But Sara had been talking to this floater only a few minutes ago...and "it" had been a living, breathing human being.

"This night isn't over," Red Hawk said, "Hold on."

A sudden wave carried them high into the air. Her feet were planted on the dock before she could manage a scream. Red Hawk stood beside her.

Carnage awaited them. The security team's car idled. What was left of its occupants littered the dock in bloody pools of shattered bone and gristle.

Four skinwalkers stood nearby, sizing them up.

"We stay near the lake for now."

"We've got to save that girl!"

Sara ran to the rung ladder – a fire hose blast of water rebounded off the wall and forced her back.

"What are you doing!?"

He folded his arms.

"We *stay."*

-=-=-=-=-=-=-=-

"Baby, please. Please...look at me."

"I'm afraid, Daddy."

"I know. I know you are. Honey...I need you to...to just sit down. Very slowly now, just sit."

Below them, battles for life had been waged and lost.

But this was the only battle that mattered. Cassie's was the only life that mattered.

The Senate, the Presidency, he didn't care about any of it now. *His little girl stood on the edge of her life.*

Worwick slipped, barely caught himself in time. His body shook. The adrenaline that had sent him all the way up here was gone, he was spent.

Below them lay death. If they didn't back down, exactly the way he'd just come, death awaited them on either side of the dam.

But he could *do* this. *He could do anything. Could get away with anything. Could fix anything.*

And now, he would fix this.

"Honey...just bend your knees. Easy...just sit..."

She faced him now.

"I love you, Daddy."

"I know you do, honey. Sit down now, honey...okay."

"I used to tell *my* Daddy I loved him. *I told him just like that."*

Todd blinked.

"Honey, this is *me.* This is your Daddy, I'm here."

She crouched, reached her hand toward him. He stretched out to take it, but somehow she remained just...*out of reach.*

"My daddy's heart broke. He died when they couldn't find me. I didn't know until I woke up tonight."

"Honey...you're scared, I know. You need to take my hand, this is real. This isn't a dream."

She took his hand. *Her grip was powerful. Unimaginably powerful.*

Raindrops splashed his face. He blinked them away.

Blood, not rain, had spattered him. His hand ran red with it.

The girl holding him there, staring down at him; had long, black hair.

"Haseya!"

"You left me for dead...*but you never forgot me."*

The hand that gripped him was bone, *nothing but bone. Her hair slipped from her caved-in skull, floating past him like dry feathers in a breeze...*

As Haseya released him Todd did remember...remembered it all!

All the way to the boulders at the bottom of the dam.

-=-=-=-=-=-=-=-

The spinning wall of water dropped away. Donovan was exhausted, spent.

"No!"

The water that had once cascaded down the hillside had faded to a trickle. *He couldn't protect them without the water.*

He was barely strong enough to stand. *Who knew doing super things made you weak?* He collapsed against a boulder and hung there, waiting to be eaten alive.

But no more silver orbs floated in the night, no more giant coyotes stood ready to pounce. The pink glow of sunrise began to show itself.

Thank God.

Terry snored. He snuffled violently awake.

"Ow, crap, *my ankle!"*

"Come on, let's get you back."

"I had a *nightmare!"*

"No. You didn't."

Tahoma said wait. But what if Tahoma hadn't made it? He put Terry's hand around his shoulder to lift him, and they both nearly fell.

"I don't know...if I can get you back up the hill."

"That was *real?" Terry asked,* "Those...*things? The ghost?"*

"Yeah."

"And *you..?."*

Donovan nodded.

"What…*are you?"* Terry asked.

Donovan shook his head.

"Where's that Indian guy?"

"I saw him jump into the spillway, after that…I don't know."

"What is he?"

"All I know is I need to get help. I can't move you."

"Okay...just go. If those things come back – being eaten can't hurt any worse than my ankle does." He tried to laugh but it was more a pained chortle.

"Stay put."

"Got nowhere to go."

So much for being a superhero.

Before he started up the hill, Donovan unhooked the scout knife from his belt and tossed it to Terry.

"It they come back…go for the spoon."

Now Terry did laugh.

A scream for help nearly blew out Donovan's badly weakened heart. It echoed across the boulder-strewn valley.

It *had* to be Cassandra. *She was alive!*

But where was she?

"Cassandra!"

"Help me! I...I can't move."

He picked his way up the hillside, hoisted himself onto the biggest boulder he could find and stood. He turned completely around. *No sign of her anywhere.*

"Cassie! What can you see?"

"Nothing! It's dark and I can't move!"

The voice had come from a small pile of rocks...not far from where the ill-advised campsite had been.

"You're okay! I'm coming!"

But as he made his way to her warming light crept across the valley to reveal more of its secrets, more of the rotten fruit of last night's horrors.

A half-mile down the trail gouged out by the flash flood, he could make out the mud-covered wheels and undercarriage of the car that had brought Cassie here. Several yards downstream of that, the roots of an overturned Palo Verde held a broken scarecrow...the skinnier boy, the one who'd told him about the Boondocker. The big one was nowhere to be seen.

Yes, it was real. Not a nightmare.

He reached the rock pile.

"Help me!"

"I'm here, Cass. Don't move. Breathe easy, and stay still."

He was thankful to hear the roar of an engine. Up near the dam, a car crested the hill, then made its way slowly down the small access road toward them.

But now, at the foot of the dam…he saw two more broken bodies. Skid marks of their own blood on that wall pointed them out like arrows on a chart.

What had he lived through?

He quickly looked for balance points in the pile of rocks, and carefully moved them aside.

Finally, he saw Cassandra's face, covered in mud and sand.

Her eyes opened wide. She was terrified. *Who wouldn't be terrified?*

"Keep your eyes closed, Cass. Let me wash this off." He uncapped his canteen and poured the water over her face and eyes. He pulled off his shirt and wiped the grit and mud away."

There was a nasty burn on her throat. He carefully cleaned the mud away and saw a sunburst of seven arrows arranged like the spokes of a wheel.

Haseya had branded her.

"Hold on Cassie. You're almost free."

He pulled away the last of the stones that held her, and she wrapped her arms around him.

Then Donovan saw what lay beneath Cassandra...*what she'd been lying on top of ever since Haseya's ghost had taken her away...*

A skeleton; its face was crushed. *Haseya's skeleton.*

"Let's get out of here."

"Dark Warrior."

Donovan had never been so happy to hear someone in his life. *Tahoma was back.*

Sara saw the skeleton too...and Cassandra's fresh tattoo. Dead and gone but not to be forgotten... Haseya Avery had left her mark.

The girl had her arms wrapped so tightly around the boy who'd pulled her from the beneath the rocks, it looked as if she'd never let him go. Sadly, Sara thought, *but you will, won't you? Stupid girl.*

Tahoma clasped the boy's forearm roughly and smiled.

"You did well."

The boy took a deep breath, he could barely say, "Thank you."

And now, a random thought that wasn't really random at all - the *waterspout* she'd seen...it had been very near where they stood now – Tahoma had been all the way on the other side of the dam.

Sara took a quick look at the other boy who sat in awed silence beside them.

"We've got first aid kits back at the camp," the boy said, hopefully, "it's just over the hill."

"That ankle needs professional -"

"We'll take care of him," the tall boy said, "I'm Donovan."

"Sara." She glanced at Tahoma, and back to the boy. "Let me guess. Donovan means, *Dark Warrior*?"

He smiled. Even with that smile, the terrors of the night had left him looking about twenty years too old to be wearing a Boy Scout uniform.

"Good work," she said.

"I can smell their coffee from here," Tahoma said.

"I didn't think you were welcome in this land."

"Temporary, truce." He said. "Enough time for coffee."

"I need to watch this area until the examiners get here. Can you take them to the camp? You can drive, right?"

He laughed. "Yes, I can drive. What do you think I am?"

"I...have no idea." The three kids were helping each other, holding so tight they were like one crippled beast limping toward her car. She looked to the bloody figures below the dam.

"Wait. Please, don't let her see...her dad."

He looked to dam and then back up the hill.

"Keep your keys. I have another way."

He strode up to the group and lifted the injured boy and Cassandra as though they were nothing. Moments later they were at the top of the hill.

Sara dropped beside the makeshift grave. By rote, she made the obvious and easy assessment; death by blunt trauma.

It angered her now that such a sterile phrase had been her first thought.

What you see is not a phrase. What you see is a little girl, a beautiful life cut short.

Haseya, *she rises.* Her ghost could sleep peacefully now. Sara wondered if she, on the other hand, would ever sleep peacefully again, and she wanted sleep more than anything right now.

Sirens in the distance; *the cavalry is on the way. Thank God for the cavalry. Late as they are.*

But it was the red Starfire making its way down the narrow access road into the valley that breathed life into her soul again.

Sara stumped up to the road as quickly as her worn legs could carry her.

Deanne looked as battered and tired as Sara felt. She struggled slowly and painfully from her car.

The tearful bear hug felt good, so good.

"You're soaked," Deanne said. "Go for a swim?"

"Of course – it's a lake. So...how was *your* night, Miss Mulhenney?"

Deanne's eyes went from Sara's, to the blood-streaked concrete of the dam and the crumpled figures below, to the makeshift grave and the body beyond.

"Just as shitty as yours, I think."

Sara nodded. "Susan and Joey are dead and you saw it all."

"How did *you* know?"

"Tahoma told me. Don't ask how *he* knew."

"My guess would be Joey's *spirit* told him." Deanne took a deep breath, "*Todd?"*

"I'm sorry." She glanced to the bodies below the dam.

Deanne said nothing. On the hill, the familiar examiner's panel truck and two patrol cars made their way into the valley.

"I made a call to Sergeant Henry. You need to talk to them?"

Sara sighed. "Yeah, this could take a while."

Eventually, they trudged back to their cars like two battle-weary soldiers.

"Tahoma and Worwick's daughter are at the scout camp," Sara said, "Coffee's brewing."

Deanne could barely open her door.

"What do we do about him?" She asked.

Sara shook her head, wearily.

"It's going to take more than Boy Scout sludge brewed over a campfire to figure *that one* out."

Deanne dropped like a sack of potatoes onto the driver's seat, the sheer effort of shutting the door behind her drained the last bit of energy she had.

"I happen to know a bar that opens really, really early." She said, "But…do I detect a change in your tone toward the *murderous* Mister Red Hawk?"

Sara leaned against the side of Deanne's car. For a while, neither seemed able to move or speak. Finally, Sara sighed.

"That bar…is it near your house?"

"It *is* my house."

Sara nodded.

"Screw the coffee, let's go."

-=-=-=-=-=-=-=-

Phoenix, June 2, 1969

A cooling breeze began a chatter of leaves from the mulberry shading Haseya's grave.

It did little to cool the heat that burned inside Donovan O'Malley.

He sat back against the concrete bench – a bench that had been moved away and back again twice in the last year...and now, seemed to be permanently set here.

Empty for over fifteen years, this was now truly the final resting place of Haseya Avery.

One year from the night that should have changed everything for Donovan.

One year later and *very little* had changed for Donovan.

Without guidance, the little power Tahoma had placed in Donovan's hands had amounted to nothing more than a few funny "tricks" to amuse himself and Terry. No one else knew...other than Cassandra.

Cassandra lived with relatives in Upstate New York now; her letters had gone from daily, to monthly…and then dried up completely.

Cindy ignored him.

Still, Donovan knew none of that would matter in the long run. *With the right training, he could be the hero he knew he was meant to be.*

Donovan leaned forward, focused all of his energy on the water behind her grave.

"*Tahoma!*"

He'd tried this many times before and had always given up and left.

Donovan wasn't giving up today. He wasn't leaving until he made contact.

"Tahoma, show me how!"

A dull throbbing in his temples became a pulsing ache, and still he pushed his energy toward that water.

Every muscle, every fiber in him was drawn tight as a bow.

His body began to vibrate, to shake.

And just when it seemed he couldn't hold that focus a moment longer...

A ripple across the surface. Slight…but there.

He pushed on.

"Tahoma, *please!"*

The ripple became a wave; the wave crested the bank then drew suddenly into itself.

Tahoma's head and shoulders rose above the pond.

"Teach me! Show me how to use this."

"Why?"

"I'm meant for more!"

"There *is* nothing more."

Donovan stood, shocked…and then *angry.*

"This life, this…*has to have a point."*

"If I train you to use this power, many years from now you'll understand the only point was to have been a boy, to have made mistakes, to have been with a girl and discovered the pleasures and secrets of each other. That is *all* there is. All there *should* be."

The form dropped back into the pool. A last ripple lapped the sides, and the pool was still again.

Donovan stood stock straight, stunned.

Finally, he shook his head.

"No," he whispered. His body shook, *"No!"*

He clenched his fists, ran toward the pool and as he dove into it *the pool rose up to meet him.*

And then there was only the water.

THE END

About the Author:

Steve Zell is a former animator, digital animation tools instructor and session vocalist. He was the first graduate of the University of Arizona's, Interdisciplinary Studies program, where his studies included Studio Art, Chemistry, Journalism, Drama and Vocal Performance. He was an early member of Tucson's Invisible Theatre Company, the "voice of doom" on the television series Baywatch, an editorial cartoonist for *The Tombstone Epitaph*, and, while working for Intel® Corporation, began Intel's partnership with DreamWorks and co-founded the Intel Audio Alliance, whose members included Billy Bob Thornton, Graham Nash, Rory Kaplan, George Massenburg, Michael Boddicker, Nathaniel Kunkel, Allen Sides and other music industry professionals.

Other Titles by Steve Zell

WiZrD by Steve Zell
Pub: Macmillan, St. Martin's Press, Hodder|Headline

Best of Backlist, 2019 Feathered Quill Book Awards, All Genres
"A perfect 50 out of 50 – this author knows his stuff and delivers great stories."
"The author's ability to draw strong characters must have given him a legion of fans already. I expect him to be the next James Dashner ("The Maze Runner") if he's not already."
- *Feathered Quill Book Awards Judge's Comments*

Caught in a centuries-old cycle of boom and bust, the northern Arizona ghost town, Pinon Rim, is booming once more, but ominous signs are beginning to emerge. It's up to thirteen-year-old Bryce Willems and his stepsister, Megan, to end that lethal cycle…or not.

Running Cold by Steve Zell

Pub: Tales From Zell, Inc. ™

An ancient gift turns deadly in the hands of a young boy. It's the mid-1960s, and Brit Helm, mourning the recent death of her eldest son, struggles to make a new life with her youngest, Michael, in a small, southern California beach town. But lingering suspicions about the horrific "accident" that took her eldest begin to rise, and soon Brit realizes she must control Michael's anger at all costs. A pretty surfer threatens to break her tenuous hold…

Urban Limit by Steve Zell
Pub: Tales From Zell, Inc. ™
Members of an Oregon family move to the mountains hoping to escape city life, only to find themselves fighting for their own lives and, possibly, for civilization itself.

Twins Kristi and Reed Carroll could not be more different. While Kristi trains for her shot at Olympic glory in the winter games, Reed spends his days in the cyber world of video games. But something sinister has found its way into both worlds that will soon bring them together, or tear them apart forever.

www.ingramcontent.com/pod-product-compliance
Lightning Source LLC
Chambersburg PA
CBHW060557310726
48982CB00008B/1152/J

* 9 7 8 0 9 8 4 7 4 6 8 7 3 *